About the Author

The author is a circuit judge and lives with his family in south east London.

Sawson's Quest

Charles Gratwicke

Sawson's Quest

Olympia Publishers
London

www.olympiapublishers.com
OLYMPIA PAPERBACK EDITION

A CIP catalogue record for this title is
available from the British Library.

ISBN: 978-1-78830-251-7

This is a work of fiction.
Names, characters, places and incidents originate from the writer's
imagination. Any resemblance to actual persons, living or dead, is purely
coincidental.

First Published in 2019

Olympia Publishers
60 Cannon Street
London
EC4N 6NP
Printed in Great Britain

Dedication

To my wife, Jane, without whose constant support and encouragement this book would never have been written, and in memory of my grandfather, Walter, who sowed the seeds in me, of my love for London and the sea.

"The man who has experienced shipwreck shudders even at a calm sea."

OVID

THE BEGINNING

The boy shivered and wrapped his ragged coat tighter about him. Ahead stretched the muddy cart-rutted lane that led down through Henderson's wood to the coast road. In spring and summer the path through the wood which led off to the right, was an attractive short cut to anyone coming down from the Downs intending to travel onto the road towards Portsmouth or to quench their thirst at the Talbot Arms which lay just beyond the end of the path set back from the road.

The cold wind and rain that had set in from the west showed no sign of abating and at times the gusts of wind caught the boy full in the face, causing him to gasp for breath while the icy rain stung his cheeks. It was not a night to be abroad and as he approached the wood, he bemoaned his ill luck in being out on a night like this, wishing he was at home in the rough stone cottage up in the Downs above. His destination was Malsters Farm that lay about half a mile off the coast road towards the sea. To get there he had to reach the end of the lane and then turn right onto the road a quarter of a mile before turning left onto a track that led to the farm.

Malsters Farm was inhabited by the Sawson family who held it as tenants of Lord Ridgemont, who owned it and much of the land in that part of the country. Edward Sawson had arrived in the area some twenty-five years before with nothing but the clothes in which he stood. He was, in those days, a man of very few words and he had not changed. He was over six foot in height with a mass of black hair now turned to silver. His features were heavy; a large hooked nose seemed to sprout out of the centre of his face as the main branch of an oak might leave the trunk, whilst two large brown eyes, heavily cowled, stood like sentries on either side of a face which, despite the years of toil on the land, still retained the sallow complexion that it had when he first appeared in the neighbourhood. His lips were thick and bulbous and when opened, revealed a strong set of white teeth. It was, however, his ears that were his most distinctive feature: his left ear was pink and fleshy and large, sticking out of his head at a right angle. Its brother on the right was similar in colour, texture and size but the top of it was missing. It looked as if it had been clipped as one might dock the ear of sheep or cattle. How the injury to the ear had occurred, no one knew. When he had first come to the area people had asked, but they soon learnt the question was not welcome and it remained a mystery, as did his earlier life.

In the five years following his arrival, Sawson had lodged at the cottage of old Mrs Barry, a widow who at the time was well into her seventies. Most of the country folk regarded her at best as slightly touched whilst the more simple-minded whispered amongst themselves about strange happenings (always witnessed by others), that were said to have occurred at her home. As a result, children thought she was a witch and the adults gave her a wide berth. In truth, she was just a lonely old woman given to talking to herself and to her animals as there was no one else. How it came to be that Sawson took lodgings with her is not known, but her isolation from others no doubt suited him well.

During the time that he lodged at Mrs Barry's, Sawson worked as a farm labourer. He was a hard worker and much sought after by the local farmers for he was prepared to work at all times and in all weather, though no matter how hot it became he was never known to remove his shirt. He was not, however, popular with his fellow workers: he declined to enter into any more conversation with them than was necessary to carry out the work in hand. His size and strength was such that that others soon learnt that it was best to leave him to himself. Of an evening, he would, like many of his fellow labourers, make his way to the Talbot. But he would remain apart from them, choosing to sit alone on an old oak kitchen chair in the alcove which commanded a view, during the hours of daylight, of the road from Portsmouth as it wound down from the gap through the Downs. The positioning of the alcove was such that anyone sitting there had a clear view into the centre of the inn and the main door and yet could not be seen immediately by those entering. The regular patrons of the Talbot soon came to realise that that was Sawson's seat and except when the occasional traveller inadvertently sat there, it was never occupied by anyone else. On those rare occasions when a stranger did sit there, they soon realised that their presence was resented and they moved. Sawson himself would not say anything, but a look from him was enough for them to realise that they were trespassing.

The ale at the Talbot, brewed by the landlord, Tom Merington, was renowned by locals and travellers alike. In a time when most taverns brewed their own, the quality of ale varied greatly and many who were making their way along the Portsmouth road preferred to travel the extra mile to get to

"Tom's" not only to slake their thirst but also to enjoy the mutton pies, roast meats, fresh bread and home-made cheeses and more, all made by Tom's wife, Kate. As a consequence, the Talbot was far busier than one might have expected given its location.

Sawson would sit in the recess with a pot of ale before him on the rough table along with a quart jug with which he would refill the pot when he had drained it. He drank not like other men: taking the pot into his large hands he would take large, audible gulps from it as if he had not had refreshment for days. As he did so his eyes would remain focussed on the road as an eagle might scour the country below it for its prey. If a strange figure appeared on the road, his eyes would remain fixed on it until the person either passed by or entered into the inn, where Sawson would gaze upon the visitor intently before resuming his watch on the road. On one occasion a Frenchman, who was from the south of that country and dark skinned, came down the road. Sawson watched him as he had watched hundreds of others: as he came closer and his colour and features became clearer, an observer would have seen Sawson stiffen. His right hand which had been nursing his pot of ale grasped it tightly with such force that if it had been a glass it would have shattered under the pressure, his left hand was clamped to the table top, his neck muscles were taunt and protruding as he continued to watch the man approach. The Frenchman entered the inn and approached the pot man. Sawson's eyes bored into his back. It was only when the man ordered refreshment in a mixture of broken English and his native tongue that Sawson seemed to relax, though he continued to watch the Frenchman throughout the time he was in the inn and when the man left, Sawson stood up and went outside and watched him until he was out of sight.

Five years after Sawson's arrival, old Jack Cowper, the tenant of Malsters farm, died without an heir. Over the next few months the burning question in the tap room at the Talbot and in many a farmhouse kitchen was who would get the tenancy of 'Malsters'. The farm was only one hundred and twenty acres. The land was good, though a little neglected in Cowper's last years, but under the hand of a hardworking farmer everyone agreed it would become again the profitable farm that it had been before sickness and old age had laid old Jack low. Mr Riverston, Lord Ridgemont's land agent, was of the same view and the rent that was asked for was higher than was expected. Many of the local farmers had designs on the farm either as an addition to their own or to set up a second son, but of course they kept such plans to themselves. At the auction of old Jack's stock and effects, which took place at the farm, many of them attended ostensibly to bid, but in reality to cast an experienced and calculating eye over the land. At the same time, they all solemnly agreed Riverston would never get that rent. He would have to come down.

Some two weeks later came the news that Malsters was let. The disappointment that many of the farmers felt soon gave way to amazement that was shared with the countryside at large when it was revealed that Sawson was the new tenant. "Sawson, who was only a labourer, how could he afford it?" was but one of the questions asked. In truth there was no mystery as to how Sawson could afford the rent. Five years of working every hour that he could, combined with spending little on himself and nothing on others had left him with enough for the first year's rent and more.

Sawson, as was his wont, said nothing. He left Mrs Barry's cottage and moved to Malsters as soon as the ink on the lease was dry.

To reach Malsters farm a visitor had to turn off the coast road onto a track through a plantation of young oak trees. The track opened out onto a stony sunken lane not visible from the road. The lane descended gently for a quarter of a mile before turning sharply to the right. Thereafter it dropped sharply down before levelling out at the entrance to the farmyard. The banks of the lane were steep so that the head of a man passing along the lane would be well below the level of the surrounding fields and they were lined by the gnarled roots of the small trees and gorse bushes that marked the boundaries of the fields above. In winter, the lane was frequently blocked by snow drifting from the fields, cutting the farm off. When that occurred, the only way to reach or leave the farm was across the fields providing the level of snow was not too high. In spring, the banks were lined with snowdrops, which soon gave way to a mass of primroses and cowslips and all the time there was a trickle of water down the banks from the fields. When summer was at its height, the smell of the gorse in full bloom filled the lane, and the branches of the trees that stretched over the lane provided welcome shade from the sun high in the sky.

***

On reaching the farmyard the lane petered out. To the left, a path dropped away but its descent was short and soon it started to climb to the top of the Down known as Gypsy's Fall. Malsters farm stood in a fold in the Downs, sheltered from the prevailing westerly winds. On entering through the old and rusty gates, the visitor found himself in the pebbled farmyard, the territory of Harry, a particularly large Bull Mastiff, who was not partial to strangers and did not hesitate to let them know it. To the left stood two large stone-faced barns whilst to the right there was a row of stables faced with the same material. At the end of the stables a gate marked the entrance to an enclosed yard surrounded by a variety of farm buildings.

Across the farmyard stood the farmhouse. It was a handsome building solidly constructed of the stone and flints found in these parts. The house had a sturdy storm porch large enough for a man to remove wet and soiled clothing with ease before entering into the house through an old and heavy wooden door which opened into a spacious hallway. The dining room and living room were to the left and right respectively of the hall, whilst an oak-panelled staircase ascended steeply to the first floor and the four bedrooms of the house. Two of the bedrooms looked out through windows set in the eaves to the front of the house giving it a pleasant symmetrical appearance whilst the remaining two bedrooms looked out through windows of identical construction, over a walled orchard at the rear of the house and the fields beyond. A broad passageway to the side of the stairs led to the large kitchen and its adjoining scullery at the rear of the house. The back door of the kitchen opened directly into the walled orchard that contained a small kitchen garden. At the far end of the orchard, a door in the wall led directly into the fields. It was an attractive house in an attractive but secluded setting. It was, however, the seclusion that Sawson found attractive.

**

Six months after Sawson moved to the farm and just after his taking of the tenancy had ceased to be the main topic of conversation in the neighbourhood, a fresh piece of news concerning him once again set everyone's tongues wagging: "Have you heard, Sawson has married?" The fact that he had married was surprising enough given his apparent desire for solitude but if the truth be known the bigger surprise to those who thought they knew what was going on in the community, was that there had not been the slightest suggestion that Sawson had been contemplating marriage to anyone, let alone Molly Garvey, the daughter of Dick Garvey, a shepherd who lived at Dusters' cottage in the Downs above the Talbot. The new Mrs Sawson was one of three sisters; Kate who had married Tom Merington who we have already met and Joan who at the time was still living at home with her father. In the fullness of time Joan herself married Bob Pearce, a young shepherd himself who came to live at Dusters with her and her father. Sawson and Molly had met on the Downs where Sawson, when not at work or at the Talbot, would spend his free time pacing along the chalky paths like a caged tiger, always with an eye on the coast road below. As their friendship developed and blossomed into love, Sawson no longer walked at his previous speed, but except in their most intimate moments, he continued to watch the road below.

AN UNFORTUNATE ENCOUNTER

Some twenty years had passed since Sawson's marriage. During that time three children had been born to Molly: Robert, who was now eighteen, Ben, now sixteen and 'little Anne', who was fourteen and the apple of Sawson's eye. Sawson had, through sheer hard work, improved Malsters so that it could now support him and his growing family. Indeed, the income from the farm had enabled him to send Anne to a small school for young ladies run by two elderly spinsters in the nearby market town of Rorton. Anne would be picked up by a local carter every Monday morning at the bottom of the track where it reached the coast road and she would return in the same manner on a Friday night to be met by her father. Sawson himself seldom left Malsters. On those occasions when farm business required a visit to town, Molly would go, or in the last year or so, Robert.

It was a warm sunny day in June. The air was still and the only noise to be heard was the distant murmur of the sea and the song of the skylarks as they hovered in the blue sky above the fields of the farm. Sawson made his way slowly down from Gypsy's Fall where he had been standing for ten minutes or so looking out to sea. As he approached the farmyard, Harry, who had been lying outstretched on the warm pebbles of the yard, sensing his master's approach, stood up and bounded towards him. Sawson affectionately patted him before passing briefly into the farmhouse to speak to Molly. He emerged from the house and set off up the lane accompanied by Harry. It was Friday and Sawson was going to meet Anne. As he made his way between the steep banks of the lane up towards the road, anyone observing him would have been surprised to hear him softly whistling a jaunty tune. Sawson was happy as he always was when going to meet his 'little Anne'. On reaching the plantation of oaks, Sawson sat down with his back against an oak trunk and waited. In this position he had a clear view of the road along which the cart carrying Anne would come.

About half an hour later the cart carrying Anne came into view and Sawson made his way to the end of the track and onto the road to meet it. As soon as the cart pulled up Sawson lifted Anne out of it. As he did so, she placed her arms around her father's neck and embraced him as she always did. Sawson was at peace with the world. He placed Anne gently onto the road and reached into the cart to remove her trunk. As he did so, he noted a coach moving slowly along the road from the opposite direction that the cart had come from. Pulling the coach were four magnificent pitch-black horses. Sawson paid it little attention for his mind was on his Anne who was chattering away beside him about the events of the week at school. He did, however, note that the horses were tired and surmised that the coach would no doubt stop at the Talbot to rest and water them. As the coach drew level with the cart, a curtain was drawn aside and a man's head looked out to speak to the coachman. The man was in his early sixties: he had a neatly-clipped grey beard and closely-cropped hair of the same colour, a swarthy dark skin and a cruel-looking hooked nose. His eyes were, however, his most striking feature: small and brown they shone out from his face as beams of light from a lighthouse might stab the darkness over the sea. As he looked to speak to the coachman, those eyes alighted on Sawson and remained locked upon him whilst his mouth curled in a sinister smile. Sawson, busying himself with Anne's luggage, looked across and caught the man's look. He stood as if transfixed and shivered as a broad oak might in the light wind that precedes a storm and then the coach was gone and so was Sawson's peace.

Sawson made his way back down the lane. Anne started to question him about things at home, but sensing that her father had something on his mind she soon fell silent. Glancing up at her father, she saw a haunted look in his eyes. "What is it Papa?" she asked. He made no reply but gripped her hand tightly and as he did so she felt a great tremor pass through his body. On reaching the farm, Sawson went into the house with her, but he soon emerged and strode out to the fields and onto Gypsy's Fall where out of earshot of all but the crows croaking overhead and the sheep chewing thoughtfully, he let out an almighty cry of anger and anguish and tears poured down his weathered cheeks. He remained on the headland for over an hour and then having composed himself, he returned home. On reaching the house, Sawson spoke briefly to Molly to inform her that he was going to the Talbot and not to wait up for him. Such a visit was highly unusual, for since his removal to Malsters, Sawson had only visited the Talbot on about half a dozen occasions. Molly, seeing the look in her husband's eyes and sensitive to the agitation he was trying to hide, declined to question him and he left, accompanied by the faithful Harry. Once again they strode up the lane but whereas a few hours before he had taken the same route with happiness in his heart, now there were very different thoughts in his head and breast.

Having reached the road, Sawson made his way to the Talbot where he was greeted with surprise by his sister-in-law Kate. After exchanging pleasantries with her, he asked her about the coach with the black horses. "Oh yes," she informed him, it had stopped at the inn for an hour whilst the horses were rested and "yes", two men who were in a hurry had come in for a quick meal. She had busied herself and other than that they spoke English with a foreign accent, there was nothing else that she had noted.

Sawson made his way outside to the stables at the rear of the inn. Having entered the building, he walked down the central passageway with stalls on either side to the tack room where he found Jethro Maybank, the ostler. He was a small, wizened man in his early seventies and what he did not know about horses was not worth knowing. Like Sawson, he was not given to idle chatter, but recognising in Sawson a kindred spirit, he soon told him everything he wanted to know. He had, of course, noted the fine black horses. They must, he mused, be worth a pretty penny. He had spoken with the coachman who had told him that they were travelling to Portsmouth where his master was going to embark for Spain. Whilst talking with the coachman, they had been joined by the master who Jethro described as a 'real gentleman', no doubt because he had tipped him well! He had appeared very interested in the area and, in fact, said Jethro, "He asked me about a man he had seen earlier on the road. From the description he gave I knew it must have been you, so I gave him your name and told him where you lived." At this news, Sawson groaned inwardly though it was what he had expected to hear. Jethro continued to talk but Sawson, who had learnt what he wanted to know, made his excuses and left.

On leaving the Talbot Sawson walked purposefully along the road in the direction of home. On reaching the track he turned down it, but he did not pass down the lane. Instead he turned left into the fields and reached a secluded position on top of the bank from where he had a clear unobstructed view down into the lane and up to its end where it met the track. Making himself as comfortable as he could, Sawson lay down and waited. It was a warm June night with a bright half-moon and a canopy of stars above. Sawson, however, had eyes for nothing other than the lane below. In the beginning the silence was punctuated by the sound of birds calling goodnight to each other and then there was total stillness and quiet broken only by the occasional screech of an owl as it set out on its evening hunting expedition, or the bark of a fox in the fields beyond. But Sawson had ears for none of this as he continued to concentrate on the lane. The sound of a twig breaking caused him to tense himself, his eyes peered into the darkness as he strained to see what it was that had caused it to break and while his right hand gripped tightly a stout wooden branch he had picked up in the field, his left hand held a long-bladed knife. What it was that caused the sound we shall never know but nothing happened and Sawson relaxed his grip on both branch and knife as everything fell silent once more. Sawson remained on top of the bank until the birds in the surrounding hedgerows and trees started to call to each other and then as the dawn broke and the sun started its daily ascent, he stood up and made his way stiffly down the lane to Malsters and bed. He awoke in the mid-afternoon with the sun streaming in through his bedroom window. He looked out into the orchard below where Anne and Molly sat talking to each other, while in the fields beyond he could see Robert and Ben bringing the cows down to the farm for milking. It was an ideal world and everything and everyone in it was at peace except Sawson.

He dressed himself and went downstairs where he had a hasty meal before busying himself about the farmyard until the family gathered for the evening meal. At the close of the meal, Sawson pushed back his chair and gazed for a while into the fire for a few moments before turning towards his wife and children who were watching him intently. He spoke to them quietly and calmly telling them that he feared that the farm might be visited by those who would wish to do harm to him and those he loved. They must all be vigilant of strangers in the area. The farm and its buildings must be secured at night. When Anne returned to school on Sunday, she was to be accompanied by Robert who would also travel to the town on a Friday to bring her home. He gave no reasons for his fear and Molly and the children, knowing him as they did, asked no questions of him.

Over the next few weeks, Sawson slept during the day and maintained his lonely vigil at the top of the lane at night. But nobody came and as June gave way to July he ceased to keep watch at night, though he continued to ensure that the farm was locked and bolted at night and Anne was escorted to and from school by Robert until the summer holidays arrived. Life at the farm gradually returned to normal and by harvest time all but Sawson had put the events of June out of their minds though Molly, on occasions catching a look on Sawson's face, would start to worry again. Sawson for his part remained as alert as ever. He seemed, however, to be much calmer than he had been for many a year. It was as if he had been waiting for something to happen for a long time and was now resigned to it. In truth, he knew that this was just a period of calm before the storm, which had been brewing for many years, would suddenly burst upon and envelop him and those he loved. Until that happened there was nothing further that he could do and he threw himself back into the work of the farm.

August came and went and the harvest was safely gathered in, when Molly heard from her sister, Joan, that their father, Dick Garvey, had been taken ill. Reluctant though she was to leave her husband and family at this time, she removed herself to Dusters' cottage to assist her sisters, Kate having returned as well, in the care of their father. Whilst she was away, Anne took over the running of the farmhouse and the preparing of meals for the family. Notwithstanding the worries that he had, these were happy days for Sawson as he watched his beloved Anne developing from a girl into a young woman. Molly was away for some two weeks nursing her father. Fortunately, Dick's health improved and she returned home in mid-September, some two weeks before Anne was due to return to school. Life went on as usual at the farm. With the approach of autumn, there were preparations to be made for the colder and darker months to follow. The first mists came and the swallows got ready to leave, and all the time Sawson waited.

THE DEATH OF AN OLD FRIEND

It was a night like any other night: at dusk Sawson and Robert secured the farm and entered the farmhouse to join the rest of the family. The bolts to the oak door were thrown and the heavy iron bar placed into the brackets positioned on the back of the door and on each of the adjoining walls. After the evening meal Sawson sat before the fire with Molly and the children until nine o'clock when he retired to bed. Outside, the wind was blowing strongly, but it soon died down and all was calm and peaceful. Harry yelped, no doubt dreaming of chasing rabbits and then all was quiet again. Sawson awoke as normal at six and having called Robert and Ben, he went downstairs where he was joined by his sons in preparation for the many tasks that needed to be carried out before breakfast. He opened the door and stood in the yard, as was his custom, breathing in the cool morning air. Unusually he was not joined by Harry. Looking across the yard he saw him lying where he always slept outside the stable door closest to the farmhouse. Sawson called out to him but he did not move. Ben, who was devoted to Harry, walked across to rouse him but as he got near he let out a cry. Sawson ran across the yard. Poor Harry lay in a pool of blood. He would not chase rabbits or dream of them ever again. Sawson bent down and carefully turned him over. The yelp in the night had been his last: Harry's throat had been cut from ear to ear. Sawson stood up and looked down on his old friend. As he did so, Ben exclaimed "look" and pointed. Sawson followed his gaze and saw that the top of Harry's right ear had been cut off and was missing. And as the blood had flowed out of the gaping hole that had been Harry's throat, so the colour drained from Sawson's face. He let out a cry of anguish followed by an almighty oath the like of which neither Robert nor Ben had ever heard their father utter, before bending down and tenderly lifting Harry up and carrying him to the field behind the orchard, where with tears streaming down his weather-beaten face, he laid him to rest in the earth.

On his return from the field, Sawson, without a word, strolled grimly up the lane looking for clues as to where whoever had killed Harry had come from. Nothing escaped his keen eyes, but there were no signs of the killer's route. He strode on to the Talbot. But his enquiries there drew a blank: no strangers had been seen in the area the day before or that morning. He returned back along the road, passing the track, looking for signs of where horses or wheeled vehicles might have waited, but he found no such signs. On returning to Malsters, he collected his telescope and made for Gypsy's Fall where he scoured the countryside, concentrating in particular on the south west. Again he found nothing. He remained there for an hour or so before turning and striding purposefully back to the farm where he summoned his family to him.

The family gathered in the sitting room. Robert and Ben looked expectantly at their father, whilst Molly and Anne, their faces pale and tear-stained at Harry's savage killing, sat nervously beside the old stone fireplace where Sawson stood, gazing out of the mullioned windows to the fields beyond. Outside, the autumn sun shone warmly. The rooks in the surrounding trees, who acted as unpaid sentries during the hours of daylight, cawing out as anyone approached the farm, called to each other. Inside all was still, the only sound was the steady tick of the old longcase clock in the corner. Sawson turned to his family and began to speak.

"I have never spoken to you all," he said, "in any detail about my early life. It is a period that I have tried to forget. But after what has happened it is important that I do, for we are all in great danger. Let me start at the beginning: I was born in the Magpie ale house in Old Gravel Lane in Wapping where my mother, who died in childbirth, worked as a cook. My father, who was a sailmaker on the 'Roxburgh Castle' left me with his sister, who kept a distiller's shop in Worcester Street, while he returned to sea. My aunt was a kindly woman but her husband, a one-armed veteran of the wars with France, treated me abominably. My earliest memories are of him the worst for drink, kicking me around the shabby shop and cursing my father for leaving him with an extra useless mouth to feed. When my aunt tried to intervene, he hit her across the face with such force that two of her teeth were knocked out and she joined me on the floor where the two of us cowered like beaten dogs before his rage. My aunt did not survive such cruel usage for long, and when I was but five years old she died following a drunken assault on her of more than usual severity, leaving me without a blood relation in the world, for the 'Roxburgh Castle' and my poor father had been lost at sea."

Sawson stopped speaking for a moment and looked once again out of the windows before reverting his gaze to his anxious family and resuming his history of his earlier life.

"My aunt's funeral took place on a cold and windy morning in February. Such was the weather, that only those who had essential business had left the shelter of their homes: the wind was whipping up the muddy waters of the Thames causing those vessels anchored out in the river to strain at their anchors as if desirous of rushing to the bank to embrace their fellows moored on the wharves, who in turn were rising up and down on the foaming waters, seemingly trying to snap the tarry coils of hemp that tethered them. Having failed in its attempt to cause bedlam on the river, the wind turned its attention to the land, whistling mournfully through the narrow, mean and squalid streets of Wapping, dislodging chimney pots, tiles, fences, anything that was not solid or securely fastened. There was at the same time, such a cacophony of noise, the sound of the tortured ropes as they restrained the rebellious vessels, doors and shutters swinging on creaking hinges before banging onto walls and doorframes and dogs howling as if it were the end of the world and, periodically, the crash of yet another piece of tile or building as it plummeted into the street. Through all this noise, my uncle, who had commenced an assault on the contents of the shop the previous night, lay on the floor where he had collapsed in a drunken stupor, oblivious to it being the morning of his wife's funeral."

"Thus it was that I alone followed the rickety cart carrying the roughly-hewn wooden coffin in which the remains of my aunt lay. The wind picked up and it was with considerable difficulty that the old and stooped carter persuaded his bony horse to do battle with the elements. The gusts of wind were such as to take one's breath away and all the time the rain that had set in since early morning, lashed and stung my face. The cart eventually turned into Scandrett Street and after passing St John's school with its statues of a boy and a girl, stopped outside the tower to St John's Church. There, with much difficulty, the coffin was lifted off and carried into the churchyard where the clergyman, whose words were lost in the buffeting wind and rain, read the funeral service as quickly as decency and respect would allow before bowing to me and scuttling away to the shelter and relative warmth of the church, leaving me alone in the churchyard and in the world."

Sawson remained silent at this point as if transported back to that harrowing day of his childhood long ago before addressing his family.

"I stood in the churchyard not knowing what to do or where to go. The only certain thing in my life was that I was not going back to my uncle's house. I found shelter in the porch of the church until the wind and the rain abated in the mid afternoon and then I made my way to Frying Pan Stairs on the river, where I joined with the other urchins of the street and many older members of the parish, in salvaging items which had been swept off ships in the river during the morning's storm. Though I was small and the richer pickings went to those older, stronger and more streetwise than me, I managed to gather up enough of the spoils, which I then sold in order to be able to buy food. That night I slept in a tumble-down shed at the back of the old sugar house at King George's stairs. I was wet, miserable and frightened, fortified only by my determination that I would from now on be the master of my own destiny. I awoke the following morning and the true reality of my situation dawned upon me: I had no money, food or shelter. Indeed, all I had to call my own were the clothes upon my back. For the first time in my life, I knew the full meaning of despair. It was not to be the last."

Once again Sawson paused and looked upon his family, and Molly in particular, who gazed at him with tear-filled eyes. He swallowed and went on.

"I made my way through the narrow streets of Wapping. It was early, but the streets were busy, for the river does not wait for anyone. Geordie sailors from the colliers, Russians, Finns and Swedes from the Baltic trades together with the native British sailors joined the flow of lightermen, coal heavers, lumpers, labourers and dockyard workers bound for the dockyard at Deptford. Tidewatchers, sail makers, coopers, rope makers, foundry workers, tally clerks and numerous other trades made their way towards the river, whilst at the same time came the shouts and oaths and the cracking of whips as the drivers of the lumbering creaking carts tried to navigate their way to the wharves, quays and riverside works. The air was full of a rich mixture of smells: the sweet but cloying odours from the sugar factories intermingled with sudden wafts of cinnamon and nutmeg from the wharves and the delicious smells of freshly baked pies and bread combined with the smell of tar and the pungent smell of the river itself. Those in the crowd moved at different speeds: a few pressed on with the determination and purpose that denoted urgent business at hand. Most, however, not long from their beds, walked slowly and quietly enjoying the last few minutes when their time was their own. Now and again there would come a shout followed by a curse as a sailor, who had not recovered from the delights of strong spirits and ales in the tavern the previous night, staggered into someone or fell to the ground before being shepherded on down the street by his mates. Everyone in the street that morning had, however, one thing in common: they had a reason for their being there and a destination. I had neither.

"On reaching Alderman's stairs, I leaned against the old stone parapet and surveyed the busy river. There was a continuous flow of small craft arriving and leaving: wherries, boats and gigs conveying officers and crews between the vessels moored in the river and the riverbank, watermen who plied their trade from the steps deposited their passengers at the foot of the steps before picking up a new passenger for transit across the river to the dockyard or downstream to Greenwich. Now and again, a capstan chant could be heard as a crew made ready to sail. The odour of the river was strong but it was as nothing compared with a sudden smell that assaulted my nostrils. I turned to my side and looked upon a man dressed in a filthy long black coat which was tied with string across the front thereby constraining a massive stomach which threatened at any moment to break out and cause him to fall forward. His trousers were cut from old sailcloth that had once been white but they were now so heavily stained that the politest description that one could now give them was mud-coloured.

His shoes were of different types, but consistent in that they were both held together with twine. At the front of the right one three of the blackest toes I have ever seen peered out as a mole might do when it first protrudes its nose into the sunshine. Around his neck he wore a green and white kerchief which bore witness to countless long-forgotten greasy meals. On his head he wore what I can only describe as a tightly fitting inverted black woollen stocking. His face was fat, two little piggy eyes peered out of deeply set sockets, his nose was squat and broad. On his cheeks and chin, a white and unkempt beard played host to the remains of the morning's breakfast. He smelt as if he had fallen into a cesspit and then dried off in the sun, so it was that I first made the acquaintance of Solomon Fenn, the rat catcher, and his terrier, Nutmeg.

"He turned his head towards me and then looked me up and down before addressing me in a deep rasping voice. "Do yer want a day's work boy?" he said. "Doing what?" I asked. "Ratting," he replied. His smell and appearance were such that my first reaction was to get away from him as quickly as I could, but hunger is a hard master and I had not eaten since the previous evening and the desires of my empty stomach to be filled were overwhelming. It was moreover clear from looking at Solomon's great belly that there was money in ratting. So I accepted his offer and agreed a day's wages. Solomon hailed a waterman and soon he and I, together with Nutmeg, were upon the river.

"It was the first time that I had been in a boat and I gazed in wonder at all around me. We were soon alongside a large merchant ship moored in the middle of the river and I scrambled up a rope that had been let down over the side. Solomon's entrance took rather longer. He stood up in the boat and grabbed at the swinging rope. He missed and fell upon the startled waterman who collapsed in a stream of oaths under him. Recovering himself, Solomon took hold of the rope and placed one of his large feet on the side of the boat in order to commence his climb, but such was his weight that he drove the side of the boat down into the river almost capsizing it, and the result of this attempt at boarding was that he once again fell back on the wretched waterman. Meanwhile Nutmeg, who had clearly seen it all before, sat quietly in the stern of the boat watching the fun. The noise from the boat drew a number of the crew to the vessel's side and eventually a rope was thrown which Solomon tied stoutly around his considerable girth. He then placed Nutmeg on his shoulder and holding tightly onto the rope, they were hauled by two straining sailors and myself over the ship's rails and onto the deck. The boat, relieved of Solomon's weight, shot away like a cork out of a bottle. Solomon picked himself up as if nothing had happened and readied himself, or more strictly Nutmeg and I, for work.

"The vessel was infested with rats. For the first few hours Nutmeg did all the work flushing them out from all over the two upper decks where the rats had brazenly made their homes. He moved quickly and efficiently: a rat would break from its cover, Nutmeg would pursue it and then with a lightning flash of his jaws, bite it at the back of the neck and shake it before dropping it dead at the feet of Solomon. Soon a pile of dead rats lay upon the deck. Solomon picked each up in turn and cut their tails off which he placed in a large canvas bag with the intention, no doubt, of claiming the bounty offered by the parish for rats killed within the parish. The dead rats, he then threw over the side. He and Nutmeg were clearly an effective team and I began to wonder what use I could possibly be. Soon the two upper decks were cleared, the rats were either dead or they had retreated to their natural territory; the lower deck, the hold and the bilges of the vessel. Access to these areas was confined and there was no way that Solomon's vast frame could enter. I, on the other hand, was small and wiry. Solomon took from the depths of his pockets two small wooden boxes with holes in the top and sides. The boxes contained an evil-smelling powder into which he placed pieces of charcoal that he lit before closing the lids tightly. The evil-smelling smoke which coiled out through the holes explained in part the smell I had first noted when we met.

"Solomon explained to me that I was to place the smouldering boxes deep in the bowels of the ship and that the noxious fumes would soon drive the rats from their homes up into the upper decks where Nutmeg would await them. I descended down to the lowest deck of the vessel and pulled open a small trap door that gave entry to the bilges of the ship. The smell of the filthy water in the bilges, combined with the smoke from the boxes, almost overwhelmed me. I lowered myself gingerly down into the bilges. There was only about eighteen inches of headroom between the keel of the ship and the deck above. Then, as instructed, I crawled on my stomach in pitch blackness with one of the boxes for about twenty yards before depositing it. I then had to slither backwards in the dark, paying out a stout rope which was tied to a ring on the top of the box. The smell was overpowering. I could hear the squeals of the rats as the smoke started to take effect, and before I reached the trapdoor a number of the more ferocious of their number scrabbled by me in the narrow passage, scratching and biting me as they passed. It was with great relief that I reached the trapdoor and climbed out before slamming it shut. I then ran up to the upper deck and gulped in the fresh air. When I had recovered, I went down to the bottom of the other end of the ship with the second box which I placed in the same manner as the first before returning to the upper deck and emptying my lungs of the foul smoke. For the next few hours there was mayhem on the lower deck as the rats were driven from their ancestral homes by the fumes only to meet Nutmeg. Nothing could be heard other than the squealing of the terrified rats, the excited barking of Nutmeg as he went about his work, and the thud of a lifeless rat as it hit the deck once Nutmeg had released it from his jaws. Eventually all was quiet and Solomon eased his massive frame down to the lower deck and I followed him. A scene of carnage met our eyes: there were dead rats everywhere. Some of them were the biggest I had ever seen. Nutmeg lay on a coil of rope, his sides panting with his exertions. Solomon took out a large marrow bone from within the depths of his voluminous coat and tossed it to Nutmeg, who fell upon it and started to gnaw on it with relish and satisfaction, though how he managed to do so given the work his jaws had already done, I shall never know. Solomon set about cutting off the rats' tails whilst I went and recovered the two boxes, the contents of which had burnt out although the boxes still smelt vile. That done, I had the unpleasant job of taking the dead and bloody rat corpses up onto the main deck and throwing them in the river.

"Our work over, Solomon hailed a passing waterman, but he, no doubt warned on the river of the earlier events of our boarding the vessel, sculled quickly away, to a stream of mighty oaths from Solomon who was anxious to get ashore to slake his thirst and feed his mighty belly. After sometime, an unsuspecting waterman came by and the troubles of our boarding the vessel were repeated in Solomon's descent into the boat below. Having climbed with difficulty over the side of the vessel, he took hold of the rope that led to the water's edge and started to lower himself down. As his feet reached the side of the boat below, the tide lifted the vessel we were leaving and Solomon went up before crashing down again into the bottom of the boat, narrowly missing the waterman and landing on top of myself and Nutmeg. Once he had composed himself, Solomon ordered the waterman to land us at the Cherry Garden Stairs at Rotherhithe. On clambering to the top of the stairs, he stopped and paid me fairly for my day's efforts and said, "See you here in the morning at ten." With that, he made off in the direction of the Angel public house. So it was that I first earned any wages in this world and I wish to God that I had always been treated as fairly in my employment as I was then and thereafter by Solomon.

"By now, I was almost faint with hunger and I made haste to a pie shop where I purchased two mutton pies and a jam tart which I ate greedily. Never had food tasted so good as this simple fare. Having eaten, I went to a bakers and purchased half a loaf which I placed under my shirt for the morrow. That night I slept in a shop doorway, sheltered from the rain which had set in. I awoke, stiff and cramped, on the arrival of the shopkeeper who sent me on my way with a cuff around my ears and made my way through the drizzle to the stairs to meet Solomon and to eat my bread. True to his word Solomon arrived, though from his gait and his speech he had clearly not recovered from his excesses of the previous evening. He acknowledged me with no more than a nod and we set off to a nearby warehouse where we set about work in the same manner as the previous day. Solomon and Nutmeg were clearly very good at what they did and were much in demand in the rat-infested wharves, warehouses, granaries and ships along the river."

Sawson stopped his narrative for a moment and again peered anxiously out of the sitting room window before continuing with his history.

"I continued to work as 'the rat catcher's boy' for over four years. It was a hard life but Solomon, for all his faults, was not a hard master and always paid me fairly and after a few weeks when he came to realise my true situation, he agreed that I could sleep in the back room of a wretched house that he lived in at the bottom of Deptford High Street. It was, in truth, the filthiest hovel imaginable and smelt dreadful, but it had a roof and I was protected from the elements. In the heat of summer, the stench was such that I preferred to sleep out in the small yard at the rear. During this time, I became accustomed to the ways of the street and made the acquaintance of a variety of unsavoury characters and street urchins and I am ashamed to say, it was not long before I found myself engaged in petty crime, though the penalties for such misdemeanours were anything but petty.

"It was Solomon himself who first encouraged me to steal. I soon noticed that his long black coat was not only used to carry the tools of his trade but it had within it numerous pockets into which he could quickly slip any small article which took his fancy as he went about his business, and it was not long before I was assisting him in his thievery. As my part of the work often involved me working in confined spaces with the evil-smelling boxes, opportunities to steal presented themselves to me and I soon became extremely light-fingered in my own right. The stolen items had, of course, to be disposed of and converted into money and thus it was that Solomon introduced me to Bully Turner. It was that fatal introduction which was eventually to cause me to flee England and lead indirectly to the dangers we face today."

A QUART OF GIN

Sawson, having gone to the kitchen and taken a long drink of water, returned to his family and continued:

"Midway up Deptford High Street on the right hand side stands 'The Seven Seas'. It was at the time, and no doubt still is, a favourite haunt of sailors and dockyard workers. But it was also frequented by thieves, cut-throats, doxies, horse thieves, footpads and others of ill repute. The landlord was Bully Turner. He was, at first meeting, a charming and quietly spoken man, but appearances can be deceptive, for he was without doubt one of the most evil and dangerous men that I have ever met. Though he looked as if butter would not melt in his mouth, cross him and there was every chance that you would be set upon in a dark alleyway by a band of ruffians and beaten within an inch of your life and that would be if you were lucky; your most likely fate would be a knife in the ribs and a splash as your corpse went into the river. There was no crime that occurred in Deptford or Greenwich or up on 'The Heath' that Bully was unaware of, and most of it occurred with his sanction.

"The Seven Seas was a bow-fronted building. The main door led into a large, wood-panelled room with a long bar at one end. On each side of the room two wooden doors in the panelling opened into two smaller rooms: when the doors were closed, there was absolute privacy for those inside, indeed it was difficult to make out where the panelling ended and the doors started.

Within these rooms, all manner of crimes were planned and subsequently celebrated. When he was not in the bar area, Bully held court in the furthest room on the right. In the right hand corner of the main bar room a broad staircase led to a first floor eating room, whilst a further staircase led to the second floor where there was a bawdy house. To the side of the tavern, a narrow lane led to stables sufficient for twenty horses. The first occasion that I entered the Seven Seas was in the company of Solomon. Having called the pot man and ordered a tankard of foaming ale for himself and bread and meat for the two of us, he turned to me and said, "Watch, listen and learn." Once we had finished our meal he called out to the pot man, "Bring me a quart of gin!" I took no real notice of his request, taking it to mean simply a request for a further drink, but no drink arrived. A short while later the pot man approached us and said in a low voice, "Bully will see you." With that, Solomon stood up and opened the door in the panelling to Bully's room. On entering the room, I looked about me: it was also panelled and I thought, though I could not be sure, that that there was a door concealed in it similar to that through which we had entered. Bully sat on one side of a small table, to his left on the floor sat Major, the fattest bulldog I had ever seen. As we approached the table, Major tensed but quickly realising that the canine visitor was Nutmeg who he clearly knew well, he relaxed and reverted to the heavy panting that is common to dogs of his breed. Bully looked at me suspiciously, but was reassured by Solomon saying, "He's with me, Bully." With that, Solomon took a number of items out of his coat, some of which I had seen earlier that day at our place of work. Without a word he handed them to Bully who examined them carefully before offering Solomon a price. After a small amount of haggling, a price was agreed and Bully withdrew a number of coins from a large money bag which hung around his waist and handed them to Solomon who, having counted them, turned without a word and left, no doubt to the relief of Bully, for to be in a small room with him was not kind to the nose. As we left, I saw out of the corner of my eye Bully placing the items we had brought into a hole in the wood panelling that had suddenly appeared.

"Following this visit, I was a frequent visitor to the Seven Seas both on my own account and often on Solomon's, when the items he had to sell, such as a silk handkerchief or a gentleman's shirt, commanded a set price. The procedure was always the same: on entering I would sit down and await the arrival of the pot man and then say, "Bring me a quart of gin." Such words always effecting an entrance to Bully's room. On one such occasion, having completed a sale of some tallow candles that I had 'found' in St Paul's Church in Deptford and being about to leave, Bully called me back and asked me if I would be interested in doing a little bit of work for him. There was, he told me, a horse of his at the Green Man at the top of Blackheath Hill that he wanted brought to the Seven Seas that night. I was in no doubt that the horse was stolen and I was confirmed in that belief when Bully told me that if questioned about the horse, I was to say that I had been asked by a man who I had met at Deptford Green, to fetch the horse and take it to the Seven Seas where he would meet me. When I got to the Green Man I was to ask the landlord, an Irishman called Jimmy Power, "if he had anything for Bully." I agreed and set off. Having crossed the Ravensbourne that runs into Deptford Creek and then into the Thames, I was soon making my way up Blackheath Hill. My progress was fast, not so the many carriages and stagecoaches making their way up the rutted road to the top of the hill to the wide, open space that is Blackheath. Such is the climb that the labouring and straining horses had to be changed when they reached the top. It was this need for fresh horses that gave the Green Man such importance.

It was a large, ramshackle building set back on the right hand side of the road, just after the brow of the hill; it had stabling for over two hundred horse at the rear. I made my way into the inn and inquired of Power. I eventually found him at the rear of the premises, supervising the shoeing of a carriage horse. He was a villainous-looking man with a broken nose and a massive sabre scar down the left side of his face, no doubt a souvenir of the wars with the French, he having served, so I later learnt, as a cavalry trooper. He appeared none too pleased to see me in the stable area and swore violently at me, telling me to leave at once or he would have my liver out. I stood my ground and looked at him straight in the eye. "Have you anything for Bully?" I said. The question brought about an immediate change in his demeanour: he smiled as best he could with the limitations of his scar. That I have," he said. "Come with me." I followed him to a long stable block, one of two which stood on either side of a wide yard sufficient for a coach to turn in. On entering the block, he continued down a central walkway with stables on both sides. The block was a hive of activity: horses were being brought in to be brushed down, fed, watered and rested. Others were being taken out to be harnessed to carriages, hired to travellers or, if they had thrown a shoe or needed a fresh set of shoes, to the farrier's forge at the end of the block. Everywhere there were grooms, ostlers, coachmen, stable boys darting in and out of the stables, tack rooms and haylofts. To the outsider, it seemed a picture of total confusion, the reality was that it was anything but. It was a busy and thriving business and Jimmy Power ruled over it with a rod of iron. It was also, as I soon came to find out, the centre of a profitable horse stealing business: with horses entering and leaving every hour of the night, it was the perfect place to bring a stolen horse. Once there, it could be easily concealed. Its coat could be dyed, its shoes changed to avoid detection (for every farrier or blacksmith can recognise a shoe made by him). After a while, the horse would be moved on either to the Seven Seas where Bully, with his many contacts, would quickly pass it on, or it would be taken across the horse ferry at Greenwich to be sold in Essex.

"Half the way down the block, Power stopped outside a stable in which a brood mare stood. He was quickly joined by a small, wiry man. He did not introduce me to him at the time, but I came to know him well: he was a Scotsman, Tommy Darroch, a renowned horse thief who subsequently ended his life on the scaffold outside Newgate prison as a result of the events I am about to recall. Tommy was the scourge of horse owners in Kent. It was said that he only had to look at a horse and it would follow him and that on one occasion, having travelled to Chelmsford in Essex on market day, he almost caused a riot when a number of former 'Kent horses' recognised and tried to follow him. Tommy opened the stable door and led out the brood mare. He looked at Jimmy Power who nodded and said, "Bully sent him." With that, Tommy went back into the stable and approached and pulled at the wooden manger that was attached to the back of the stable.

To my surprise, the manger moved as did the wooden wall to which it was attached, revealing a further stable in which a chestnut-coloured hunter was tethered. He attached a halter to the horse and then led it out into the yard, all the time stroking the horse and whispering to it. After a minute or so he handed the short reins to the halter to me and I set out.

"It was a warm spring evening as I made my way down Blackheath Hill with my charge. The sun was setting to the west over London. There were still carriages and horsemen on the hill, but nobody paid any attention to a boy leading a horse. The journey passed without trouble and the horse was soon secure in a stable at the Seven Seas and I was well paid for 'my little bit of work' by Bully.

"For the next year or so I continued to work with Solomon, though at the same time I continued to do 'little bits of work' for Bully. One summer evening, having gone to the Seven Seas to dispose of some items on behalf of Solomon, Bully asked if I would be interested in some different work. It would not be dangerous, he said, but it required a lad with steady nerves. I was then all of ten years of age, but given the hard lessons of life I had experienced, I was as hard a little urchin as had ever walked the streets of Deptford and the adjoining river parishes and I was flattered that Bully should think of me thus. I immediately said that I was interested and I agreed to return the following evening at eight when the 'business in hand' was to be discussed. I wish to God I hadn't agreed.

"I arrived at the Seven Seas the following evening and having called for a "quart of gin," I gained entry to Bully's room where I found him in company with Tommy and a younger man,

Bob Chandler. I had never spoken with Chandler before but I was aware of him, for it was said of him that he made his living on the highway preying on travellers and coaches on Blackheath and Shooters Hill. He was about twenty-five years of age and was always well dressed with plenty of money, popular with the younger women of Deptford and the surrounding area. He had, however, a reputation for hard drinking and violence, especially if he was in drink and most people steered well clear of him. On my arrival, Bully got down to business.

"You all know Samuel Clegg," he said and indeed everyone did. Samuel Clegg lived at 26, Albury Street in Deptford: it was a fine house as befitted the bailiff to Sir Gregory Page who owned a large amount of land and property in the area. Sir Gregory lived in Wricklemarsh House, a stately residence surrounded by acres of parkland that bordered the southern side of Blackheath. Samuel Clegg would collect the tenants' rents on the usual quarter days and then on the following day he would ride to Wricklemarsh House to account for and deliver the rents that he had received. The sums collected were large, and Bully had resolved that he would have them.

"Samuel Clegg was a short, stocky, red-faced man in his early sixties. It was known that he had been a soldier in his early years and he was said to be a good horseman. He would, said Bully, put up a fight. The obvious and indeed the only place to rob him was after he left the Dover Road which crossed the heath east to west and rode off to the south across the heath on the track through the gorse bushes that led to the gates of the Wrinklemarsh estate. There was, said Bully, little doubt that if he caught sight of a horseman as he rode across the heath with a

45

large sum of money, his natural caution would lead him to flight: he must therefore be taken by surprise and that is where I came in. Half the way along the track travelling south, there was a natural indentation in the sandy soil close to the track. It was obscured by the gorse and there was room for two men to lie there unobserved by a horseman on the track. The plan was that I should station myself on the track and cause Clegg to stop by pretending that I was lost, whilst hiding my face as much as possible. As I did so, Darroch and Chandler, both masked, were to quickly approach him from behind with Darroch taking hold of the horse's reins, while Chandler was to pull Clegg to the ground where he would be robbed by Darroch and Chandler whilst I held the horse, having pulled a handkerchief up over my lower face. The plan then was that Darroch should ride off on the horse with the money, whilst Chandler and I were to make our escape on foot across the heath to the Green Man and hide in the concealed stable and remain there until word came from Bully that the coast was clear, following which we were to return to the Seven Stars. In case it was necessary to rapidly change our plans of escape and lie up somewhere else, Bully advanced each of us a small sum of money against our expected share of the plunder.

"The next day was quarter day, so that evening Darroch, Chandler and I slept in the concealed stable at the Green Man, leaving early the following morning to take up our positions. Thus it was that at eleven in the morning I climbed out of our hiding place and awaited the arrival of Samuel Clegg. Shortly after, the sound of trotting hooves could be heard and Clegg, whom I immediately recognised, came into sight. I played my part as he came towards me: I stood in the middle of the track and called out, "Please sir, I am lost." He drew his horse up, but at the same time, whether through instinct or natural caution, he looked sharply about him and saw a movement in the bushes at which he pulled his horse around in the direction of the road and dug in his spurs. As he did so, Darroch made a desperate but unsuccessful lunge at the reins, causing the horse to rear up at which point Chandler who, unknown to me, had a pistol upon him, discharged it at Clegg at a range of no more than six feet. The ball hit him full in the face killing him instantly whilst the horse bolted, dragging with it Clegg's body, his left foot being caught in the stirrup. Darroch and Chandler, eager to get the money and knowing that the body would cause it to slow down, set off in pursuit whilst I, overcome with shock and the enormity of what had happened, threw myself into the hiding place from which we had sprung and sobbed and sobbed with regret and despair.

"My decision not to pursue the horse was my salvation. I did not witness what happened next, but from what I could hear and was subsequently told, it ended like this. The shot had been heard by a troop of Hussars en route to Chatham. They set off in the direction of the sound and came upon Darroch and Chandler as they were plundering Clegg's corpse. On seeing the soldiers, the two men fled. Chandler, in attempting to escape and no doubt knowing the fate that awaited him, fired upon a pursuing trooper. He missed and was run through with a sabre and died there and then. Darroch was eventually hung for the wilful murder of Samuel Clegg, 'a murder committed with Robert Chandler deceased.' Of my name there was no mention. At the time, I had no idea of what had happened to my companions in crime and I lay on the heath all that day crying and vowing that I would never again involve myself in crime, a vow that I have kept to this day.

At nightfall I left my hiding place. A sixth sense warned me to keep away from The Seven Seas, for I had little doubt that if things had gone badly, Bully would not welcome me and indeed he was quite capable of organising my disposal if it was necessary. I waited till the road across the heath was quiet and made for Crooms Hill and from there descended down into Greenwich and then via the Creek Road to St Nicholas' church in Deptford. As I made my way through the gates into the churchyard, the stone skull and crossbones that surmount the pillars to the gates seemed to grin at me in welcome and I thought of Samuel Clegg and cried as if my heart would break.

"I slept that night and the following two nights in the charnel house at St Nicholas'. I got word of my predicament to Solomon through old Ted Joyce, the night watchman, and late in the evening of the fourth day, I made my way across the green outside the church to the river steps by the shipwright's house. Here a waterman, sent by Solomon, picked me up and rowed me to the 'Lichfield' moored in the river awaiting the morning tide before sailing for Gibraltar. As I looked back to the dark riverbank and at the ripe old age of ten, my heart lifted at the thought of the new life before me."

AFLOAT

"I scrambled up the side of the Lichfield and on reaching the deck I became aware of a young sailor approaching a member of the starboard watch, who were preparing to weigh anchor as soon as the tide turned. "You will be the new ship's boy?" he asked. This was news to me, for I had no idea in what capacity Solomon had arranged for me be taken on, but I readily agreed. "The captain told me to tell you to keep out of the way until he has time to sign you on and tell you your duties," he said, introducing himself as Richard Ball. "But everyone calls me Bounce," he said with a grin. I followed him towards the quarter deck and at his direction positioned myself on a coil of rope beneath the starboard ladder. "Wait there," he said and disappeared. It was a balmy night with a full moon. On the bank the buildings of the dockyard were silhouetted in the moonlight, the river flowed sluggishly towards the city, the tide was about to turn and as I looked about the ship I became aware of the crew, both watches being on deck, standing at their appointed stations ready for the moment when the tide turned.

"A shrill whistle from the quarter deck above pierced the silence, followed by much shouting of orders. One of the sailors started a shanty: "As I was walking down Paradise Street". The crew joined in lustily with the chorus: "Blow the man down bullies", as they strained at the capstan bars to lift the anchor out of the muddy embraces of the London river. Once the anchor was on its way up through the flowing waters, there were further shouts and whistles as some sailors climbed onto the lower rigging where gaskets were untied and sails unfurled, while others pulled at a bewildering combination of ropes. The Lichfield, now freed of her shackles, came alive and taken by the ebbing tide, started her voyage to Gibraltar. I remained at my appointed station and watched familiar landmarks glide by: Deptford Creek gave way to Greenwich with the spire of St Alfege's church bathed in the first rays of the rising sun. The magnificent buildings of the Greenwich Hospital, where ancient seamen lay snoring with contentment, dreaming of foreign lands, exotic ports and the girls, now grandmothers, who they had met there, loved and promised faithfully to return to, but never had. Onwards to Blackwall Point and the vast stretch of Bugsby's reach. Soon Charlton house could be seen high on the hill. The Lichfield sailed on past the Arsenal at Woolwich, where a warship with warning flags flying was taking on gun powder and shot.

"That's the Tryton," said Bounce as we passed by. "She's a sixth-rate frigate with twenty-four guns." The Lichfield progressed on, passing the marshes bordering Gallions Reach, before reaching that broad loop in the river on which sits Erith village; ahead the muddy waters of the river Darenth, having flowed lazily from Otford through Farningham and Dartford now reluctantly, as if afraid to lose their identity, joined the Thames. A favourable breeze now filled the lower canvas and her speed through the water increased as, anxious to escape the confines of the river and the land which had held her, she raced to meet the sea."

Sawson paused, outside all was quiet, inside you could have heard a pin drop, he continued:

"Once the Lichfield had passed Tilbury Fort and the busy riverside town of Gravesend and as the estuary opened up, Bounce called me and I moved out onto the deck and followed him through the double doors under the starboard side of the quarter deck which led to the captain's cabin. He knocked and was bidden to enter. Captain Hayward was a tall bluff man in his late fifties. He was a man of few words, but what he did say was always to the point and woe betides anyone who did not immediately jump to when he gave an order. He had been at sea, man and boy, all his life: what he did not know about the sea and the sailing of ships was not worth knowing. He had formerly served with the East India Company and in common with many of the masters of their vessels, he would, as nightfall approached, take in sail, no matter how favourable the conditions, before retiring to his cabin and cot, with standing orders to the first and second mates that he should be called if there was a change in the prevailing weather and sea conditions in their respective watches. He was, in short, a careful and cautious sailor and although the crew might, on occasions, grumble as sail was taken in and the Lichfield's speed through the waters was reduced, many of them had sailed with him on previous voyages and his reputation was such that he never had any difficulty in finding a crew.

"In truth there was no need for a speedy passage: The Lichfield's owners had chartered her to carry stores from the naval dockyards at Deptford and Plymouth to the dockyard at Gibraltar which supplied the needs of His Majesty's Ships in the Mediterranean. She had for this voyage loaded a cargo of barrels of salted pork and beef, and cases of ship's biscuits and sacks of flour from the great warehouses at Deptford. On other voyages from Plymouth she carried gunpowder, spars, rope and canvas, together with wood that was in short supply in Gibraltar. Captain Hayward looked up from a chart he was studying and eyed me carefully. "Have you been to sea before boy?" he asked. "No," I replied. "I have two pieces of advice for you, mark them well. Firstly, just do as you are instructed and there will be no complaints. If you don't, you will feel the weight of my hand. Secondly, as you go about your duties on deck and in the rigging, always have one hand for the ship and one for yourself." He then proceeded to tell me what my duties were as a ship's boy. Many of them were expressed in nautical terms, the meaning of which was lost on me though I nodded vigorously at what I thought were appropriate moments. It seemed to come down to this: I was to do whatever anyone on the ship told me to do as and when instructed. The captain made no mention of what I was to be paid and I was too frightened and tongue-tied to ask. I need not have worried, for as I was to learn, he was an honourable man and I was paid my due wages at the end of the voyage, less the cost of the necessary items of seafarer's clothing which I had of necessity to purchase from the slop chest, which left me with precious little. I was then signed on as a member of the crew, which I did by making a cross where he directed me to, for I could not at that time read or write. That done, he ordered Bounce to show me to my quarters and turned back to his chart.

"I followed Bounce along the deck to the fo'c'sle and descending a short ladder, found myself in almost total darkness, the only light coming from the hatch through which I had climbed. As my eyes adjusted, I became aware of what appeared to be rough wooden shelves to the left, right and immediately in front of me, on some of which the starboard watch were sleeping. Bounce pointed out an empty top shelf. "That's your bunk," he said and left. I climbed up to the bunk that required me to use the two occupied bunks below as steps. As I did so, the Lichfield lurched, causing me to fall back onto the deck. In doing so, I managed to kick the head of the occupant of the bunk below, who cursed me in low German before returning to his slumbers. I managed to reach my lofty perch and to crawl over the wooden lip on the side which prevented its user from falling out when the ship heaved and rolled. The foscle was already wet and damp, the air was foul, but I had not slept since the previous night in the charnel house and with the gentle movement of the ship as she rode over a calm sea, I fell into a deep refreshing slumber.

"I was awoken by the sound of the ship's bell being rung and the curses and shouts of the starboard watch as they awoke and prepared to go on deck and relieve the port watch. The watches had been selected by the mates as the Lichfield had come down the river, when I was keeping out of the way, and I was not therefore a member of either, it was tempting to return to my slumbers, but I sensed that I should be on deck and I was right. I climbed up the ladder to find it was early morning. The Lichfield had left the estuary, passed the Nore and was sailing down the North Sea with Kent to starboard, towards the Channel. The wind was slight and gradually died away and we found ourselves becalmed in the Downs off Deal, along with many other vessels awaiting a favourable wind for our passage down the Channel. I stood for a moment wondering what to do. I need not have worried, the ship's cook stuck his head out from his galley in the small deckhouse amidships and ordered me to carry a bowl of hot water to the captain so that he might shave. That completed, I returned with his breakfast. That set the pattern for the rest of the day: helping the cook in the galley, the carpenter in his shop and below deck, the sail maker, an old and kindly German called Goldstaub, as well as being at the beck and call of the first mate, Mr Hawksworth, who had the starboard watch and the second mate, Mr Newton, who had the port watch.

"I worked from dawn to dusk and longer if necessary. As the ship's boy my duties at this stage did not include any involvement in the actual sailing of the ship other than pulling at a rope as and when directed. I was not allowed to go aloft, but this soon changed. As a result, like the cook, sail maker and carpenter, who all slept in the small deckhouse, I did not belong to either watch, and did not have to turn out with the watch at night, unless conditions required it and the order was given: "All hands on deck!" at which everyone would turn to. The Lichfield lay with other vessels waiting for the wind for over a week, during which time the stout boatmen of Deal rowed out on two or three occasions to sell produce to the assembled ships. As each day passed, I learned more and slowly the sense of bewilderment that I had felt when I first came on board left me. I began to understand the nautical terms that had originally seemed like double dutch to me, but as yet with the ship becalmed, the numerous ropes, blocks, pulleys and the rigging and sails remained a mystery.

"On the evening of the eighth day, I was standing at the door of the galley talking with the cook and Goldstaub when I felt a breeze. Mr Hawksworth, who was on deck, felt it too and sent me to tell the captain. On hearing the news, Captain Hayward came on deck, looked about him and immediately ordered, "All hands on deck!" The men went to the capstan and the sea anchor was soon hauled aboard and catted, men sprung into the rigging, the sails started to fill and the Lichfield was on her way down the Channel, accompanied by the shouts and shanties from the vessels all around as they set sail. The wind continued to blow favourably and the Lichfield, though heavily laden, under full sail made a good run down the Channel. During the first few days I was frequently taken by surprise and lost my footing as the Lichfield rode up on a wave and plunged down into a trough before rising up to meet the next wave. As I picked myself up out of the scuppers, the sailors would laugh and tell me that this was nothing: "Just wait till we are in the bay," they would say, "then you will see some real waves." I soon gained my sea legs but not before I had spilt the captain's shaving water and dropped his breakfast on the deck, which I then had to scrub clean.

"My stomach at this time was reluctant to entertain any of the food that I forced myself to eat, but it eventually capitulated and I never again suffered from sea sickness, though I have never been sure to this date whether this early sickness was due to the rolling of the ship or the vile food that old Hepburn the cook produced. He had been a sailor all his life until a fall from the deck into the hold had smashed both his legs leaving him crippled and unable to follow his former calling. That he had formerly been a sailor seemed to be his only qualification for being a cook and it showed: his efforts at cooking were bad enough with the fresh produce, but when that ran out, his attempts at cooking the salt pork and salt beef from the ship's stores resulted in an ungodly mess which was eaten with bad grace by the crew as was the stodgy and lumpy bread he baked. In fairness to him, the food that was provided to him to cook was revolting. Not long into the voyage, I helped him open a barrel of salt pork. The smell that came from it was overpowering, but that was nothing as to the appearance of the contents, great globules of yellow fat floated on the brine. Hepburn fished out a large piece of pork. It was green and slimy and smelt to high heaven. I did not eat that day.

"The winds continued to be favourable: soon Ushant was off our port quarter and the Lichfield was in the Bay of Biscay, which I had been awaiting with trepidation. I need not have worried, for the big seas I feared did not arrive, though I was to experience them with all their might and fury on subsequent voyages. The Bay was traversed without mishap and the Lichfield was soon off the south western coast of Spain, sailing south towards the straits of Gibraltar where the waters of the Atlantic meet those of the Mediterranean. As we sailed south, the days became warmer. Many of the sailors abandoned their dark and damp quarters below and slept on deck under the stars. The horrors of that day on Blackheath started to fade and for the first time in my life I was happy with my lot.

"One morning I was sitting with old Goldstaub on the main deck as he patched a sail. He was short in stature with close-cropped silver hair and was brown as a berry with twinkling eyes. He was a native of Rostock on the Baltic Sea and spoke with a heavy German accent. Earlier on in the voyage he had asked me if I could read and write. When I said that I could not, he replied,

"Vell then, I vill teach you." Thereafter, whenever I was working with him and sometimes in the dog watches at sea when he and I had no pressing tasks, he would instruct me in reading and writing. So thorough was he, that sometimes I spell a word with a German pronunciation! One day, as he sat there teaching me my letters, sewing and chewing a quid of tobacco, the first mate approached. Mr Hawksworth was a stocky bearded man of prodigious strength: he came from Yorkshire and had sailed from Whitby in colliers for many years. He was a good seaman and had once been a ship's master but his one failing was a love of beer and spirits and he had long since lost his command. He was as good a first mate as the captain could have wanted when at sea, but as soon as he was in port he became a different kettle of fish when he succumbed to the delights of the dockside taverns and girls.

"Looking up he saw Bounce high on the lower yard arm with two sailors tying the gaskets on a sail which they had just furled. "Get up there and help them!" he ordered. I did not wait to consider his order and climbed at once into the rigging. I did not look down and on reaching the yard arm I placed my feet on the futtocks and edged my way gingerly out onto the yard, all the time mindful of the captain's second piece of advice: "One hand for the ship and one for yourself." If truth be told, the work was over by the time I got out on the yard as Mr Hawksworth knew it would be, but I had been aloft, albeit only as far up as the lower yard arm. Higher climbs would come later. On reaching the safety of the rigging and looking down at the ship below and seeing old Hepburn hobbling along the deck never again to soar high above the ship, I was elated. I was afloat! I was a sailor! I had found my world. I descended to the deck to a gruff "Well done boy" from Mr Hawksworth and a roar from old Hepburn to fetch some fresh water.

"The Litchfield continued to be blessed with fair winds and calm seas and it was with great excitement that I stood on her decks as she entered the straits with Spain on her port side and to the starboard through the heat haze I could see Africa and the Barbary coast. It was a long way from catching rats in Wapping. The excitement continued as we approached the harbour at Gibraltar, where twelve ships of the line from our Mediterranean fleet lay moored. The Litchfield sailed slowly through the anchorage with the great rock towering above and late on a sunny afternoon she was securely moored alongside the stone quay of the dockyard warehouses. There was, to my disappointment, to be no early shore leave for the crew, for there was work to be done in the cool early hours of the morning. Dawn broke and with it, the Litchfield became a hive of activity as the olive-skinned dockyard workers came aboard to unload the ship, whilst the sailors half-heartedly went about their duties, overhauling the rigging, cleaning the hold as the cargo was unloaded and a hundred and one other jobs that the mates had found for them. At last the unloading was completed and the crew who had signed on for the round trip were given an advance on their wages and two days shore leave. I was desperate to go ashore, but I was required to remain on board to carry on with my duties, as well as carrying messages from the captain to a variety of dockyard officials as the Litchfield was provisioned for the voyage back to England. I began to fear that I would never get beyond the dockyard gates, when I was summoned by the captain to accompany him to the governor's residence where he had business.

"Having left the ship and the dockyard we passed through a gate in the casement and we were soon walking up the narrow street that leads to the convent where the governor's residence is. As I walked through the streets, my senses were assaulted by a rich variety of sounds and smells. It was like England, but it was not England. A file of marines marched by, resplendent in their scarlet, whilst coming the other way a group of dark-skinned children called to each other in a tongue I did not know. Street vendors offered exotic fruits, whilst cheek by jowl with The Albion Tavern stood an eating house from which came the smell of delicious spicy food and all the time the sun beat down, causing the captain to sweat profusely and to buy two cups of delicious sweet water and two oranges. Thus refreshed, we arrived at the convent. From the outside, it was an unassuming building marked only by the sentries who stood stiffly in the burning sun in uniforms which would have kept them warm on an autumn day in England. On passing through the wooden gates, we entered a beautiful shaded courtyard full of exotic flowers and shrubs giving off delicious scents, the like of which I had never smelt. I remained there listening to the splashing fountain, it was the most beautiful place I had ever seen. The captain having finished his business, we retraced our steps through the bustling streets to the ship.

"The following day, the captain, who did not like the heat, advanced me a small sum from my wages and sent me ashore with a letter to the owner's agents. It would take a few hours for a reply, he said, and I might remain ashore in the meantime. I hurried ashore and having delivered the letter, I set about exploring the town and purchasing peaches, oranges and a bunch of fat juicy grapes to refresh myself when the heat became too much. I climbed through streets so narrow that two people could not walk abreast, to a shady spot above the town and looked out across the bay to Spain and further to my left across the straits to where the dark mountains of Africa emerged from the sea. On descending to the town to collect the captain's reply, I passed the Albion, where a drunken Yorkshire voice and a woman's laugh showed Mr Hawksworth to be at home.

"The Litchfield commenced loading. Usually there was little cargo for home, but on this occasion she was heavily loaded with the equipment of a battalion of infantry who were returning to England by a separate ship after service on the Rock. Mr Hawksworth still being ashore to the annoyance of the captain, the loading was supervised by the second mate in his stead. The day before she sailed, whilst the loading continued, I was given a day's shore leave and together with Bounce we climbed slowly in the heat along a winding road, passing gun emplacements and the entrance to a tunnel driven deep in the rock, inside which the muzzles of cannons peered wickedly towards Spain. Eventually we stopped and the deep inviting blue sea of the Mediterranean lay below and beyond and I wondered if I would ever sail those waters. Little did I know.

"We returned to the ship to find the loading complete and Mr Hawksworth on board in a foul mood, no doubt caused by a sore head and a lashing from the captain's tongue. Early the next morning the stout hawsers tethering the Litchfield to the quay were loosened and she commenced her voyage back to England."

SHIPWRECKED

Sawson stopped his tale while Molly and Anne bought refreshment. Then fortified by a large wedge of cheese and thick slices of crusty bread, he continued:

"The voyage back to London was everything the voyage out had not been. On entering the Bay of Biscay, we experienced persistent heavy rain and heavy seas, it was if the Bay was saying, "you had it easy last time, now you will pay". The Litchfield, heavily laden, made slow progress through the waves. Lifelines were rigged to prevent those of the crew who had to be on deck being swept away when she shipped a heavy sea and they had not made the safety of the lower rigging, whilst the helmsman was lashed to the wheel. She rose on the enormous waves and her bow then crashed down and was engulfed in the foaming waters, before slowly rising with water pouring out of the scuppers. The captain remained on deck without sleep for two days and nights and the sight of him standing there calmly gave me hope and reassured me that we would make port. I was not at all certain now that I had in fact 'found my world'.

"The winds abated and the seas moderated, though the rain continued. Old Hepburn and I managed to light the galley fire that had been out for three days when the galley was flooded. Hot food even such as Hepburn produced revitalised the crew who were soaked to the skin with no dry clothes to put on. There was still a foot of water swilling around in the fo'c'sle. The Litchfield entered the Channel and sailed into heavy fog. It was an anxious time for all concerned, as ears were strained for the sound of waves breaking on rocks, for these were dangerous waters. All the time the Litchfield's bell rang mournfully, warning other vessels of her presence so as to avoid collision. Gradually the fog lifted and the captain, after taking sightings, found us to be south of the Lizard. The voyage proceeded without incident and days later I found myself looking at familiar views as the Litchfield rounded Blackwall Point and Greenwich and Deptford came in sight. Soon we were alongside at Deptford with sails furled. The crew lined up at a table on the deck where the captain paid them their dues and they rushed ashore where the delights of Deptford awaited. When my turn came, I was paid what was owing to me, but I was reluctant to go ashore as I still did not know what had occurred after Darroch and Chandler had left me in pursuit of Samuel Clegg's horse and I was frightened that I might be wanted for the murder by the authorities or that Bully might wish to silence me. The captain, perceiving my reluctance to leave and assuming that it was because I had nowhere to go, said I might stay on board and assist the watchman, who would be on board to deter thieves. I gratefully accepted his offer.

"That night I slept alone in the fo'c'sle. It was cold and miserable without the crew who had been my shipmates. The Litchfield, deprived of the men who brought her to life, was like a ghost ship. The next morning as I sat on deck watching the river traffic, I saw a waterman rowing towards me. In the stern of the boat sat a familiar figure, whilst in the bow stood a familiar dog. I ran to the side of the ship and threw a rope ladder over the side and minutes later, having left the boat with his normal difficulty,

I was reunited with Solomon and Nutmeg. Solomon soon reassured me that nothing was known of my presence at the murder and that Bully had assumed I had fled. For the rest of the morning, I told him of my voyage until it was time for them to go ratting. Solomon hailed a passing boat, and as he stood to leave I looked at him closely and he sheepishly removed from that smelly coat a number of items that he had "found" as he walked around the ship. With a wink he was over the side and I waved the two of them out of sight.

"I continued to sail on the Litchfield under Captain Hayward for the next five years on her voyages to and from Gibraltar. During this period, despite the food served up by a succession of cooks, I grew into a tall and muscular youth, no longer the ship's boy, but a young and nimble seaman who could run up and down the rigging like a monkey and out onto the yards in all weathers without a second thought. Bounce and I had become firm friends and when an order was given to go aloft we would race each other up into our world above the old ship, and disdaining the rigging once the job was done descend to the deck by rope. When the ship arrived home at Deptford, I would spend my days ashore at the village of Lee beyond Blackheath, where Bounce's widowed mother was the landlady of the Old Tiger's Head on the Folkestone road. It was an idyllic spot: in the garden behind the inn, the waters of the Quaggy flowed languidly on their way to meet the Ravensbourne at the village of Lewisham. Across the Folkestone road lay 'the Bright Field', where Bounce's uncle grew vegetables to sell in the markets in London and where Bounce and I spent many a happy hour rabbiting.

"I was sixteen when I made my final voyage on the Litchfield. By this time old Goldstaub had left the sea, while Bounce remained at home: his mother having fallen ill, he was needed in the inn. Captain Hayward was not a well man and although Mr Hawksworth was still the first mate, he did not as usual come aboard until the ship was ready to sail and the loading was supervised by the new second mate, Mr Faulkner, a martinet and thoroughly unpopular with the crew. The Litchfield on this voyage was bound for Palermo in Sicily with a mixed cargo of wool, grain and hides, her owners having become fed up with the lack of homeward cargoes from Gibraltar. Under the lash of Faulkner's tongue, the loading was quickly finished and Mr Hawksworth having come on board, she sailed with the tide from the London river a day early. As the Litchfield sailed by the familiar landmarks on the riverbank, I little knew how long it would be before I saw them again.

"The voyage to the Mediterranean was uneventful and having passed through the straits and with the familiar sight of the Rock of Gibraltar disappearing to port, Captain Hayward set a course to pass south of Sardinia to the Tyrrhenian Sea and Sicily. A week later the Litchfield was south of Cape Teuleda on Sardinia when the clouds darkened. Captain Hayward immediately ordered that sail be taken in and I and the starboard watch went aloft but we had hardly completed our climb when a ferocious wind, the like of which I had never experienced and never wish to experience again, hit the ship on her portside and with an almighty crack the mainsail was ripped to shreds. The wind did not abate and with it came blinding rain that stung the face and limited visibility to a few yards. The heavens were lit by forks of lighting and thunder roared, the sea was whipped up into a hissing and furious maelstrom; we were in the most almighty storm. For six hours the two watches struggled to take in all sail, for Captain Hayward had resolved that the only course was to run before the wind under bare poles. As the wind whistled through the rigging and the Litchfield rolled to an alarming degree, we struggled to get the canvas off her with one hand whilst with the other we hung on for dear life, all the time conscious that a mast or the yardarms we were out on might snap and pitch onto the deck below or the boiling waters that surrounded us. At last we had such sails as had survived tightly furled and we descended exhausted from that hell in the air to the hell below where the Litchfield pitched and rolled in the mighty seas.

"The storm continued and the Litchfield was driven eastward before the wind through the Sicilian channel. There was little we could do but pray for the storm to ease. The Litchfield, buffeted by the heavy seas, struggled manfully on, when all of a sudden a rumbling sound was heard deep down in the ship; the cargo had moved and she took a heavy list to port. Faulkner's speedy loading had been achieved at the price of not properly securing the cargo and we were now to pay the price. With the list to port the Litchfield started to ship water, the carpenter sounded the well and reported that the level of water was rising. I went below with the starboard watch to try and trim the cargo whilst Mr Hawksworth, gathering an axe and a few members of the crew, set about cutting the main mast down to relieve the pressure of weight on the Litchfield's port side. All the remaining crew members continued to pump furiously. The scene below deck was like something out of hell as we tried to shift the cargo to the starboard side. A number of heavy barrels broke loose and started to pommel the portside timbers. With difficulty we managed to secure them without anyone being crushed and then continued to try and move the cargo to the starboard side, all the time conscious that the ship might roll over at any time. Our efforts were all in vain and the Litchfield developed a further list. We were called on deck where it was clear that despite the Herculean efforts of Mr Hawksworth and his party in cutting away the main mast, all was lost and that the ship would go at any minute. Captain Hayward gave the order to abandon ship and to launch the two ship's boats, but before it could be done, the Litchfield gave a final lurch and started to roll over and I was thrown into the sea.

"I have little recollection of what immediately followed other than finding myself in the stormy water, clinging to a spar of the dear old Litchfield and of my shipmates there was no sight. I was alone in the stormy sea clinging desperately to a piece of wreckage; once again, still only sixteen, I knew the meaning of despair.

"I do not know how long I remained in the water clinging to that spar: I remember tying a piece of rope that was still attached to it to my wrists, so that I would not lose it. I knew that I could not remain in the water without support, for swimming or treading water would soon leave me exhausted and my only hope was that there was land nearby and the spar would carry me to it. The storm had now passed and the sun beat down on me and I started to suffer from a terrible thirst. I seemed to drift in the water for hours and I became resigned to the fact that my life was to end here, far from home. It was at this point that I saw what appeared to be a tiny sail upon the waves and my spirits rose momentarily. Clinging to the spar, I kicked in the direction of the sail. After a time, I came close enough to it to see that that it was a triangle made of three pieces of reed to which was attached a small sail about the size of a shirt. On reaching it, I found that attached to it there were a number of short lines with hooks attached. It was, I was later to find out, a Mrejkba. Hauling in one of the lines, I found that a number of fish had bitten and I quenched my burning thirst by eating raw fish. Attached to the Mrejkba there was a length of strong twine which I tied to the spar.

"The discovery of the Mrejkba buoyed my spirits, for I reasoned that it belonged to a fisherman and that land must be near, but I could see no sight of it and I lapsed into despair for the Mrejkba could have travelled many miles from land on the waves. I strained my weary bloodshot eyes, but I could see no land and I bowed my weary head with resignation and held onto the drifting spar. I do not know how long I drifted, but on looking up I thought that I could see a faint line on the horizon. I continued to stare in that direction. The line did not move and gradually I could make out a definite coastline and mercifully the spar was drifting in that direction. The hours passed agonisingly slowly but eventually I found myself drifting towards a rocky coastline with tall cliffs that stood stiffly and proudly like a line of soldiers looking disdainfully at the waves that crashed against their feet. As I drifted closer, I saw to my right a high cliff through which the sea had broken creating a mighty arch. I was now at the foot of the cliffs and the waves rose up and dissipated their energy against them before subsiding in a mass of foam.

Before the next wave rose up, I had mercifully reached the land, but I might as well have been out at sea for there was nowhere to come ashore. I drifted further to my right along the foot of the cliffs. Such was the power of the sea that it had over the centuries cut into the base of the cliffs creating caves. I drifted into one, but there was no way to land under the rocky outcrop and the spar was swept out by the water and pushed further along the foot of the cliffs. As I hung on, I saw the entrance to what appeared to be another cave, but to my amazement I could see light beyond. I kicked with all my strength and found myself in a rocky tunnel that the sea had cut through the cliff. With one final kick I was through and found myself in a shallow turquoise bay with the shore only fifty yards away. I struggled through the shallow water and threw myself on the land and gave thanks. I had reached, though I did not then know it, 'the Inland Sea' at Dwejra on the western coast of the island of Gozo which itself lies north of the island of Malta.

"I lay exhausted on the pebbled beach. It was late afternoon and the sun was still hot, but I was so weak and tired that I could not move to find shade, and I soon fell into a deep sleep. I awoke to feel someone sitting me up and placing a goatskin bottle of water to my lips. My lips were swollen and my mouth and throat were parched, but never did water taste as good. In between my greedy gulps, I looked upon the face of the owner of the water bottle. He was, as I was later to learn, eighteen years old. He had olive-coloured skin with a kindly open face and when he smiled, as he frequently did, he displayed a set of glistening white teeth, contrasting with his jet black hair that was tied back with a bright red scarf. Around his waist he wore a thick leather belt attached to which were a large number of fish hooks, along with two villainous looking knives. Thus I first met Joe Gafa the fisherman; never was there a truer friend.

"My thirst quenched, I looked about me: immediately before me was the shallow bay into which providence had taken me. On the far side of it a cliff of grey-coloured limestone rose up over a hundred feet where it was topped by a cream-coloured layer of the same rock, whilst at its bottom was the entrance to the cave through which I had passed. In the bay bobbed a small fishing boat in which Joe had sailed in through the same cave. He spoke to me but it was in a tongue that I did not understand. On realising this, he pulled me up by the arm and motioned me to follow him. Though it was early evening the sun beat down relentlessly and after my time in the sea without sustenance my progress, though assisted by Joe, was slow. We climbed up a path to our left and after a few minutes I could see the sea which had carried me to the west coast of the island on which I now stood. The waves had abated and the blue of the sea and the blue of the sky seemed to merge into one as if we were in a gigantic blue tent. On reaching a small plateau, I stopped to look back to where the limestone cliff plunged down to meet the sea: its head where it met the ocean was shaped like a crocodile and I noted with amazement that there was a wide arch through it so that one could see the sea beyond. This was my first view of the Azure Window, which with the nearby Fungus Rock, was to play a major part in my adventures on the island.

"We continued to climb up the path which became very steep. It would have been easier to take a more gentle route that opened up to the right but that would have involved approaching a small fortified tower known as the Qawra Tower that was perched on the cliff top looking out on Dwejra Bay and the Fungus Rock which stood proudly in the sea in front of it, whilst at the same time giving its occupants a commanding view over the Azure Window behind us. Joe, by a variety of signs, made it clear to me that we should not show ourselves to anyone who might have been looking inland in our direction. We continued our climb, skirting a dry ravine that led down to the sea before climbing down it and up the other side. The ground was dry and dusty with little vegetation and the heat was more than I could bear. Of human activity there was no sign, save a small quarry to our right. The path gradually widened into a rough track and the land became more level with small fields each surrounded by low limestone walls. The soil within them seemed to my eyes thin and stony but there were a variety of vegetables and fruits growing there. Immediately ahead the dome of the Church of San Lawrenz came into view surrounded by small houses like chickens around a mother hen. It was now getting dark and we entered into the village which bore the same name through a street called Trig Wied Merril that led into the Triq Langura, where a number of more prosperous-looking stone built houses had enclosed balconies at first floor level, from where the owners could observe the street without being seen. We passed slowly down the street, with Joe greeting the few inhabitants who were about, before arriving in the wide square in front of the church called Pjazza San Lawrenz. Joe motioned me to stop and I collapsed to the ground utterly exhausted where he left me. He returned a few minutes later with a pitcher of ice cold water and a basket of sweet plums and peaches. The fruit was the first food to pass my lips since the raw fish I had eaten in the sea and I wolfed it down like a dog. After I had eaten the fruit and drunk deeply of the refreshing water, we remained seated in silence on the steps of the church under a star-filled sky, the stillness only broken by the occasional dog bark and by the great bell of the church as it struck on the quarter, to be answered by its brothers in the church of the village of Gharb half a mile further to the west.

"We remained seated until Joe stood up and beckoned me to follow him. To the north east of San Lawrenz the land fell gently away and we descended through the fields to the village of Gharb which was dominated by the twin towers of the new church of The Visitation on the Hill at the centre of the village. We reached a road called Il Madonna Tal Virtu and turned right up towards the church. Halfway up the street, Joe stopped outside a small stone house on the right and beckoned me to follow him in through a heavy wooden door. On entering, Joe bolted the door. As he did so, I looked around me: it was dark, but by the light of a single candle that burned in an alcove in the wall, I could see that I was in a narrow passageway with a stone floor. A narrow staircase led up to a floor above; ahead was a further heavy wooden door (which I later learnt led to where sheep and goats were kept in winter), but Joe directed me through an open doorway to my right. I found myself in a large chamber with a vaulted ceiling with a small shuttered window that looked out onto the street from which we had come. The room was sparsely furnished with two pallet beds. Joe motioned towards one of them and I collapsed gratefully onto it. Never had a bed seemed more inviting and within minutes I fell into a deep slumber, dead to all the world. So exhausted was I, that I slept all that night and all through the following day and night, though my sleep was disturbed by vivid recollections of the shipwreck and my time in the sea."

THE AZURE WINDOW

"I awoke on that second morning to the sound of a cockerel crowing. Within seconds or so it seemed he was answered by his brethren, each it seemed trying to out-crow the other. They were soon joined by a chorus of dogs who seemed to be involved in a similar competition. This cacophony of animal sound was only interrupted by the regular booming and chiming of church bells, it was clearly not expected in Gozo that anyone should lie in their bed after dawn. I looked about the room: the other bed was unoccupied and all was quiet in the house, though not outside. As I was wondering what to do, the door opened quietly and a round, smiley-faced, middle-aged woman looked in. It was (though I did not know it at the time), Carmela, Joe's mother, who during my time on the island was to be the mother that I had never had. Seeing that I was awake, she beckoned me to follow her. Carmela and her farmer husband, Guzepp, together with their two sons, lived on the first floor, access to which was via the staircase that I had noted on my arrival and by stone steps from the farmyard at the rear. On reaching the first floor, Carmela directed me into the kitchen where she motioned me to sit at a rough wooden table. She then placed before me a bowl of steaming soup along with a hot loaf of crusty bread (ftira). This was the first hot food that I had had since before the shipwreck and I needed no second bidding to eat. Whilst I did so, Carmela busied herself about the kitchen and the farmyard below. Looking out of an open window,

I noted how hot it was already, though it was not yet eight in the morning. As I was to come to learn, the sun was so hot in Gozo that everyone started work at dawn and worked until midday, when they would retire home to avoid the heat before returning to their labours in the early evening. Thus it was that a few hours later I met Guzepp and Joe's older brother, Georgi, who had returned from their labours in the small terraced fields that lay behind the house and San Lawrenz. Of Joe there was no sight, but Georgi indicated to me by hand gestures that he was out fishing. Guzepp was a short muscular man: his skin was dark, tanned by years of labour in the fields under the hot sun. He was, as I came to learn, a man of few words, perhaps because Carmela and Georgi were given to continuous talking so that he could not get a word in, or maybe because he genuinely was one of life's foot soldiers, content to follow in the wake of the bustling Carmela. When he did speak, however, it was worth listening to, for he was a fountain of common sense and experience. Not so Georgi, who was, I was soon to learn, a loud-mouthed wastrel, more interested in enjoying himself than assisting his parents on the small farm that would one day be his. He was quite unlike his younger brother in appearance, short and squat with hooded eyes and a swarthy complexion. His face seemed fixed in a permanent scowl. He was now some twenty-five years of age and was running to fat which was not surprising given the amount of food that he managed to put away at the table that first morning, whilst his parents, who worked hard all day to put food on the table for this fat cuckoo, ate sparingly.

"I was now in a difficult position: I had been saved from the sea and cared for through the kindness of Joe and his parents, but

I was in a foreign land far from home and unable to speak the language. I clearly could not remain living with them, though I had nowhere else to go. My home had been the Litchfield and she was gone and I had no family to return to. All I could think of was finding a ship somewhere and returning to England, but where would I find such a ship when I did not even know where the nearest port was or that I was on an island? I was embarrassed to stay any longer and be a burden on the kind people who had taken me in and yet I did not want to leave without saying goodbye to Joe. I stood up as if to leave, trying to communicate to Carmela that she should pass onto Joe my thanks when he returned. She waved away my attempts to explain and indicated that I should stay until he returned which I gratefully agreed to do, having no desire to set forth immediately on the rough road of life that I had travelled on so much in my short time on this earth.

"Guzepp stood up to return to the fields followed reluctantly by Georgi, who clearly would have preferred to have remained at home and rested. I followed them both out into the farmyard and from there into the furthest field where Guzepp was harvesting onions that he had grown. Observing what they were doing, I endeavoured to assist but lacking a sharp knife I was not much use. Guzepp, seeing that I was prepared to work, handed me a knife and showed me how to cut and tie. It was back-breaking work, but I was fit and strong, hardened by the life I had led and it was not long before I got the hang of it and noted with satisfaction that I was making better progress than Georgi, not that it appeared to bother him. We continued to toil under the hot sun, the perspiration dripped down my face so that I was nearly blinded, but at last the day's work was done and we trudged home with a heavy load of onions and a welcome bucket of cool water over the head from the well in the farmyard. Then after shutting the animals away for the night, we climbed wearily to the kitchen where a dish of baked macaroni (timpana) awaited us along with honey rings (qaghaq ta'l-ghasel) and rough red wine from Guzepp's vines. The night fell quickly and I retired to my chamber and slept soundly.

"The next day, Joe not having returned, I again worked in the fields. The work was hard and monotonous and at times I found the heat unbearable but I had and have always been a hard worker and I did my best to be so, in return for the board and lodging which I had. On the evening of the third day Joe returned from fishing and after the evening meal of rabbit stew, I endeavoured to express my thanks and to explain that in the morning I would be on my way. To my surprise Carmela again insisted that I should stay and she was joined in insistence by Guzepp who I believed, I hope modestly, was more than happy to have a hard worker to assist him given the reluctance of Georgi to put his back into anything. Thus it was that I settled down to life as farm labourer on Gozo.

"I remained living with the Gafa family for over three years. During this time, I continued to work on the farm and when the workload permitted, to go fishing with Joe. As the weeks passed into months, I learnt to speak Maltese, falteringly at first but I became fluent. I continued to grow and fill out and by the time I reached nineteen years of age, with the combination of wholesome food and hard toil, I was a strong and healthy young man capable of doing any work required on the farm, which was just as well for the family's sake, for as my usefulness increased, Georgi's declined. He had developed a taste for his father's wine or indeed any alcohol that came his way and to the despair of his long-suffering parents, it was not unusual for him to lie in bed until late morning, sleeping off the excesses of the previous night. When he did eventually join Guzepp and I in the fields, his contribution to the required labour became less and less.

"Gozo, together with the islands of Malta and Comino are ruled by the Knights of St John from the fortified city of Valletta in Malta, with the Gozitans (as the inhabitants of Gozo are called), administered by the knights from the citadel high on a hill in Rabat, the capital of Gozo. Working on the farm and living in Gharb, I saw little of the Knights or their men-at-arms, but when I went fishing with Joe, as I shall relate, their presence was very much felt. The villagers of Gharb and San Lawrenz were kind and friendly people and though I was not one of them, nor indeed of the same religion, I was shown nothing but kindness by them during my time there. In the cool of the evenings they would sit outside their homes and talk whilst I and the other young men would congregate in the village square by an old stone cross and play skittles and other games. After about eighteen months, however, instead of turning right of an evening after I came out of the house, I began turning left and walking down to the old Church of the Visitation, now known as the cemetery chapel, which stood at the bottom of Triq San Pietru. Between the chapel and the first house as you walk up the hill there is a small stream, dry in summer and no more than a shallow pond for the geese and ducks of the adjoining house. Here, when it was flowing, I used to collect water for the fields rather than undergo the exertions of drawing water from the deep well at the farmhouse. I used to go there in the evening in the hope of seeing Katarina Axiaq who lived in that house with her widowed father Victor."

Here Sawson stopped and looked at Molly, who from those long walks on the Downs knew everything of his past life and how painful this memory was for him. She smiled and said, "Go on." Sawson continued:

"Katarina was sixteen when I first saw her and I was immediately smitten. She was high-spirited and full of laughter, long-legged and slim. Her skin was olive-coloured, she had long black hair with dazzling green eyes and when she smiled her face lit up the world and my heart. She kept house for her father and helped him in the small field opposite where he grew melons which she, as he had injured his leg a number of years earlier and could not walk long distances, would take to Rabat once a week when in season, along with other produce from the small fields at the back of the house. Katarina had many admirers in the village, including Georgi who was not pleased when he found out that she was the object of my affections and that those affections were reciprocated. Her father was, however, not at all pleased. He was resigned to the fact that he would lose his daughter, but not to a ship-wrecked sailor with nothing in the world. Far better it be Georgi, who at least stood to inherit a farm. Fortunately, Katarina knew her own mind and a drunkard like him was not for her.

"One evening, as I stood in the grounds of the small chapel quietly talking across the stream to Katarina, a familiar whistle pierced the silence. It was Joe coming back across the field from his fishing. I responded in the same vein and he altered his course and joined me in the churchyard. After a few minutes, we took our leave of Katarina and walked down the little lane that led from the chapel to the 'Il Madonna Tal Virtu'. Joe was in high spirits and before reaching the junction, he took me by the arm and having satisfied himself that there was nobody about, he opened the bag he was carrying and from underneath two large Lampuki fish he was bringing home for Carmela, he took out what seemed to me to be a handful of dried seaweed or moss. I looked at it but it meant nothing to me. "What is it?" I asked. "It's fungus from the Rock," he said triumphantly. I looked carefully at the dried plant and wondered: access to the rock was forbidden by the knights who guarded it closely from the Qwara Tower, for the fungus was said to have medicinal properties and was therefore highly valued by them. Those who attempted to take it without their consent did so at their peril, for the penalties were severe. Joe explained to me that the seas had been stormy and that he had been driven in close to the rock as he returned from fishing. For a short period of time, his boat, which was well known to the watchers from the tower, was obscured from their vision by the rock itself and he had seized the opportunity to grab at a handful of the fungus growing on an inaccessible ledge. Knowing that his boat had been seen close to the rock and that it was likely that he and it would be searched when he landed, he had concealed the fungus in the throats of the fish that he had caught. He was searched, but the fish did not speak and the fungus was not discovered. "What are you going to do with it?" I asked Joe. He told me that he had heard of an old apothecary in

Rabat who lived in one of the tiny lanes in the warren of streets behind St George's Basilica who might be interested in it.

"The next morning Joe set off for Rabat. He returned in the evening and could hardly contain himself. Once we were alone, he told me that not only was the apothecary, old Louis Vella, interested, but he had purchased the fungus there and then and closing the door to his shop he had whispered to Joe that he would purchase any more fungus that might come Joe's way. The amount that Joe had received for the small amount of fungus was more than he made from a day's fishing and he was resolved to gather some more from the Rock. The enterprise would be difficult and dangerous, of that there could be no doubt, and I tried to persuade him not to become involved in such an escapade, but it was all to no avail, his heart was set on it and what was more, he wanted me to help him. I remembered the vow that I had made never to become involved in crime following the murder of Samuel Clegg and I explained that to Joe. This was quite different, he said. The fungus had not been put there by the knights any more than the fish in the sea had been. They had no more right than any other man and indeed far less than a native Gozitan, for the knights were foreigners who for the time being held sway. I was, to my everlasting regret, persuaded by his argument and his enthusiasm, for though I still do not believe what we did was a crime, the consequences were terrible, but that we were not to know and we were young.

"Having agreed to help him, we settled down to work out a plan. The rock was constantly watched and all approaches to it from the land guarded, with the road to San Lawrenz and the paths from the Inland Sea patrolled. The only approach possible had to be from the sea, but how? Joe's fishing boat could not just sail up to it in full view of those on the land. The fact, however, that Joe regularly sailed past it was to our advantage, for the watchers would see nothing unusual in that. But how to use that advantage? And then we hit upon an idea: Joe and I would make our way separately to the Inland Sea, and Joe, who was a strong swimmer, would swim out to the mouth of the cave that led to the open sea. I would sail the boat (I was after all, as Joe kept reminding me, a sailor). Once I had got the boat into the cave, Joe would get into it for the short passage to the open sea. On reaching the sea, as I turned the vessel to port to sail along past the Rock, Joe would slip over the starboard side holding onto a small piece of rope that to an onlooker would appear to be dangling casually over the side. Thus Joe would be concealed from the watchers on the land who would just see me, the sole fisherman. On passing as near to the Rock as was possible without causing alarm, I would gently tug the rope. Joe would let go and with a sharp knife and a bag tied to his waist, swim underwater to the Rock, obscured from prying eyes. He would then climb onto a small ledge he had noted and proceed to climb part of the Rock hidden from above by an overhang and gather fungus. He would have to remain concealed on the Rock for the day. I, meanwhile, would proceed to sea for a day's fishing. On my return, we would repeat the process with the small rope, this time dangling over the port side. Once the boat entered the cave leading to the Inland Sea, Joe would put the bag into the boat. We both believed that in this way we could obtain the fungus, but the difficulty remained that we had no way of knowing whether there might be men at arms waiting to search the boat when we sailed into the Inland Sea. If there were, the fungus was likely to be discovered, whereas if we knew that there were going to be men there, then the fungus could be hidden in the cave by Joe ready to be picked up later when it was safer. After thinking about this difficulty we decided that we needed a third person to help us. That evening, with some reservation, I decided to ask Katarina if she would help. She did not need much persuading, though I wish to God now that I never asked her. Her role was simple and without risk: on the day when we were to make the trip, she would come at five in the evening, as any sweetheart might to greet her fisherman. If there was no danger of being met by men at arms at the Inland Sea, she was to stand on the rocks in front of the Azure Window, as if she was in a portrait. From there, she could be seen by me without difficulty as I sailed home. If there was danger, then she was to stand on top of the arch to the window, in which case the fungus would be left in the cave. Finally, we agreed that if any of us were in trouble, we should try and make our way to the remote north-west corner of Gozo, some two miles from Gharb, and hide in the old quarry near to the isolated and remote chapel of San Dimitri, which looked out over the blue sea beyond.

"The next morning I set out at six o'clock for the inland sea, having arranged with Katarina the previous evening that she should be at the 'Window' at five in the afternoon. As I strode across the fields from Gharb to San Lawrenz with the sun rising in the east behind me, silence was broken by the strangulated crowing and isolated barks as the animal chorus tuned up to greet the new day, much as an orchestra might before the arrival of the conductor on the stage. My head was full of the adventure that I was to have, whilst my heart thought of nothing but Katarina. I was young, carefree, happy and in love. Would that time had stood still.

"On reaching the Inland Sea I set sail and on entering the cave I picked up Joe who had hidden there the previous night under cover of darkness. Thereafter, everything went as we had planned and as I sailed home in the evening with a full bag of fungus, there was Katarina silhouetted by the arch. On reaching the shore, I embraced Katarina, who concealed part of the contents of the bag beneath her skirts whilst I concealed the remainder within my catch in the same manner as Joe had done previously. Arm in arm, we made our way back to Gharb, leaving Joe to make his way back during the night. Two days later Katarina made her way to the market at Rabat with baskets of vegetables but on this occasion she also visited the apothecary who paid her well for the goods she delivered.

"Life went on without incident, for Joe and I had resolved that the success of our enterprise required that we did not engage too frequently in it. I continued to work on the farm and to walk out with Katarina, though old Victor could hardly bring himself to utter a word to me. One afternoon, however, an event occurred, the full significance of which was lost on me at the time. Returning one lunchtime from the fields where I had been working alone, I heard the sound of raised voices which I recognised as that of Georgi and Guzepp. There was nothing unusual in this, for over the past few months there had been frequent arguments as Guzepp became more and more angry over Georgi's drinking and refusal to do any meaningful work about the farm, but this was different: returning from the fields and finding Georgi in a drunken stupor still in bed, Guzepp had repaired to the well and filled a heavy wooden bucket to the brim. Returning to the bed, he emptied its contents over the sleeping Georgi, who on being aroused from his slumbers in such a fashion, raised his fist to Guzepp, further angering his father who set about him with a leather belt. I arrived to the accompaniment of Carmela's cries in time to see Guzepp throwing Georgi out into the lane and shouting to him not to return until he was sober and prepared to work. Georgi clearly was not prepared to work for he did not return, but took himself off to Rabat, though where he lodged or how he still managed to get money to drink nobody knew. With Georgi gone, nothing changed at the farm, as the work had been done by Guzepp and I. What did change, however, was people's view of me. Joe had always made known that farming was not for him. As a result, people assumed that I would one day take over the farm and it was noticeable that very shortly after, Victor started to talk to me! More importantly, however (and this I did not know), Georgi believed bitterly that he had been thrown out of the nest and his birthright stolen by the ship-wrecked sailor. This unjustified grievance was to cost me dear."

IN THE QUARRY

"Joe and I, assisted by Katarina, continued with our occasional visits to the Rock. We made five or six successful visits, though sometimes with Katarina appearing on top of the arch, it was necessary to hide the fungus in the cave and recover it later when the coast seemed clear. One evening, having worked in the fields, I made my way down to the Inland Sea and having swam out to the cave and recovered the Fungus which I had placed in my shirt, I started to make my way towards San Lawrenz. It was a fine moonlit night; the air was still warm after the heat of the day. All was still as I came to the outskirts of San Lawrenz and then all of a sudden, I don't know why, I thought, "It is too quiet." I stopped and instinctively darted into the nearest field to my left and lay face down on the earth, still warm from the day's heat and listened. I heard nothing and it was this lack of sound that heightened my sense of danger. Not a dog barked, when normally one would hear at least a yelp as a dog in slumber chased its dreamy prey. I lay on the ground for a good ten minutes but all remained quiet. I was just about to get up and make my way into the village, when I heard a horse whinny. Though there were horses in the village, the sound came from the direction of the village square where it was unlikely that any of the village horses would be at this time of night. I instinctively thought that the knights and their men must be about. I froze and pressed myself to the earth whilst my heart pounded in fright. I heard the horse whinny again and my worst fears were realised when I heard at the same time the sound of what I believed to be a chain bridle and horses' hooves coming closer through the night air, followed by the sound of men's voices. I lay motionless and within a minute, three men on horseback attended by a body of men on foot, appeared from the direction of the village. If I had not left the road on which I had been travelling, I would have walked straight into them. I instinctively rolled further into the field, oblivious to the stony soil. The horsemen stopped and three foot soldiers were ordered into the entrance to the very field in which I lay, where they took up a position crouched behind the stone wall which divided it from the road. The rest of the party moved on towards the Inland Sea. I lay still for the men were only about thirty yards from me. They spoke in low whispers, but I distinctly heard one say: "He said, they always come this way." I immediately thought, who is 'he'? Was it the man on horseback who had posted them there? Or was it a reference to someone else and if so, who? It was a question I was to come back to over and over again during the next few days.

"I lay as still as a tombstone. I had little doubt that the men were looking for Joe or me. Why this was so would have to wait, for clearly I could not remain in the field with the fungus concealed in my shirt. If I did nothing, then with the coming of dawn, I was bound to be discovered. Clearly San Lawrenz and, I had no doubt, Gharb and the surrounding fields were being watched. I started to roll slowly away from the men, frightened that any movement would be noticed. After what seemed an age, I reached the far boundary of the field. The field beyond was at a lower level and I dropped down over the terraced stone wall into it and held my breath. There was no sound. I sat with my back to the wall, out of sight of the watchers in the field I had just left and gathered my thoughts. First I must get rid of the fungus, for to be caught with it would be damning evidence of my activity. I immediately dug a hole in the soil with my bare hands and buried it. I then considered my position: clearly I could not risk trying to return to the farm as all the routes were no doubt being watched and even if I did manage to return home without being caught, it was clear from what I had heard in the field that the knights had some information and there was every likelihood that that included where I lived. I resolved, therefore, to make for the old quarry where Joe and I had agreed to meet in the event of things going wrong.

"Resolving to go to the old quarry was one thing, getting there was another, for I was still in close proximity to San Lawrenz: I dared not stand up in case I was seen silhouetted in the moonlight. I, therefore, crawled on my belly across the rugged terrain until I reached a point where the land started to fall away toward the sea. I was then in a position I judged to be safe to get to my feet and commence the tortuous journey towards the north-east corner of the island where it should be safe. I arrived at the quarry just as dawn was breaking. I approached it warily, given the events of the night, half hoping that Joe would be there, but it was empty. I was exhausted by my journey but I dared not sleep until I had found a safe place to do so. Looking about, I noticed a bush on a ledge some twenty feet above the quarry floor. It appeared from where I was standing that there might be space behind the ledge in which I could hide. With difficulty, for my strength had all but gone, I climbed to the ledge and found that there was sufficient space for me to lie down concealed. I did so and soon fell into a deep sleep. I awoke at midday, stiff and sore, my throat was dry and the sun beat down on me. The quarry was silent and it appeared to be empty, but I took no chances and resolved to remain concealed until dusk. As I lay on that ledge, I cursed myself for my stupidity in getting myself into this mess and not for the first time in my young life I shed tears of despair. I had arrived on Gozo with nothing, I had worked hard and settled down, and I thought of Katarina; I was in love with her, she loved me and I had put all this at risk for some pieces of fungus.

"I lay on the ledge for the rest of the day, tortured by thirst but I dared not make a move. To satisfy my thirst, I was driven to chewing the bitter leaves of the bush which only made my thirst worse as the taste left in my mouth was revolting. As soon as darkness arrived I descended to the quarry floor in search of water but there was none to be found. I was loathe to venture out of the quarry, but my thirst was such that I had to. I crawled on my hands and knees into a nearby field but I found no water. The next field again had no water and I was in despair, but I dared go no further and I turned back towards the quarry. On reaching the wall between the two fields I noticed a small gnarled and ancient olive bush. It had produced a pitiful crop of olives which I devoured with gusto before climbing back up onto the ledge, where I spent a restless night. I spent the next two days on that ledge only moving at night in search of liquid to soothe my parched throat: the first night I finished the remains of the olives whilst on the next I had to make do with the leaves from the bush. Throughout my time on the ledge I was racked by doubts: why had Joe or Katerina not come? Had he and Katerina been caught by the knights? Had old Louis confessed? Why were the Knights out on the road that night?

"On the morning of my fourth day on the ledge I heard the sound of dogs barking. It was from a long way off and I did not really pay much attention to it. Gradually, however, the sound started to come nearer and it suddenly dawned on me that it might be that the dogs were searching for me. I froze and lay completely still and listened. At first I could hear nothing but the dogs, but then as they drew nearer I heard once again the sound of a horse neighing followed soon after by the sound of men shouting to each other. The sound of the barking grew louder and then suddenly, without warning, three huge mastiffs with heavy metal chains around their necks came bounding into the quarry. They stood below my ledge snarling and baring their teeth as they leapt into the air below the ledge. They were soon followed into the quarry by their handlers, one of whom I noticed was carrying a piece of red material which I immediately recognised as a shirt of mine. Clearly the dogs had been following my scent, but how was it that my pursuers had possession of it? I did not have to wait long for an answer, for as a number of knights and their footmen came into the quarry I saw following in their wake Georgi. At once all became clear: he had somehow got wind of what Joe and I were doing with the fungus. He had clearly betrayed me to the knights in order to remove me from the farm and I had little doubt to remove me from the island so that he could press his attentions on Katerina with me out of the way.

"The dogs continued to bark and snarl but I did not move a muscle in the vain hope that I would remain undiscovered but it was not to be. Someone shouted to me to come out and show myself. I remained still, whereupon one of the dog handlers started climbing up the quarry wall. Realising capture was inevitable, I showed myself and climbed down to the quarry floor, where the dogs were in a frenzy to sink their teeth into me and tear me to pieces. But the knights had a different fate in store for me and a sharp word from one of them caused the dogs to be withdrawn, while I was savagely kicked and beaten by my pursuers (the most violent blows inflicted on me coming from Georgi), before having my hands tied tightly in front of me. One end of a rope was then tied around my chest with the other end attached to the saddle of one of the knights' horses. In this manner, I walked and stumbled out of the quarry as we began the hot and dusty journey to Rabat. As soon as we reached the road above Gharb, I realised why Joe and Katerina had not come: the knights had blocked the roads leading to the village and, as I was to learn subsequently, they had imposed a curfew on all the surrounding villages.

"On entering Gharb, we passed up Il Madonna Tal Virtu and as we passed the Gafa house, I glanced up and out of the corner of my eye saw Joe at an upstairs window. He winked at me before ducking down to avoid being seen by my captors. That wink filled me with hope when I most needed it, for with such a loyal and staunch friend at liberty, everything was possible. We processed on through Gharb, the sun was beating down, sweat filled my eyes and I had not eaten for four days, nor had a drop of water passed my lips and on more than one occasion I fell to the ground. But the knights showed no mercy, the horse walked on, pulling me along the rough and dusty road until I regained my feet, assisted by hefty kicks from my captors. In this manner we continued on towards Rabat, which we reached with me more dead than alive in the late afternoon.

THE CITADEL

"The citadel in Rabat sits high above the town like a large brooding bird watching over the narrow streets that lap up against the rock on which it stands. It dominates the town and the surrounding countryside. From the citadel, the knights controlled the island and of course the town and the main island road which runs through the centre of the town passing in front of St George's Cathedral, the other major building in the town. Having passed through the town gates, I was taken along the Triq Saint Orsala (the main road). We then turned up the steep Triq il Kastell to reach the huge wooden gates of the citadel that slowly creaked open as if to devour their prey. We passed through and the gates swung back to be followed by the sound of large metal bolts being slid back into place. I looked ahead to see the steps leading up to the knights' Church of the Assumption. My escort turned right and then after about twenty yards, left into a narrow passageway. Passing a flight of steps that led up to the ramparts, we paused at the second wooden door on the left. One of my captors slid open the three metal bolts which secured it before taking a heavy iron key and inserting it into the large metal lock. While this was happening, my hands were unbound but I had no time to enjoy the sensation of my limbs being free before the door swung open to reveal a small, evil-smelling cell into which I was flung, landing on some filthy straw, while the door was slammed shut behind me. I lay on my back in total darkness for the only light that came into the foul hole into which I had been thrown came from a small opening in the door at head height. This enabled the guard who patrolled the passageway to look in without having to open the door. The opening itself contained three metal bars placed so close to each other that a man's clenched fist could not pass through. At night and during the day, if the guard choose to do so, a small, hinged slat of wood would be dropped down over the opening and no light would penetrate the cell. Fortunately, my captors had not closed the slat and with the limited light that came in I was able to take stock of my new quarters, though if the truth be told there was very little to them. The cell was about eight-foot-high by ten foot wide. The walls were made of solid stone and the ceiling consisted of two massive, roughly-hewn pieces of timber, across which stone slabs had been laid. The floor was again of stone with straw strewn over it. In one corner there was a stone manger which was half full of water whether it was clean or not I could not tell and indeed I was past caring so great was my thirst and plunging my head into it I drank as an animal might. That done, I laid down exhausted. But I had not been on the straw for more than a few minutes, before I realised that I was not alone, as a succession of hungry fleas introduced themselves to me. I scratched and slapped at myself to try and gain some respite from their attentions but it was all to no avail I continued to itch all over. Mercifully the exhaustion of the past few days came to my aid and notwithstanding the attack on my body, I fell into a deep sleep.

"I was awoken the next morning with a kick in the ribs, having slept through the noisy opening of the cell door. Above me stood my jailer, 'Old John' who, along with 'Fat John' his nephew (as I came to call them), was responsible for my security. He poured a pitcher of water into the manger and threw a half a loaf of stale bread in my direction before slamming the door shot and locking it. I drank the water greedily and made a start on the loaf, eating each mouthful carefully as I did not know whether this was all I might receive that day. All the time I continued to scratch myself to try and gain some peace from the numerous flea bites on my body. As I ate, I thought anxiously of the inevitable interrogation that I knew must come soon. How much did the knights know? Clearly Georgi had betrayed me, but not, I guessed, Katerina or Joe. I knew the knights would not believe I had acted alone: they would want to know who my accomplices were and to whom the fungus had been sold. I resolved to maintain that I had acted alone and that the fungus was for my own use to try and relieve a constant nagging stomach pain that I was suffering from. I did not believe that the knights would believe me, but it was the best I could do in the circumstances and I hoped that that in the course of my questioning I might discover how much my captors knew.

"I had not long to wait for within the hour the cell door was unlocked and I was seized roughly by Old John, who despite his years had the strength of an ox. He pinned my arms behind my back, whilst Fat John tied my wrists tightly with rope. Thus prepared, I was marched out of my cell. They then each took hold of one of my arms and propelled me left past the steps leading to the ramparts. We turned right through an arch and passing in front of the steps leading up to the knights' church, crossed the courtyard and climbed a flight of steps that led to the treasury and the knights' quarters. At a large wooden door with rusty iron studs in it stood two men at arms holding long metal halberds that they held across the door preventing passage through it. On our approach they withdrew their halberds and we passed through into a guardroom, where my escort was joined by four further men at arms. Our enlarged party now passed through several chambers before arriving at a very large door that was again guarded by two men at arms. Old John struck the door with his fist. "Enter," shouted a voice from within. The two guards pushed the door open and our party passed through it into a great hall. At the far end on a raised platform there was a semi-circular table with a number of richly-carved chairs behind it. Around the walls there were portraits of previous knights who had governed the island. The room was illuminated by sunlight that poured in through coloured glass windows high up in the walls, depicting the coats of arms of the knights. I looked around in amazement. I had never been in such a magnificent room before. But I had no time to admire it, as I was brought in front of a stern-looking man who sat alone behind the table, while his secretary sat at a small desk immediately in front of the platform. My interrogator was (as I was to learn later, for there was no introduction), an Italian knight from Genoa. He was a short, jowly man with deeply inset eyes, a bald head and large nose, giving him a pig-like appearance. He was not the Governor of Gozo but his deputy, the governor having left for Valletta on the morning I was captured in order to attend a meeting of the Grand Council of the Knights. He was not due to return for a fortnight. This, though I did not realise it at the time, was a stroke of good fortune for me.

"My questioning started immediately and was much as I had expected. I maintained that I had acted alone at all times and for my own purposes. My interrogator became angry and shouted at me to tell the truth or I would be put to the rack to loosen my tongue. He repeated his questions and I continued to stick to my story. By this stage I was convinced that they did not know the identities of Katerina, Joe or old Louis but clearly they knew that I had not acted alone. I resolved not to betray my companions but I knew that I would not be able to hold out long under torture. All I could hope was that I could resist long enough for Katerina, Joe and old Louis to make their escape. The questioning continued; I repeated my answers. Old John pushed me to the floor, where he and Fat John kicked me savagely. Still I stuck to my story. The secretary, who had been quietly noting my answers, looked at me keenly and passed a note up to the deputy, who read it and asked: "Where were you born?"

"London," I replied, for I did not think that the Magpie alehouse in Wapping would mean much to them.

"You are English?"

"Yes," I replied. The effect and the significance of my answers were not immediately apparent to me as I answered questions as to how I had come to be on Gozo. But with this revelation as to my nationality, what had clearly appeared to my interrogator to be a simple case of dealing with a thief, now had an international dimension and notwithstanding my explanation that I was no more than a shipwrecked sailor, I was clearly now seen as a spy who had stolen the fungus on behalf of England. This was clearly a much more important matter than the deputy was prepared to deal with and the interrogation ceased to await the return of the governor. I was marched from the hall back to my cell. "You were lucky," Old John growled in my ear. "If the governor had been here you would have talked by now, or your liver would be feeding the birds." I did not doubt him nor did I doubt that it would be him who would have racked me and cut out my liver if I had not talked.

"Back in my cell, I rejoiced that I had unexpectedly gained sufficient time for my companions to make good their escape. On the other hand, I was in even deeper trouble than I had been. I lay on the floor of my cell and thought how I might escape. But the walls were so strong and the citadel so well guarded, that I quickly realised that without the assistance of others there was no chance and once again, as I had in the quarry and previously, I shed tears of despair. I then heard the sound of the key in the door and quickly wiped my eyes so that my captors might not see my tears. The door was opened by Fat John, but he was not alone. By his side stood a wizened little old man dressed in rags, carrying a wooden bowl of foul-smelling soup, some lettuce leaves and a jug of water. He moved slowly but instinctively into the cell, for he was almost bent double, in order to pour the water into the manger. But it was not only his infirmity that caused him to walk slowly, for as he painfully turned his face towards me, I saw that his eyes were lifeless and yet he had the most beautiful smile. As he poured the water, he whispered out of the corner of his mouth, "Your friends are nearby." Turning, the poor creature shuffled towards the door as Fat John bellowed from without: "Carmelo, you old fool. Come along or you will feel my boot." In an instant he was gone and the door slammed shut. Those four words lifted me from depression to elation, so much so, that I managed to consume the soup without throwing up.

"The next morning I lay in my cell waiting for something to happen, but nothing did. Then at midday, as the noon-day bell rang from Saint George's Cathedral, the door was opened by Fat John. He stood at the entrance of the cell. "Hold out your hands," he grunted. I did so and he tied them together with rope before pulling me out into the sunlit passage where to my right Old John was sitting on a stone seat, sheltering from the sun. He joined the two of us. "Work," he said with a sneer. We turned left from the cell and after a short distance left again up a flight of stone steps. At the top of the steps, I found myself on the broad ramparts of the citadel. Straight ahead and below I could see the cathedral, whilst to the right to the north, though not in sight, was Gharb and Katerina. The three of us then turned right and walked towards the edge of the rampart, passing a sentry who was marching to exchange places with his fellow who was advancing from the left hand side. We halted some five yards from the edge of the ramparts. "That's enough!" said Old John. "We don't want you to jump to your death do we? Well, at least not till the governor comes back and orders us to throw you over." At the spot where we had stopped, iron manacles were attached to the floor. Fat John attached them to my ankles and pointed to a large pile of rocks: "They need to be cut and shaped into building blocks," he said, freeing my hands and handing me a wooden mallet and a blunt chisel. I set to work and laboured for the next five hours in the scorching heat, my eyes half blinded by the sweat which poured from my brow and the dust from the stone. At the end of 'work', Fat John took the mallet and chisel from me, tied my hands again and removed the manacles. We then returned down the steps to the passageway and my cell.

"The next morning Carmelo again brought me my daily rations. He smiled but said nothing. Once again at the stroke of the noon-day bell, Fat John unlocked the cell and I was marched off to work in a similar fashion. This routine continued over the next few days, save on the Sunday, when I remained locked in my cell. As I lay on the filthy straw, by now oblivious to the fleas, a germ of an idea came into my mind as to how I might escape. The next morning, after Fat John had unlocked the cell, I counted out carefully the number of paces along the passageway to the stone steps. There were twenty-two. There were twenty-eight steps up to the ramparts and forty-two paces to my place of work, which was about five yards (three paces) from the rampart wall which was approximately four feet high. On the way back to the cell, I confirmed my measurements. That evening I calculated that if I were free and able to run from the door of my cell to the edge of the western rampart, I could do so in just under twenty-five seconds. That was all very well, but that still left me with a number of problems: firstly, and fundamentally, I had to be free to do so. Secondly, I did not know how far the drop was from the ramparts, though clearly it was a large one. Thirdly, even if I knew how far the drop was, how was I to make my escape from the ramparts to the town below? The answer to the second problem was unexpectedly answered for me the following day, for just after I had been unshackled and my hands tied in preparation for the walk back to the cell, there was a loud crash, followed by shouting and much swearing from below the ramparts. The two Johns, anxious to see what had occurred, took hold of me tightly and rushed to the ramparts. A cart, which had been travelling up the steep road below the ramparts that led to the citadel (It Telgha tal Belt), had broken free and collided with a cart that was following it, injuring the two mules that were pulling the second cart. As I looked down, I noted that there was a sheer drop of between forty to fifty feet from the ramparts to the top of a bastion that was about thirty feet wide. There was a drop from that bastion into It Telgha tal Belt of about twelve feet. As I lay in my cell that night, I calculated that if a man could get on top of the bastion with a rope and a grappling iron, he could, if he had sufficient skill, throw the grappling iron onto the ramparts. There was only one man I could think who might be able to do it and that was Joe the fisherman, skilled with ropes. Time would be of the essence for the grappling iron would have to be thrown at the precise moment that I reached the ramparts to avoid the sentry taking hold of it and clearly there would only be time for one throw before my pursuers caught up with me.

"The next morning as Carmelo was pouring the water into the manger, I whispered: "Can Joe throw a grappling iron onto the western rampart?" He gave no acknowledgement that he had heard and left the cell. The following morning as he held out a mouldy piece of bread for me to take, he said out of the corner of his mouth, "Yes. When and at what time?" "Tomorrow," I replied. "Just after the noon-day bell, when I shout." He nodded and left. That night I could hardly sleep with the tension of what was to happen: this was to be my only chance, there could be no second attempt. Carmelo arrived as usual the following morning, but for some unknown reason, Fat John chose to come into the cell with him. There could clearly be no whispering now and yet I needed to know if today was to be the day. My heart sank. I could not take the risk of trying to escape to the ramparts if Joe was not going to throw the grappling iron. Carmelo turned to leave. As he reached the door, he turned his head slightly and said, "Goodbye." The door swung shut, but I knew that the attempt was on.

"I paced up and down the cell that morning like a caged animal. As the noon-day bell sounded, I made ready. The door was unlocked by Fat John. As it swung open, I sprang forward and kicked him with all my might between the legs. He staggered back and as he did so, I punched him in the face. Old John jumped up from his stone seat, but it was too late. I bounded past the crumpled Fat John, down the passageway and ran at full pelt up the twenty-eight steps followed by the Johns, but by reason of age and weight they were never going to catch me. As I reached the top of the stairs, the sentry who had already passed turned, alerted by the shouts of the two Johns, but I was already twenty yards ahead of him running at speed. "Now!" I bellowed. Almost instantaneously the grappling iron snaked through the air and caught on the rampart. The rope was pulled tightly by Joe. I ran to it, blessing Mr Hawksworth for ordering me into the rigging all those years ago. Taking hold of the rope, I slid down it sailor fashion and gained the roof of the bastion and Joe in seconds. Without pausing, we ran across the bastion to where Joe had placed a second grappling iron and rope and dropped down into It Telgha ta Beltwe, we ran down the steep road at speed and crossed over the main street. As we did so, a cannon fired from the citadel. We ran through the market into the square in front of the cathedral. Passing to the right of it, we gained the security of the labyrinth of tiny narrow streets. On we ran until Joe stopped suddenly at an old wooden door in the Triq San Georg. He pushed it open and we ran in, whilst the door was quietly but quickly closed and bolted by other hands."

A TRAGIC DEPARTURE

"I had reached, though I did not realise it, 30 Triq San Georg, the home of old Louis Vella, the apothecary. Joe ran through the house into a small courtyard filled with plants and caged songbirds and I followed him. He stopped and lifted a wooden hatch on the ground that revealed a well from which the house drew its water. He then took up a length of stout rope to which a wooden bucket was attached. He threw the bucket into the well, holding the rope tightly in his hand. "Climb onto the bucket!" he whispered. I did as he bid and he started to lower me down the deep shaft. After the bucket had descended about fifteen feet, he stopped lowering. "Look to your right," he called. I did so and saw a narrow hole in the well shaft and a flickering light. "Climb in," he called. I did so and the bucket started to ascend. I found myself in a small cave in the sandstone underneath the courtyard. A candle burned in a small lantern attached to the cave walls. As my eyes became accustomed to the dark, I could see that a comfortable bed of fresh straw and a blanket had been prepared for me. There was a stone pitcher of cold water and a bucket and chain that I could use to replenish it from the well. Beside the pitcher was a basket containing figs, cheese and bread which I started to consume, reflecting what a change there had been in my circumstances in the past twenty minutes.

"I remained in the cave for three or more hours until I heard a sound in the well shaft. I moved cautiously towards it and saw

Joe descending on a rope. Within a few seconds he climbed into the cave and we embraced as brothers. I listened eagerly to the news: the whole town was in an uproar. The firing of the cannon was a signal to close the gates. A search of the town was underway and he could not remain with me long. He would, however, return as soon as it was safe. He gave me a supply of candles and a fresh loaf. Before departing he gave me two further pieces of news: Katerina would come when it was safe. That news filled me with joy. The second piece of news had come from poor Carmelo who was a cousin of old Louis. As he had left the citadel kitchen where he worked, he had heard that the two Johns were now making friends with the fleas in my old quarters, awaiting the return of the governor. With that news, Joe climbed up the rope, warning me to extinguish the candle if I did not hear a stone splash in the well when the hatch was opened. Joe reached the top of the well and the hatch was closed, leaving me in darkness save for the flickering candle. I lay down to sleep, wishing the fleas a good dinner.

"I stayed in the cave for three days and nights. Each morning the hatch was opened and a stone splashed in the water below. The bucket would come down with food in it that I would take. It would then return to the surface, nothing was said and the hatch was closed. On the morning of the fourth day the hatch was opened but there was no splash. I extinguished my candle and lay still. I could hear the sound of voices and of dogs, but not the rasping, growling sounds that I had heard in the quarry. Rather it was the sound of whimpering, subservient, fawning dogs. A little later the hatch was closed, but I still lay still. Hours passed. Then the hatch opened and rope was lowered down the well. An unknown but kindly voice whispered, "It's safe to come up."

"I took hold of the rope and quickly climbed up. On reaching the rim of the well, I found it to be early evening. The caged birds were singing goodnight to each other in the coolness of the courtyard. Standing next to an old palm tree to which the rope was attached was a little old man dressed in a richly embroidered green dressing gown with rabbit fur around the edges. Around his middle he wore a bright red sash, while on his feet he wore slippers of the same material as the gown. On his head he wore a bright blue fez with a gold tassle. He had a full grey beard which matched the colour of his hair. He looked at me with twinkling eyes and smiled. "Welcome to my house," he said and thus it was that I met for the first time the charming and genial apothecary, Louis Vella. "The door to the shop is locked," he said as he led me inside. "If anyone knocks, then take hold of the rope and go back down the well." On entering the house, I saw that the whole of the ground floor was given over to his shop. On the heavy wooden counter and on the shelves that ran all around the room there were hundreds of bottles and glass jars of different colours containing medicines, potions, powders, pills, creams, ointments and liquids. The room was lit by numerous candles that reflected in the glass, giving the impression of being in the middle of a rainbow. From a cage on the counter an old parrot lifted its head and gazed at me quizzically and then, satisfied that I meant no harm, returned to glare at a tabby cat that was sleeping peacefully near its cage, dreaming no doubt of parrot for tea. A strong but not unpleasant smell enveloped the shop. Louis smiled and said,

"A potion for the dogs, it takes their minds off things," which explained the whimpering I had heard earlier.

"I followed Louis up a flight of stairs to a richly-furnished room. On a table a meal of rabbit stew, cheese, bread and peaches was set out. Louis motioned me to sit down at the table. "Eat," he said, before leaving to return with a glass jug of red wine. I needed no second bidding and set to with relish. When I had finished and Louis had cleared the table, I asked him for news of Joe and Katerina. "Joe will be here in three days' time," he said. "He must do nothing to draw attention to himself, for he is probably being watched and he must continue as a fisherman. It is the same for Katerina. Joe will bring you news of her when he comes." I was, of course, disappointed but I could see the good sense in what he said. I would have to lie low and wait for matters to calm down. There were still roadblocks on the roads and houses were being searched as his had been that morning and a large reward offered for the capture of the English spy.

"At the end of the evening, I retired to the courtyard and climbed down the rope to my cave where I slept soundly. The following morning my breakfast was lowered down to me in the bucket. I remained concealed throughout the day, only climbing up the rope after Louis had closed the shop and whispered to me that it was safe to come up. I continued to spend my days in this manner while I awaited Joe's arrival. So I had plenty of time to think of my future: clearly I could not remain on Gozo, or indeed on Malta, for if I did so, the knights were bound eventually to catch me and I had no doubt that that would be the end of me. On the evening of the third day, Joe's cheery voice called softly down the well. I climbed up the rope and was reunited with him.

The news he brought was sombre; the governor had returned and had flown into a black fury at the news of what had happened in his absence. He had ordered that the hunt for me was to be stepped up. The reward for my capture had been doubled and more particularly, he had decreed that anyone found harbouring me would be put to death. This news served to reinforce my view that I must leave the island quickly and not put others, particularly Louis, at risk. The news from Joe was not, however, all bad: Katerina was coming to the market in two days' time and would be at the house once she had sold her father's produce.

"That evening I sat with Joe and Louis and we discussed my future. All agreed that I must leave as quickly as possible, but how and where to was another matter. Louis suggested that I should make my way to Mdina on Malta where he had a brother, but Joe and I felt that the risks were too great. "No," said Joe eventually, "there is only one course open to us; I must sail you to Sicily." I protested that this was too far a voyage for his boat, but he brushed aside my concerns: "No, it can be done and it will make a change for me not to keep having to look over my shoulder all the time. Besides, I got you into this and I will get you out of it." But how was I to get to Joe's boat? For all the little fishing harbours were being watched by the knights. Eventually Joe said, "I shall pick you up from Mgarr ix-Xini (the port of the galleys), the night after next at four in the morning." Mgarr ix-Xini is a tiny inlet on the south of Gozo, not far from the village of Sannat. Legend has it on the island that the Romans had used it as a safe anchorage to refit their galleys. Joe and I had, on occasions, sailed into this tiny natural harbour and swum in its clear waters. It had the advantage that it was remote and approached by a long winding steep path from the direction of Sannat. But it had the disadvantage that on the south side of the entrance on a rocky brow stood the Mgarr ix-xini tower built by the knights to watch that part of the coast after the Turk, Dragut Reis had used the inlet when he had stormed Gozo in 1551 and carried off a large number of its inhabitants into slavery.

"I voiced my concerns about the tower to Joe, but he soon laid my fears to rest: "I shall be sailing from the west," he said, "It will be pitch dark. I know these waters well; it is deep at the foot of the cliffs as you approach the mouth of the inlet and the current will be in my favour. I will sail close to the coast and when I am two hundred yards from the entrance I will drop the sail and let the sea take me to the entrance. Then I will quietly row into the inlet on the south side, where I will be sheltered by the lie of the land from any prying eyes from the tower. I will then anchor there and wait for you to swim out. Once you are on board we can row out, keeping to the south side of the inlet until we reach the open sea and safety. If I am unlucky and a sharp-eyed watchman does spot me as I approach from the west, then all he will see is a small fishing boat with one man in it which is not unusual and I doubt sufficient to cause him to raise the alarm, even in these heightened times. You, however, must approach the inlet with care in the darkness, for the sentries on the tower will have a view over the path as it leads down to the northern side of the inlet and although it will be dark, any sudden movement or noise will raise the alarm.

"Having agreed upon our plan, Joe and I embraced and he set off to Gharb, whilst I returned to the safety of the well and thought of the day after tomorrow. If all went well, I would be free and safe. But coupled with this was the thought that I would see Katerina on the day of my departure: the joy of that meeting would be tinged with sadness, for when would I see her again? It was with very mixed emotions that I fell asleep that night. The following day I remained in the well until Louis called me. That night after our meal, he opened a wooden drawer, took out an old map and traced the route that I must take from Rabat to Sannat and from there to the inlet. "Today," he said, "after I closed the shop at noon, I walked to Sannat and back. There are roadblocks everywhere. I have marked them on the map. Your journey will be difficult, for you will have to avoid the main roads and travel with care, following this map." I thanked him profusely and retired with the map to the shop, where I studied it carefully, before retiring to the well.

"The next morning I awoke with excitement: in a few hours I would see my Katerina. The minutes dragged as I lay there in a fever of excitement! At last came the whisper that I had been waiting for. I sprung onto the rope and in a few seconds I was in the courtyard holding her in my arms, as old Louis discretely engaged himself in making some form of medicine or potion in the shop. She was as beautiful as ever and my heart ached at the thought that we must soon part. That afternoon was one of the happiest of my life, as I sat with my arm around her waist in the coolness of the courtyard with the birds singing. All too soon the cathedral clock struck four and I knew that she must soon leave to be back at Gharb before nightfall. "Katerina," I said. "It is time for us to part." She looked at me and smiled. "No," she said. "I am coming with you!" I was filled with joy, but quickly realised that I could not ask this of her. I gently explained the difficult journey that I was about to undertake and that it was too dangerous for her. She should return home and wait for me. She looked at me and smiled. "Where you go, I go," she said.

"Thus it was that at eight that evening, Katerina and I said a fond goodbye to old Louis. He handed me a small bundle of rags. "For the dogs," he said. We slipped out into the dark street; our journey had begun and as we turned the corner from Louis' shop with my hand in Katarina's, I felt I could take on the world. The first part of our journey was uneventful. We passed through the little streets of Rabat following a route that I had memorised, avoiding the main thoroughfares. On a number of occasions, in order to avoid our faces being seen, we embraced whilst people approaching us walked by. But then as we came to the outskirts of the town, fate struck us a cruel blow, though how cruel I could not at that stage have imagined. We had just passed a small shop where people were drinking and making merry, when a man came out. He stopped and started walking in the same direction. We walked on, but a sixth sense made me turn sharp right up a little alley way. The man followed. We turned right again, the man did the same. We were being followed. We turned a corner and ran on. Turning another corner, a narrow passageway led into a courtyard. We went in to find a number of doorways. In front of one was a cart, we dashed behind it and knelt down and waited. Nothing happened and then a man crept silently into the courtyard entrance. His gait was unsteady, but as the moonlight played upon his face his identity became clear; it was Georgi! He looked carefully about the courtyard, but he did not venture in. He turned and left. My first instinct was to follow him and silence him forever, for he would no doubt alert the guards. Would that

I had, for it was to cost us dear, but he was Joe's brother and the son of Carmela and Guzepp who had showed me such kindness. So to spare them, to my everlasting regret, I spared him.

As soon as he had gone, we left the courtyard and soon regained our original route. But now we moved with speed, but not such as to draw attention to ourselves. The gate to the town was barred and guarded, but guided by the map, we turned down a small street and climbing a garden wall we passed through the garden and quietly came to a wooden gate. We pulled open a rusty bolt, gained access to the open fields and headed in the direction of Sannat. There was a half-moon that evening and we kept low. The going was difficult and we both stumbled and fell, but the fear of the knights drove us on. We dared not stop, for we knew that Georgi would have raised the alarm, though it was our hope that he would have led them to the courtyard and that they would concentrate on searching the houses there. But as we reached the outskirts of Sannat, we heard the distant sound of dogs. We ran across the fields and eventually gained the beginning of the tortuous path that winds its way to the inlet.

"As we commenced our descent, I was hopeful that we were far enough ahead of our pursuers that we might make the sea in time, but our progress was painfully slow: To fall and twist an ankle or break a bone would put an end to everything and each footstep had to be carefully taken. Our pursuers would have the same difficulty but not of course the dogs and they were getting closer all the time. We continued our descent. I looked back and in the distance I saw a bright light bobbing up and down and travelling in our direction. At first I did not realise what it was, but it suddenly dawned on me that it was a knight on horseback carrying a flaming torch and despite the roughness of the path, he was gaining on us. We were by now both breathless, the noise of the dogs was getting louder and we then heard shouts from the tower – the sentries, no doubt alerted by the dogs and the flaming torch. I prayed that Joe was in the inlet.

"The water was now in sight. On we struggled, the dogs were now very close having been released by their handlers. I turned and saw three giant dogs bounding down towards us, growling and showing their teeth as they had in the quarry. I turned and held out the bundle of rags. The effect was instant; they became quiet and merely ran alongside us, whining. At least we were not going to be torn to pieces. We were now about a hundred feet above the water. Soldiers were now leaving the fort in an attempt to cut us off, but they had a distance to travel and we had almost reached safety. Suddenly the knight with the torch was upon us with drawn sword. It all happened so quickly: one moment Katerina was beside me, the next she was running at the horseman raising her arms. "No Katerina!" I screamed, but it was too late. The startled horse reared up unseating its rider. As its right foreleg came down, its hoof hit her on the head and she fell lifeless to the floor. I sprang forward in anguish and anger. The knight who had been winded by his fall clutched at his side for his sword; I picked up a heavy rock and slammed it into his head; he did not move."

Sawson stopped his narrative and looked at the assembled company: "That was the first man I ever killed and he was not the last; there would and will be others," he said meaningfully, before resuming his narrative.

"I turned and ran, blinded by my tears, carrying the body of my beloved Katerina to the water's edge. I laid her gently on the sand, kissed her still warm lips and then closed her beautiful eyes forever, before running into the water and striking out for Joe's boat, just as the guards from the fort reached the water. Pistols cracked, I dived under water and swam strongly for the mouth of the inlet where Joe's strong arms hauled me into the boat. I collapsed into the bottom of the boat in tears, while Joe rowed strongly out to sea. Thus I left Gozo and the woman I loved."

A DARK ENCOUNTER

"I remember very little of the following day, as Joe sailed his little craft through the channel that separates Gozo from the island of Comino. I remained distraught, still lying at the bottom of the boat, little caring whether I lived or died. Yet again my world had collapsed. Nothing could equal the sorrow and the pain that I felt. Little did I know the tragedy that was about to befall me, which has led to the situation that we find ourselves in today. Joe sensing that there was nothing that he could do or say to ease the pain, wisely left me alone. Once we had cleared the channel, he pointed the boat's bows towards the open sea and the north-west and set a course for Sicily. The sun rose high in the sky, the breezes were light and we made slow progress on the calm turquoise sea. In the evening, I crawled up and sat next to Joe, who said nothing but handed me a piece of bread and some cheese, which I ate without relish before slumping back down into the bottom of the boat, where I slept fitfully. I awoke at three in the morning. Poor Joe, who had had no rest since the night before we had left Gozo, was exhausted and needed little persuasion to rest while I sailed the boat, though my mind was far away.

"But I had little time to mope, for it was not long before a strong wind was upon us and I had to devote all my efforts to keeping the little boat on course. At the same time I regretted that I had eaten anything, for as the boat was tossed up and down my evening meal decided that it no longer wished to be confined down below in my stomach and without asking permission, ascended back the way it had gone down, though at a far more rapid rate, and I was violently sick. The dawn came up and Joe awoke. We sailed on for the next eight hours or so through heavy seas towards Sicily. As we did so, I had plenty of time to contemplate my future and it was not a happy thought: everything I knew and loved had been taken from me. I could not return to Gozo and if I could, to what purpose? There was nothing for me there. As for Sicily, I knew nothing of it or its people and I was not anxious to reach it, for when I did, I knew I would have to part from Joe, the one true friend I had in the world. As I looked out across the open sea, I saw through the spray far astern the masts of another vessel, also no doubt on a course to Sicily and sadly concluded that it could not be long before we sighted land. The wind that had arisen without warning, now suddenly dropped and within half an hour it had disappeared altogether. We were soon becalmed in such a thick sea mist that we could scarcely see beyond the bows of our small craft.

"With no wind and engulfed in the mist with no sight of the sun, we could do little other than try and keep the head of our vessel to the course that we were steering before we lost the wind. We continued in this manner for a number of hours with no sound other than the water lapping against the side of our boat as it drifted in a lifeless sea and as we did so we both said little, overwhelmed by the events of the past forty-eight hours. It was not long before it started to get even darker and we knew, though we could not see it, that the sun had set. We drifted on in an eerie silence, engulfed in the darkness and the mist. Suddenly Joe sat up and peered into the darkness. "What is it?" I asked. "I heard voices," he replied, pointing to the port side of our boat. I strained to hear but I could hear nothing, I was about to tell him that he must have imagined it, when I heard a voice shouting in a foreign tongue and another voice responding. I looked at Joe, fearful that our little vessel might be run down by a larger ship, perhaps the one I had seen before the mist came down, but he put his finger to his lips. "It may be pirates," he said. I froze and said nothing and we both held our breath and I lay as quiet as a church mouse at the bottom of the boat, while Joe kept his hand on the rudder in order to steer clear of the other vessel, should it be on a collision course with us. We continued in this manner for an hour or so, when all of a sudden without warning, fate accursedly took a hand. A breeze got up and the mist started to lift slowly. We emerged briefly into the moonlit sea at about the same time as the other vessel, that appeared no more than fifty yards away. Joe immediately pointed our vessel back into the mist, but it was too late: a shout rang out, followed by many more and the bow of the vessel turned in our direction.

"If there had been any doubts that the other vessel would be hostile to us, there were none now: the natural manoeuvre for any peaceful vessel in such sea conditions would have been to have put its helm over and steer away in order to avoid a collision. This vessel, far larger than us, was chasing us and that could only mean that they were ill-disposed to us. Joe sailed his little vessel instinctively, with consummate skill, but it was an uneven contest. The other vessel was far faster and the mist that had been our protector was lifting fast. Try as we might to hide in the banks of mist, it was to no avail and our pursuer continued to close upon us. The chase continued for over an hour with the gap between us narrowing and as the sun started to rise in the east, we began to make out the lines of our pursuer more clearly and our hearts sank even further: She was a Zeebeck, the fast sailing ship favoured by the Barbary pirates in their murderous attacks upon shipping far from the Barbary coast. Soon we could make out the features of those on board and a more villainous crew of ruffians armed to the teeth, literally in some cases, it was difficult to imagine. Foremost among these scoundrels was a stout, heavily-bearded rascal whose face was adorned by a vicious-looking scar that stretched from his left eye down past his mouth (in which he gripped a dagger) to his chin. But the most noticeable feature of this thief of the sea was the absence of his right hand, where only a blackened stump was visible. Thus for the first time I clapped eyes on the infamous Hadji Omar Ali, the scourge of the Algerian coast.

"As the Zeebeck came up close to us, those on board shouted at us in a tongue we did not understand. But their gestures made it clear that they wanted us to heave to. Fearful that they would cut our throats and throw us into the sea, we continued to try and make our escape. At this, Hadji Omar Ali roared at a group of his cut-throats who were clustered on the bow of his vessel with knives between their teeth, at which they jumped without hesitation into the sea and swam towards our little boat. We tried to resist their attempts to clamber aboard: Joe in particular hit one of them a mighty blow on the head with one of the oars, causing him to fall back unconscious into the sea, but there were too many of them and they soon overpowered us. Within a few minutes we were manhandled aboard the Zeebeck and trussed up like chickens after which we were kicked and dragged before Hadji Omar Ali who proceeded to kick us both about the body, reserving his strongest blows for Joe for striking one of his vagabonds with the oar, whilst at the same time shouting at us in his foreign tongue. At length he became tired with his kicking and with his powerful left arm he pulled me to my feet and tried to interrogate me. But as neither of us could speak each other's language and I was loathe to reveal that I spoke English (preferring that he should think that I was a simple fisherman), this did not last long and he called for us to be manacled, both feet and hands. Once secured in this manner, we were bundled below deck and confined in a tiny, dark and damp storeroom deep down in the bowels of the vessel. The size of our new quarters was such that Joe and I were unable to fully lie down; my foul cell in Rabat was like a palace in comparison.

"How long we remained in that filthy hole we could not properly tell, as the absence of any light prevented us from knowing when night gave way to day. We were not disturbed by the pirates, save that the door would be opened on regular occasions and a bowl of foul water pushed in, but no food. We estimated that we were being given water once a day and as we counted the number of times we received our water, we calculated that we were confined there for twelve days by which time we were both at our lowest ebb. I was still distraught by what had happened on Gozo, while poor Joe had taken the loss of his boat badly, it was all he had and he loved it like a person. Now it was gone, taken from him and with it had gone his sole means of livelihood. We did not even know whether the pirates had taken it in tow or abandoned it to the ocean.

"It was with such thoughts that we became conscious of heightened activity on the vessel: voices were raised and there was much activity on deck. Eventually the door to our prison was pulled open and rough hands pulled us, in our weakened state and still in our manacles, up onto the deck in time to see that we were entering a large, fortified harbour with a lighthouse at its entrance. We did not know it at the time, but our vessel was entering the Port of Algiers, the stronghold of the Barbary pirates. On looking about me, I could see the wide and blue bay on which the city founded as "El Jesair" stands. Immediately in front of us as we sailed in was the heavily-fortified seafront with its massive stone walls and numerous forts. At each end of the seafront two large stone walls over forty feet high with a twenty-five-foot deep ditch on the outside ran up the hillside to join each other at the citadel known as the Kasbah. Within the enclosed area, like chickens seeking the protection of a mother hen, rows of brilliant white buildings rose up the hillside to reach the citadel. High above all this, dominating the citadel, the city and the harbour and the road to the south east stood the brooding Château de l'Empereur, rectangular in shape with each wall being about one hundred and seventy-five yards in length with a small bastion on each corner. In the centre of this fortress was a thick, squat, round tower from which flew the standard of the Dey of Algiers. It was clearly at first sight a beautiful city in an attractive setting, but it was rotten to the core: For within its filthy and mean streets in which the majority of its citizens struggled to eke out an existence, there was more poverty, misery, violence and degradation than can be imagined.

"As the Zeebeck approached the stone wharves beneath the towering fortification, our noses were assailed by obnoxious smells, for all the effluent and detritus of the city discharged directly into the harbour where it festered, until a storm arose and cleansed the bay. A storm was long overdue and the baking heat of the sun served only to exacerbate the assault upon our noses. Soon the Zeebeck was alongside and Joe and I were marched down the wooden gangway onto the quay to be greeted by Hadji Omar Ali with his customary kicks, following which he climbed into a waiting carriage, barking out orders to a member of his crew, a bald-headed, swarthy, one-eyed cur, before disappearing into the labyrinth of streets which ran down to the quay. 'One-Eye' marked his departure in what was clearly the time honoured fashion by kicking us both and pointing in the direction of one of the larger streets which gave out onto the quay. We shuffled along in our manacles and thus made our entry into the town. We continued along in this manner, assisted on occasions by the boots of 'One-Eye'. After a while the street opened out into a grand square where a large crowd had gathered. It was not apparent to us at first why so many were present, but 'One-Eye' clearly knew and pushed us to the front to see what was happening. It was then that we saw for the first time, but certainly not the last, a poor wretch being punished by being bastinadoed. The prisoner was dragged into the square, held fast by his captors. Others held a staff some six foot in length in the middle of which two holes had been bored. A cord was passed through each of the holes and its ends fastened on one side with knots so that it made a loop on the other side of the staff. The feet of the prisoner were placed into the loop and the staff lifted by two men, one at each end, who proceeded to twist it around until the feet were fast pinched by the ankles, they then raised the staff onto their shoulders, so that the prisoner was suspended with only his neck and his shoulder on the ground. Once this was accomplished, another man started to violently strike the soles of the unfortunate prisoner with a heavy wooden cudgel for as many times as had been ordered. What offence the man had committed we never found out, but each blow was cheered lustily by the watching crowd, none more so than 'One-Eye' who, shooting occasional glances at us out of his one functioning orb, clearly gave us to understand that any trouble from us would result in similar treatment or worse.

"Once 'One-Eye' had seen enough, we continued on our way up the winding street until we reached the square in front of the Kasbah. From there we turned to our left and entered a narrow street with high walls on either side. After some thirty yards, the street turned sharply to the right, before starting to climb once more. We carried on before stopping before a heavy metal gate set into the wall beside which stood two unsavoury individuals who greeted 'One-Eye' as one of their own, before knocking at the gate and calling to those within. The gate swung slowly open and we passed through before it swung shut behind us. I looked around: it was as if we had passed from hell to heaven. We were in a large, shaded courtyard with orange and mimosa trees giving off their fragrant perfumes. Immediately in front of us was a tiled pool fed by a small spring, while songbirds called from a small aviary to our right, whilst on the far side of the courtyard a large white house glistened in the sun. We had reached, though I did not know it at the time, the sumptuous home of Hadji Omar Ali, paid for no doubt out of his murderous attacks on merchant ships.

"Joe and I were shepherded to a corner of the courtyard where a flight of steps led down to a wooden door. This opened into a small stone room with a number of iron rings set into the walls. 'One-Eye' attached our manacles to the rings and after giving us a final kick, left the room, closing the door behind him. The sound of metal bolts being drawn leaving us in no doubt that we were securely imprisoned. What our fate was to be, we did not know and for the moment it was not uppermost in our minds: far more pressing was the fact that we had not eaten for twelve days and we were both feeling weak. There was nothing we could do other than to wait and see what our captors had in store for us.

"After about an hour, we heard the sound of the bolts being drawn and an old woman carrying a tray with a pitcher of water and bread and fruit entered. She set the tray down before us and waited for us to eat. We fell upon the food for we were ravenous, at which she motioned to us to eat and drink slowly. As we did so, she spoke to us, but I could not understand what she was saying. Joe at this stage addressed her in Maltese. She clearly recognised some of the words as being similar to her own tongue that I believe, though I never found out, was a strain of Arabic. Through a combination of words and signs we learnt that we were less likely to be taken to the slave market and sold, as because of our age and strength, Hadji Omar Ali was hoping to get a better price from selling us (and at this stage she whispered) to the 'Accursed One', who at that time was at Blida, a small inland town some thirty-two miles from Algiers. He was not due to return to the coast for a number of weeks, but it was hoped that his agent would come to view us the following day. With that, she took up the tray and left. Joe and I, at last able to lie down and stretch out after our cramped quarters, soon fell into a deep, refreshing sleep.

"We were awoken early the next morning by the return of the old woman with bread and bowls of a watery mutton soup. This time she did not stop, but gave us to understand that the agent was expected in the late afternoon. We remained in the room until mid-afternoon when 'One Eye' came for us. He was armed with a small cane. Having released our manacles from the rings, he prodded us up the stairs with the cane into the courtyard at the far end of which, under a rich woven canopy, sat Hadji Omar Ali and a thick-set man with heavy gold rings on his fingers. He was wearing a heavily embroided turban and Turkish trousers. This was clearly Abd-el-Allai, the agent. Joe and I stood in the late evening sun whilst the two men finished their coffee and conversation. During this time Abd-el Allai looked at us keenly. Eventually he stood up and came over and started to examine the two of us as one might examine a horse or a cow at a country market. He felt our arms and legs, measured our height and the width of our backs and then required us to open our mouths so that he could view our teeth, though to what purpose I could not fathom. Once he had completed his observations, he returned to join Hadji Omar Ali who had remained under the canopy whilst the inspection was carried out. Clearly there was something about Joe and I that was of interest to Abd-el Allai for soon the two men were quite clearly haggling over our price. There was much waving of arms. Hadji Omar Ali at one stage jumped up to his feet roaring at Abd-el Allai, leading me to believe that the two were about to come to blows. He strutted about the courtyard like an enraged cockerel, whilst Abd-el Allai remained seated and spoke quietly, his words, however, served only to drive Hadji Omar Ali into fresh bouts of indignation. After a while, this initial skirmishing ceased, Hadji Omar Ali regained his composure and his seat and the two men resumed haggling before a satisfactory agreement marked by an almighty spit from Hadji Omar was reached, and we were sold into slavery."

THE COUNT DE MONTAGNAC

"Abd-el Allai took a cloth bag out from under his clothing and counted out a number of coins. Having completed his business, he stood up and took his leave of Hadji Omar Ali, who looked at us wistfully as if he wanted to give us a final kick to seal the bargain. Abd-el Allai motioned to Joe and I to follow him and passed through the gate out into the small street, where a camel accompanied by two men sat nonchalantly chewing. He climbed onto its back and pulled at its reins and the camel, with the aid of a kick from one of the men, no doubt trained in the Hadji Omar Ali school of diplomacy, indignantly got to its feet. A stout rope was attached to the manacles on our wrists and then tied to the saddle of the camel. The manacles on our legs were removed and we set off. We continued in this manner and headed west on the coast road out of the city towards the setting sun. After an hour or so, we reached a large white house overlooking the sea. We passed through a stone archway into a quiet courtyard. Once he had secured our manacles to metal rings set into the ground, Abd-el Allai went into the house and we settled down to sleep on the ground. We were awoken before dawn and after being given water to drink and some oranges, we set off in the same manner as we had done previously, again travelling west. Our destination, though Joe and I did not know it at the time, was Sidi Ferruch, which is some twelve miles to the west of Algiers.

"At first the going was pleasant, but as the sun came up and started to beat down on us as we trudged along the dusty open road, we started to perspire heavily. To our right was the dazzling blue sea, while all around us the perpetual sound of the cicadas could be heard. The sweat was pouring down our faces almost blinding us, as we could only wipe our eyes with difficulty due to our hands being manacled. Every time we attempted to lift them to our faces, the rope attached to the saddle on the camel acted as a brake. Abd-el Allai was also feeling the heat and frequently slaked his thirst from a leather bottle, but he remained indifferent to our condition and we continued to march on. Joe was clearly feeling the heat and started to stumble. Abd-el Allai's response was to take up a whip from the side of the saddle and to whip him like an animal across the back and when I stumbled I received a stinging lash across my back and neck. In this manner we proceeded onwards towards Sidi Ferruch. This was the first occasion I had ever been whipped, but it was certainly not to be the last.

"At last we came in sight of Sidi Ferruch: a tongue of land some one thousand yards long and five hundred yards wide ran out into the sea with a bay either side. At the tip of the tongue a mass of rock fell into the sea. On this cape was the tomb of a Mohammedan holy man from which the place takes its name. The southern end of the tongue consisted of sand dunes which gave way to more fertile land. At the northern tip of this spit of land was a large stone fort that commanded the entrance into the western bay, whilst in the bay, two galleys and a Zeebeck rode at anchor. The eastern bay, smaller and more cramped than its western brother, was overlooked by a smaller fort on the eastern end of the promontory. In this bay a small brig could be seen, while drawn up on the sandy beaches of both bays were a number of smaller vessels including feluccas. A stout stone fortified wall with a gate in the middle ran across the lower third of the spit, behind which a number of stone buildings could be seen. We had arrived at the lair of the man who had purchased us, The Count De Montagnac 'the accursed one'. As we approached, I noted three rough crucifixes: On two of them the sun-bleached skeletons of what had once been men were nailed and on the third there was the decomposing body of another poor wretch. Birds pecked at the putrid flesh; it was a nauseating sight. "The fate of those who try to escape from their master, the Count!" shouted Abd-el Allai. We passed through the gateway and stopped at a small stone building outside of which two heavily-armed men stood. We were ushered inside and placed in an iron cage, whilst Abd-el Allai sat at a roughly-hewn wooden table to await the arrival of the Count De Montagnac.

"The Count De Montagnac had fled France some thirty years earlier whilst under sentence of death for a series of cruel murders and other depravities he had carried out in the basement of a secluded hunting lodge on one of his estates in the Haute-Garonne. He had fled to Algiers and enlisted in the army of the Dey of Algiers. A ruthless and able soldier, he soon rose to a position of authority in the Dey's forces. Uncovering a plot to murder the Dey, he dealt with the conspirators ruthlessly. The main conspirator was crucified against a wall with four large nails through his hands and feet, whilst a red hot iron was hammered through both cheeks to prevent him speaking, following which he was slowly burnt to death with faggots of wood whilst other members of the conspiracy had their legs and arms broken in three places on an anvil with a hammer before being strangled (it was said by the Count himself). His actions caused him to be feared and hated by the Algerians, but nobody moved against him for he had built up an efficient network of spies and informers and little happened without him knowing about it. At the same time, he had built up a considerable fortune and it was a great relief to the Dey when the Count expressed a wish, which was quickly granted, to leave his service and retire to his large estate at Blida. He remained, however, the most powerful man on the Barbary Coast and nothing happened without his consent.

"After half an hour had passed, a commotion outside the building announced the arrival of the Count. The door swung open and he came into the room and observed us in our cage. He nodded to a large, bearded Turk who was stripped to the waist. The cage was opened and the Turk took hold of our manacles and led us out into the open, while the Count remained with Abd-el Allai. I looked about me and saw a single storey building open to one side in which a large brazier was burning. Four men came out of the building and two took hold of Joe, whilst the other two took hold of me and held me face down to the ground. All of a sudden a heart-piecing shriek rent the air; it was Joe. I struggled to go to his aid, but strong hands held me down as a long drawn out scream came from Joe and then silence. The grip on me was lessened and I was dragged to my feet. There was no sign of Joe, but the Count was standing nearby looking towards the brazier. The two men then ripped the shirt from my back and I was dragged into the building and manhandled face down onto a wooden table. Leather straps were used to secure me, then the Turk reached into the brazier and took out a hot branding iron with the shape of a letter M which he applied to my upper back. The pain and the smell of my own burning flesh were unbearable and thus I was branded with the initial of the count whose property I now was. The Turk placed the iron into a bucket of cold water, but my ordeal was not over, for he then held my head in a vice-like grip whilst one of his assistants cut off the top of my right ear, as you can see. The Count then looked us both in the eye. "You are my property and always will be until the day you die," he said. "Should you manage to escape there will be no place for you to hide, for I shall hunt you down."

At this point Sawson paused and took off his shirt to reveal the letter M between the shoulder blades of his leathery back. "I need not describe the Count to you," he said. "He is the very man who looked out of the carriage window and saw me on the day that I went to meet Anne at the top of the lane. He saw my right docked ear and recognised me as his property. It is he and his scoundrels who killed poor Harry and will no doubt soon attack us.

"Once Jo and I had been marked and branded, we were taken to a long stone building with a red tiled roof and a stout wooden door. As we approached, the smell was overpowering and once the door was opened and our eyes adjusted to the gloom, we saw why. Inside there were over four hundred men manacled to iron rings attached to the walls and floor. These poor wretches, who we were now to join, were the galley slaves of the Count, each of them branded and docked in the same manner as Joe and I. Once inside the building, a convenient ring was found for both of us and we were left with bleeding ears and branded backs to meet our new shipmates. They were drawn from many different nationalities, mostly poor merchant seaman who had been captured whilst at sea or black Africans from the sub-Sahara who had been captured by Arab slavers and subsequently sold in the slave market in Algiers. We remained in that building for over two weeks, sleeping on the beaten earth floor, whilst the two galleys that the Count owned were being overhauled and repaired following a battle at sea with two Dutch merchant ships, who had made good their escape having put up a stout fight when attacked by the galleys. In the battle, we were told, a number of the slaves had been killed as they sat chained to their oars; clearly Joe and I together with others had been purchased to replace those that had been lost.

"Although we were confined to the building for those two weeks, we did not suffer any further ill treatment. We were in fact reasonably well fed, our staple diet being a variety of different types of couscous dishes with meat and fish along with a plentiful supply of figs, dates and water melons. We had been purchased as galley slaves and it was not in the interest of the Count that we should become weak and sick. Two weeks having passed, we were woken by the main door being flung open and a large bald man with a large beard shouting at us to get out and for the first time in my life I clapped eyes on Hashim Hamidou, the Count's overseer. He was over six feet tall, his brown piggy eyes were deeply set into a flabby fat face across which a livid scar ran from below where his left ear would have been up to his right forehead, cutting across both his lips. It was, without doubt, the most hideous face I had ever seen, becoming even more distorted when he spoke, as the injury to his lips became more apparent. While the Count had a reputation for cruelty and struck fear into the hearts of all who knew or heard of him, Hashim Hamidou ran him a close second and certainly we, who were under his direct control, had cause to fear him the most.

"We emerged, shuffling in our chains, into the bright sunlight to the sound of whips being lashed by Hamidou and his assistants onto the backs of those of the slaves who were not moving as quickly as required. As my eyes became accustomed to the light, I could see that one of the galleys was already putting to sea. The other, the Meshuda, was moored against a low stone pier, waiting to take on its guns and provisions. We were marched onto the pier, where a number of wooden derricks had already been erected with ropes and pulleys attached. Our task was to haul the vessel's twenty-four pounder guns on board. There were eighteen of them and it took us most of the day, toiling in the heat without respite, to heave them aboard. Anybody who flagged was 'encouraged' by a lash across the back to work faster. Once the guns were on board, we continued to load the galley with barrels of gunpowder and a number of small swivel guns that were mounted on the sides above the rowing decks. By now it was early evening and I was expecting to go back to the shed for the night, but it was not to be. We continued to load all the necessary stores and when that was done, we were marched onto the galley and allocated our positions on the rowing decks. Joe and I were fortunate enough to be directed to the starboard upper rowing deck: although we were subject to the elements, it had the advantage, though we did not know it at the time, of meaning that we did not have to live in the fetid conditions of the lower decks. It was six men to an oar. Joe and I sat next to each other on a sturdy wooden plank along with four others. Our ankles were manacled to the deck, whilst our wrists were shackled to the massive oar that we had to row and in that condition we were to remain as long as we were at sea. An open gangway upon which the overseers walked ran down the middle of the deck between the rows of seated slaves and if we did not put our backs into the rowing at the required rate, we soon felt the lash of the whip as the condition of my back testifies.

"Once we were chained to our oars, the most evil-looking body of men that you could imagine came on board: these scoundrels, the sweepings of the port of Algiers, had been recruited by the Count to fight for the ship and to board any unfortunate vessel that had the misfortune of encountering the Meshuda. Once they were on board, Hamidou took leave of the Count, who was not coming with us on this voyage. The gangway was lifted and the ropes that held the galley to the pier were loosened and she started to drift away from the land. Once she was some thirty yards out, a single drumbeat signalled the slaves to heave at their oars and the galley started to move under the power of the rowers, who heaved in time to the beat of the drum. We gradually began to make our way out of the bay and away from Sidi Ferruch to the open sea and our voyage of piracy began. We rowed for two hours. By now we slaves, who had toiled all through the day, were exhausted. Sails were raised, the drumbeat ceased and we collapsed forward onto our oar. Such was our tiredness that in a very short time most of us were in an exhausted sleep."

A LIFE OF PIRACY

"We awoke the following morning to the sound of oaths and the lash of whips. An old man with a leathery back tanned by sea, sun and the whip passed down the line of tethered rowers. He was almost bent double and had clearly spent years in the galleys, as the marks around his ankles and wrists testified. He carried a large wooden bucket and had by far the dirtiest hands I had ever seen which he used to scoop a foul smelling porridge into our cupped hands. This was breakfast. He then returned with a pitcher of brackish water from which he offered each rower in turn a drink. Once he had completed his breakfast duties, he returned with a bucket of seawater which he poured over our sticky hands to enable us to grip and hold the oars without slippage. Once he had accomplished his tasks, he curled up like an old dog under one of the stern guns. Our breakfast complete, the drum began to beat and we commenced rowing, whilst the sun began to rise in the sky and beat down on us. The Meshuda, powered by sail and oar, now set a westerly course towards the waters approaching the straits of Gibraltar where Hamidou hoped to find merchant shipping to plunder. For three days we sighted nothing other than a few small fishing vessels. On the morning of the fourth day we were rowing steadily (there being little wind), when we heard a shout from the lookout that he had spotted a vessel approaching from the east. At once the drumbeat rate increased and the Meshuda started to speed through the water towards a vessel sailing towards us on our starboard side. The crew of the other vessel were clearly not keeping a proper lookout and we were rapidly making ground on her. Eventually we were spotted and she altered course towards the north to try and run from us. It was, however, too late; the wind was light and she could not match the Meshuda for speed. We pursued her for about three hours: the galley was a hive of activity with Hamidou barking out orders and the whip being used liberally to encourage us to keep up our increased rowing rate.

"Whilst we bent our backs to the task in hand, the guns were run out and the pirates prepared their weapons for boarding. As the gap between the vessels narrowed, Hamidou ordered the starboard bow chasers to fire. The first few shots dropped short, but the Meshuda was soon propelled by our efforts into range. The bow chasers continued to fire and although they did not immediately hit the other vessel, it was clear to everyone that it was only a matter of time before they did and more significantly before the Meshuda could bring her main guns to bear and fire a broadside into her quarry. The captain of the other vessel clearly realised that he was not going to be able to outrun the Meshuda and that he would have to fight or surrender. He and his crew were clearly brave men, the colours of France were run up and the 'Deux Frères' of Nantes, although lightly armed with only four twenty-four pounder guns on each side and two stern guns, prepared to fight. No doubt the captain and the crew knew their likely fate if they surrendered. He ordered the man at the wheel to turn the vessel sharply to starboard to prevent the Meshuda raking his vessel with her first broadside. As the 'Deux Frères' turned to starboard she was able to bring her two stern guns to bear on the pirates, who were massing ready to board on the bow of the Meshuda. The sound of her guns firing was followed by screams of anger and pain as the canister and grape shot cut through the exposed boarders. The 'Deux Frères' continued her turn, exposing her stern to the starboard guns of The Meshuda. As each gun came to bear, it fired into her stern. She shuddered and lost all steerage as her rudder was shot away. The Meshuda, highly manoeuvrable under the power of her rowers, now moved in for the kill. Hamidou placed her alongside the starboard side of the 'Deux Frères' and fired three rapid broadsides into her. The effect was devastating: Her main mast was shot away and all her port guns were silenced, though not before one of them had fired directly into the side of the Meshuda, smashing a great hole in her side and killing over twenty of the unfortunate rowers as they sat chained to their seats. Though her guns had stopped firing and she was disabled, the 'Deux Frères' did not strike her colours. As the gap between the two vessels narrowed, the pirates, armed to the teeth with knives, swords and guns, swarmed aboard her. The remains of her crew had retreated to the stern, where they put up a gallant fight. But it was all to no avail and they were overwhelmed by the pirates who showed no mercy to those who had resisted them. With the exception of two badly wounded sailors, all the crew of the 'Deux Frères' who had seen the sun rise that morning were dead. Hamidou quickly went on board the 'Deux Frères' to examine the cargo and to ensure that it was secured for the Count and not stolen by the pirates who had gone below decks in search of plunder.

"With the fighting over and Hamidou and most of the pirates aboard the 'Deux Frères', quietness and calm fell upon the

Meshuda. The exhausted rowers, still chained, fell forward onto their oars, having given their all in the high speed chase. The calm was disturbed only by the throwing of the unfortunate slaves who been killed into the sea and the groaning and screams of those who had been wounded by the 'Deux Frères' initial broadside. The pursuit itself had taken its toll: four of the rowers had collapsed and died from exhaustion. Their bodies too were dumped without ceremony into the sea. A number of others were also in a bad way as a result of their efforts: they received no treatment other than being given the usual gruel and water that we now all received. Our bodies craved sleep and gradually most of the rowers, myself included, were slumbering at our oars. All of a sudden we were woken from our dreams by shouting and swearing. It was still light and looking across to the 'Deux Frères' I could see Hamidou confronting three of the pirates. The 'Deux Frères', though I did not know it then, was a rich prize with a cargo of spices, scents and silks that would sell well in Algiers. The three pirates I could see (I was told later) had raided the captain's cabin. There they had found, amongst other things, a small wooden box containing a number of beautiful carved Chinese ivory pieces. In addition, they had found a number of bottles of liquor which they had broached. Fortified by the liquor, they emerged on deck to be confronted by Hamidou who was engaged with a number of his henchman in securing the cargo on behalf of his master, the Count. Seeing that one of the three was carrying the wooden box, Hamidou called upon him to hand it over. The man refused, calling Hamidou a fat pig and pulled out a short boarding sword, as did his two confederates and they started to move towards him. Hamidou's response was rapid for a large man: he quickly pulled out a loaded pistol and shot one of the men in the head. He fell dead to the deck but before he even landed on it, Hamidou had thrown a dagger at the second of the two pirates: it caught him in the throat and as he lost his balance, Hamidou brought his sword down on his head, killing him instantly. He then advanced on the man with the box and with a swift movement slashed at his upper groin causing him to fall. He could have dispatched him instantly, but he did not do so, for he had other plans for him as we were swiftly to learn.

"The following day, a crew was put on the 'Deux Frères' and a line attached to it from the Meshuda and we commenced the long row back to Sidi Ferruch, towing the 'Deux Frères' behind us. Before we started to row, we were addressed by Hamidou. The unfortunate pirate who he had spared was brought up from the lower deck cage in which he had been confined. Hamidou pointed at him: "This dog tried to steal what belongs to the Count!" he shouted. "His cursed tongue insulted me, let this be a lesson!

"With that, a terrifying scream was heard as the man was dragged to the main mast, his mouth forced open and his tongue nailed to it. He remained nailed in this position until we reached Sidi Ferruch.

"The voyage back to Sidi Ferruch was uneventful. A day after our arrival, the Count arrived to survey the galley's plunder, to estimate its value and to arrange for it to be sent on for sale in Algiers. Once this had been done, the pirates who had been recruited for the voyage were paid handsomely, based upon the estimate of the cargo's worth. Most of them elected to go on the next voyage, though some decided to return to Algiers. Before any of them were paid or allowed to leave, they and the galley crew were forced to watch Hamidou personally crucifying the unfortunate pirate who had insulted him. The cross on which he was crucified was erected on the headland at Sidi Ferruch as a deterrent to all not to cross the Count or Hamidou.

"Joe and I remained as galley slaves on the Meshuda for over four years. During this time, we made many voyages and witnessed scenes of violence, cruelty and depravity; there can never have been such wicked, heartless and violent men as the Count and Hamidou. During those years we were involved in a number of violent actions, but they all pale into insignificance when compared with the fight between the Meshuda and the Hannah of Bristol. We departed from Sidi Ferruch along with the usual bunch of cut-throats that the Count had assembled. He never had any difficulties in finding recruits, such was the success that his vessels had in seizing cargoes and hostages. On this voyage, the Count had decided to accompany us, though as usual Hamidou was also aboard, along with a number of the Count's retainers.

"The two previous voyages had not yielded much in the way of prizes and on this occasion the Meshuda headed east. For the first week into the voyage we saw nothing. A storm then came upon us and we ran for cover towards the coast of North Africa. After twenty-four hours, the storm died down as quickly as it had started and we started to retrace our course. Thus it was that as dawn broke, a cry from the look-out told us that a ship had been sighted through the morning mist, in the distance to the north of us. But for the storm, we would have missed her completely. The drumbeat increased rapidly as we set off in pursuit. The sea now was calm and as the sun came up and the mist dissipated, nothing further could be heard, save the endless groan of the oars as they cut through the tranquil blue water. At first we seemed to be making good progress, but the other vessel quickly became aware of us and at once put on extra sail to make good her escape. Though at first the gap widened, we soon started to gain on her. The ease of the pursuit should have given rise to suspicion, but such was the all-consuming desire for plunder of the Count, Hamidou and the other cut-throats, that all caution was thrown to the wind and within two hours the bow chasers on the Meshuda were firing ranging shots at the slow lumbering vessel ahead of us.

"The Hannah of Bristol was in fact, as we came to learn to our cost, anything but a plump merchantman there for the taking. She was owned by The Levant Trading Company, who held the British trading monopoly in the Levant and had recently conveyed the British ambassador to Constantinople, in which city, along with Aleppo, the company had its chief trading posts and factories. She was now returning to England via Gibraltar with a cargo of silks, cotton, nutmeg, currants and spices. In addition, she was carrying a company of foot soldiers from the 58th Regiment of foot who had embarked at Gibraltar and travelled on the outward voyage as an escort to the ambassador. In addition to the soldiers, the Hannah carried eight twenty-four pounder guns on both her port and starboard sides. This armament made her a formidable opponent, a fact clearly not appreciated by the Count and Hamidou as we bore down on her.

"We were closing rapidly on the port side of the Hannah from a south-easterly direction, when without warning she turned rapidly to port and pointed her bow towards the starboard side of the Meshuda. As she bore down on us, Joe and I had a clear view of the foaming water beneath her bow. A cry went up from the ranks of the rowers as her intention to ram the Meshuda amidships became clear. The helmsman on the Meshuda steered her rapidly to port, but the manoeuvre was painfully slow and still the Hannah came on, so that it seemed the vessels must collide. At the very last minute, the stern of the Meshuda evaded the oncoming Hannah. But as she did so, the soldiers who had been lying concealed in the bow of the Hannah discharged a devastating volley of musket balls into the stern of the Meshuda, where the pirates had been massing, ready to board. As the two vessels moved apart, the air was rent by the screams of the dying and the wounded in the pirate ranks. In addition, the helmsman had been cut down and for a moment the Meshuda shuddered out of control before Hamidou, who had sprinted along the middle gangway, regained control and bought the Meshuda around onto a parallel course to the Hannah. As she came about, she was able to bring her stern port guns into play and discharge a partial broadside into the Hannah. The Meshuda, more manoeuvrable than the Hannah, was soon able to pass down her starboard side, raking her with her twenty-four pounders, whilst the Hannah gave as good as she got, pouring fire into the port side of the Meshuda which wreaked heavy losses amongst the ranks of the unfortunate rowers as they sat at their oars. The soldiers on the Hannah continued to extract a heavy toll on both the pirates and the rowers as they fired relentlessly into the Meshuda. Amidst the noise, smoke and the cries of the wounded there arose a further chorus of pain and agony as the swivel guns on the

Meshuda, which had been packed with chain shot, found their target in the closely-packed ranks of soldiers, cutting swathes through them, whilst at the same time carrying away much of the Hannah's standing rigging. Soon the decks of both vessels were slippery with the blood of the dead and the dying, who lay in heaps where they had fallen, as the two vessels continued to pour broadsides into each other. Although the rowers on the port side bore the brunt of the Hannah's fire, the starboard rowers did not escape death and injury: Four of the rowers on the bench immediately in front of where Joe and I sat were killed by a cannon-ball which had already caused devastation amongst the rowers on the port side, whilst one of the overseers who was particularly free in the use of the whip had his head removed by chain shot. Joe and I bent down on our oars in an attempt to avoid death or injury, but there was no real shelter and in any event we were still in chains, it was a miracle that we escaped injury whilst all around men fell.

"The two vessels continued to pummel each other for over an hour. Hannah's foremast came down with an almighty crash and fell across the Meshuda and the two vessels became entangled. Twenty or so of the pirates, uttering heart-stopping curses, attempted to use it as a bridge to climb aboard the Hannah, but the remnants of the 58th opened up such a withering fire that not a pirate in that party survived. By now only three of the Meshuda's port guns were firing as the two vessels fought themselves to a standstill. The noise of guns firing and the screams of the dying were so loud that you could not hear what your neighbour was saying, when all of a sudden the air was rent by the loudest explosion I had ever heard as the powder magazine on the Hannah exploded. She was soon burning fiercely from bow to stern and clearly there was a great danger that the fire would spread to the entangled Meshuda. Hamidou, who had survived the maelstrom, was the first to see the danger and arming himself with an axe he began desperately chopping at the remnants of the foremast to try and free the Meshuda. He was quickly joined by the Count and a number of the surviving pirates and after about ten minutes of desperate hacking, the Meshuda broke free and started to drift away from the screams of the burning Hannah.

"Whilst the Meshuda was still afloat after the attack, conditions aboard her were terrible: There were dead men everywhere, many mangled beyond recognition, whilst the screams of the dying and wounded pierced the air. Whole benches of rowers had been slaughtered, their remains still chained to the deck as they had been in life. The upper port side of the vessel had been blown away by cannon fire and most of the oars on that side had been reduced to matchwood. For over three hours she just drifted. Joe and I and about thirty others were released temporarily from our manacles and under the watchful eyes of the surviving pirates, we were forced to dump the twisted bodies over the side without ceremony and to wash down the blooded decks. We did so against a background of despairing screams and cries from the untreated wounded as they lay about the ship in agony. As I went about my gruesome work, I could still make out the Hannah on the horizon enveloped in dirty black smoke, breached occasionally by leaping yellow tongues of flame as the fire devoured more of her. Before long she passed out of sight over the horizon, leaving the Meshuda alone on a tranquil sea.

"At the time, the ultimate fate of the Hannah and any who were still alive on her was unbeknown to any of us aboard the Meshuda and if truth be known, little thought was given to her, as Hamidou and his remaining henchmen struggled to get the Meshuda into a condition when we could attempt to return to Sidi Ferruch. We did, however, hear later as events unfurled, that a number of her surviving crew and passengers had managed to escape from her in one of the ship's undamaged boats, whilst others clinging to pieces of wreckage were picked up by a fishing boat which had seen the smoke and altered course to investigate. Amongst those plucked from the sea was one Sergeant William Dodd, the sole survivor of the company of the 58th that had embarked on the Hannah. He and the other survivors were eventually landed at Gibraltar, where they reported the murderous attack upon the Hannah by the Meshuda. The news soon reached the governor and the Admiral of the British Mediterranean fleet and from there the Admiralty and The Levant Trading Company, with far-reaching consequences.

"The voyage back to Sidi Ferruch will live with me for the rest of my days, marked as it was by the whip lashes across our backs as Hamidou and the overseers forced us to put every last effort into our rowing. The sun beat down on us relentlessly, our tongues were parched, for water was in short supply, and we were starving, as most of our meagre rations had been destroyed in the action. The shouts and oaths of the overseers were occasionally punctured by the sound of another unfortunate who had succumbed to his wounds being thrown unceremoniously into the blue sea. We felt at the time that they were in fact the lucky ones; nobody could hurt them now and death had come as a pain-relieving comfort, whilst we who were left continued to suffer. After a few days, the rower immediately in front of us suddenly collapsed forward, dead on his oar through exhaustion and he was not the last, as the heat, lack of water and food and cruel usage took its toll. There was however no let up as Hamidou and the Count continued to drive us on. We were only spared from our labours for six hours in the night, when we collapsed on our oars into an exhausted sleep, all too soon broken by the beat of the drum as the dawn came up. I lost count of the number of days that our nightmare continued, until at last the cape of Sidi Ferruch appeared on the horizon. I had experienced nothing but pain, misery and degradation at that accursed place, but at the time it seemed to me, through sweat-streaming eyes and a parched throat, nothing short of paradise. Slowly we edged into the bay and at last that relentless drum ceased to beat as we tied up alongside the pier. Joe and I had survived but many of our fellow captives, their time on earth now spent, slept soundly with the fishes under the blue Mediterranean Sea, no more to be woken by drum or lash."

RESCUE

"The first few days after our arrival is all a haze to me now, but I'll always remember the sheer delight of slowly quenching my thirst: never had water tasted so good, nor will I ever forget the absolute enjoyment of the water as I poured it over my salt-encrusted head and body. Once we had drunk we were marched in chains to our former quarters, where even the foul gruel that was prepared for us seemed fit for a king. After that my companions and I fell to the bare earth floor and slept. We remained in our quarters for four or five days, though sadly a few of our number were so worn and weak after what we had been through that they died of exhaustion. The Count had lost a considerable number of galley slaves: These were men that he had purchased and no doubt with this in mind and anxious not to have to purchase any more replacements than necessary, we were given time to recover and our food was improved for a time. The Count left, no doubt to see Abd-el Allai and organise the purchase of replacement slaves and to go to Blida. We were left to the tender mercies of Hamidou, who was to see to the repairing and refitting of the Mashuda.

"At the time, though I did not know it, The Levant Trading Company, angered by the loss of The Hannah of Bristol and her valuable cargo, petitioned Parliament to take action against the Barbary Coast pirates and the Mashuda and her owner in particular. As a result, the Admiralty sent orders to the Admiral of the British Mediterranean fleet at Gibraltar to destroy the 'nests of pirates' on that coast. It was decided to send the third rate *HMS Lion* of sixty-four guns under Captain Edward Lynch, who was to command the expedition and the fifth rate *HMS Penelope* thirty-two guns under Captain Harry Lodge to attack Sidi Ferruch. Captain Lynch's plan of action was that *HMS Lion,* having silenced the fort that commanded the entrance to the western bay, should enter that bay and that he should land a force of marines supplemented by sailors at the bottom of the peninsula and destroy any shipping found there which had not succumbed to *HMS Lion's* guns. At the same time, *HMS Penelope* was to carry out a similar operation in the eastern bay, silencing the small fort there and that a smaller land force should then be landed at the bottom end of the peninsula. These forces would then advance and meet those of *HMS Lion*. The two forces should then combine and turn left towards the top of the peninsula and the sea, driving all before it.

"The two vessels did not have sufficient numbers of marines embarked on them for the expedition, so it was decided that the two remaining companies of the 58th Regiment stationed at Gibraltar under the command of Colonel Davis should also be embarked. It was soon known in Gibraltar that the two warships were to mount an attack on the pirates, though their exact destination was unknown. Sergeant Dodd was still recovering from his ordeal in the garrison hospital but once he heard of the expedition he begged to be allowed to take part in the action and his request was granted. He was a short muscular man with a bushy moustache who had seen much active service. Like many members of the regiment he came from Northamptonshire from where the regiment was historically recruited. He came from the village of Chelveston in that county, as had two of his closest comrades who had perished on the Hannah and he was determined to avenge their deaths.

"Captain Lynch, together with Captain Lodge and Colonel Davis were the only people who knew the exact destination of the force, thus ensuring surprise when the attack came. Thus it was that a few weeks later, the two warships sailed stealthily under cover of darkness to a position a few miles off Sidi Ferruch, where just before midnight the forces of soldiers and marines that were to mount the initial assault disembarked into the ships' boats. As soon as the boats were away, the two warships withdrew further out to sea so as to avoid being sighted from the land. The boats meanwhile were rowed with hooded oars steadily under a starry sky towards a point half a mile off the Peninsula. Once there, a masked lantern was shone out to sea three times to inform the warships that they had reached their first destination without detection. This accomplished, the attacking force divided into the two groups that were to attack the forts, whilst the warships started to move slowly towards the coast in the direction of the respective bays they were to enter. The two flotillas of boats both reached the shore close to the respective targets. They were run onto the beaches and the soldiers and marines landed without observation. Yet again, a hooded lantern was flashed out to sea, four flashes to denote the successful landing near to the west bay fort and six flashes for the east bay.

"As I was to learn later, the west bay force moved off quietly in the direction of the silent fort. They passed quickly inland before turning sharply back on themselves so that they advanced on the fort from the rear and out of the sight of any alert sentry who might be looking out to sea. The fort was approached by a stony road with a ditch on either side. The marines and soldiers quickly melted into the ditches and hardly believing their luck, they soon found themselves outside the fort still undetected. The stout wooden gates of the fort were bolted shut whilst the garrison of brigands slumbered inside. Two marines crawled forward on their stomachs, each with a small keg of gunpowder strapped to their backs. Having reached the gates, they placed one of the kegs on its side and removed its wooden bung causing some of the gunpowder to spill out onto the ground. Then opening the other keg, they slowly crawled back to their comrades leaving a trail of gunpowder behind them until they reached the safety of the ditches. Once they had done so, a flint was struck in a tinder box causing sparks to fly in the box and ignite the char cloth contained inside. A small candle was then lit from the flaming char cloth and applied to the powder trail. The marines and soldiers pressed themselves down into the bottom of the ditch while the flame hissing and crackling raced along the trail to the barrel, causing a loud explosion which could be heard all over the peninsula. Pieces of wood, rock and soil rained down on the attacking force, but within seconds a bugle called and the marines and soldiers were out of the ditches and charging through the destroyed gates into the fort. The garrison, stunned and bewildered by the explosion, were no match for the well-trained troops that that were now pouring into the fort. A few managed to take up their weapons but they were cut down by the disciplined musket fire of the attackers as they fanned steadily throughout the fort and up the stairs to spike the guns on the ramparts so as to remove any threat to the Lion which was now sailing purposefully into the bay to destroy the shipping that was anchored there and at the piers. The attack was all over in less than ten minutes with the garrison either dead or locked in a guardhouse under the grim eyes of a file of marines charged to shoot anyone who moved. Another party of marines together with a signaller from the Lion who had reached the highest ramparts spiked the guns there, whilst the signaller with his lamp signalled to the Lion that the fort was taken and no longer posed a threat to her.

"The east bay force had also moved inland in order to attack the fort there from the rear. Their progress was, however, impeded by a deep gulley that required them to move further inland than they wished. Having done so, they soon alighted on the track that led to the fort, but they were now behind schedule and they had just reached the perimeter of the fort when they heard the explosion from the west fort. Any chance of surprising the eastern fort was now gone as the shouts and cries from within made clear. They lay hidden in the scrub about one hundred yards from the fort, where they could clearly make out the anxious sentries on the ramparts looking towards them. A full frontal attack on the fort would clearly be highly dangerous as the garrison would be able to shoot down on them with impunity as they advanced and in any event the gates of the fort would still be locked to them. Faced with this dilemma, Major Black of the 58th detailed one company of the 58th to move to the west side of the fort and to lay down rapid musket fire at the ramparts in order to persuade the garrison that the attack was coming from that quarter. He then called for volunteers to run forward to the gates of the fort with small kegs of gunpowder which had slow burning fuses attached to them. Sgt Dodd stepped forward together with Marine Gray and under disciplined heavy covering fire from the remaining attackers aimed at the ramparts so as to make the defenders keep their heads down, the two of them dashed forward and reached the gates safely, though Marine Gray was shot through his left shoulder. On reaching the gate, they placed the kegs together and ran to the right and pressed themselves against the walls of the fort to await the explosion. An enormous explosion followed which blew down the gates and the ramparts above. With cheers and shouts the 58th and the Marines ran towards the breach in the fort's defences and they were soon within the fort, where fierce hand to hand fighting took place. No quarter was asked for or given. Sgt Dodd was everywhere in the action, fighting like a man possessed. He led a charge of the 58th up the stone stairs bayonetting a huge pirate who stood in his way. Soon the ramparts were cleared and the guns spiked and a signal made to the Penelope that she need not concern herself about an attack from that quarter.

"The two forts having been taken and their guns destroyed, the attacking forces withdrew from them and marched towards each other. They eventually joined together and wheeled to face the sea and the fortified wall, behind which lay the pirates' buildings, including the one in which Joe and I and the other wretched rowers lay manacled.

"The Lion and Penelope meanwhile were in total command of the two bays, their heavy guns pounding the shipping that lay therein. Soon they were all ablaze and sinking, including the Meshuda into which the Lion poured broadside after broadside before she went to the bottom and the water extinguished her burning timbers. Soon every pirate vessel was either burnt or sunk and the two warships ceased firing and started to disembark a force of sailors onto the devastated waterfront. The pirates were now sandwiched between the sailors and the combined land force which was now advancing from their rear.

"Joe and I meanwhile still lay in our manacles in the long stone hut. We had been awoken by the explosion at the west bay fort, but we had no idea what was happening. All went quiet and just as I started to slumber again, there came the explosion from the east. Soon the whole hut was wide-awake wondering what was going on. Suddenly there came the deafening sound of the first broadside of the Lion, as all of her thirty-two portside guns fired. After that, it became clear to us all that Sidi Ferruch was under attack from the sea, but by whom and why we did not know. All we could do was to lie there in our chains and anxiously await the result of the attack, as the sounds of the guns and the fighting came closer and closer.

"The stone fortified wall which separated the top of the peninsula occupied by the pirates had not been constructed to withstand an attack by a disciplined force advancing from the land. Its purpose had been to mark out the area controlled by the pirates and in particular to make it difficult for any galley slave not deterred by the crucifixes I have mentioned, to escape landwards. It was not surprising therefore, that as the 58th and the Marines advanced they met with little resistance other than a few musket shots from the remaining brigands and cut-throats who were all too aware of the impeding threat to them, not only from the land but increasingly from the sea, where the shouts and cries from the sailors grew louder and louder, striking fear in the hearts of those who would oppose them. The gates were soon forced and the 58th and the marines fanned out to hunt down the remaining pirates and to destroy the remaining buildings and their contents. Joe and I along with the other slaves remained chained in our quarters, our ears straining as we attempted to work out who was attacking those who had treated us so severely.

"As the conflict drew closer, I heard for the first time in many a long year the sound of English voices. Never did a sound so uplift a man! I and others roared out: "Here!" "Help us!" "We are captives!" "Rescue us!" and numerous other entreaties. One of the doors was flung open and three or four of our hated overseers ran in, trying to hide amongst us. One of them in his blind panic tripped and fell to the ground close to a large Swede who had felt the lash of his whip for many years. In a flash, the Swede's manacles were tightening around the man's neck. His legs kicked violently for a few seconds before he breathed his last. One of the other overseers, seeing the fate of his companion, advanced towards the Swede with his scimitar raised. An outstretched foot caused him to fall on top of a number of the galley slaves, who rapidly dispatched him from this life with his own weapon.

"Again the door flew open. Standing there, though we did not know it at the time, was Sergeant Dodd. He let out a mighty oath at the sight of what he saw; he called out to those behind him to follow and advanced into the building to the thunderous cheers of all who lay there. A musket ball whistled past his head as one of the surviving overseers fired at him in an attempt to make good his escape. The sergeant swore at him and ran forward to meet him; the overseer advanced towards him waving his sword at head height. Dodd ducked and thrust his bayonet upwards into the man's chest where he remained impaled for a few seconds, before Dodd with a violent twist of his wrist extracted the bayonet and the overseer fell lifeless at his feet. Alerted by our cries, Dodd sidestepped just in time to avoid the downward thrust of a heavy scimitar wielded by the remaining overseer. A volley of shots rang out and the remaining overseer fell, never to rise again. An almighty cheer rang out from all of us at the dispatch of those who had inflicted such pain and misery upon us. Outside the sounds of fighting ceased, the battle was over.

"Though we were now in the hands of my fellow countrymen, we were still manacled and unable to leave the building. Sergeant Dodd roared out: "Where are the keys?" We could not help. They were normally in the custody of Hamidou and of Hamidou there was no sight. Indeed, nobody I subsequently spoke to could tell me his fate. We had to await for an anxious twenty minutes, before a cheerful British sailor arrived with a strong pair of bolt cutters and cut our manacles free from the rings in the floor. As if in a dream, we were then led to the very shed where we had been branded, so that our manacles could be broken on the anvil there. We were at last free and able to take our first steps for a long time without the impediment of chains. Kind hands soon shepherded us down to the water's edge, where the ship's boats were moored. As we shuffled along, we passed a group of thirty or more pirates who had survived the fighting. Their fate was, however, sealed and as we were rowed out into the bay where the Lion lay at anchor the first of them was hung from a gibbet, as a warning to others who might be tempted to act as they had done. As I savoured those moments of freedom, a series of explosions rang out, as the remaining buildings were reduced to rubble. Minutes later Joe and I, along with many of our companions, stood on the deck of the Lion as free men.

"The soldiers and marines were soon embarked and the Lion prepared for sea. As the gap of water between the ship and the land increased, I stood on deck, safe at last, hardly able to believe that my nightmare was over. Suddenly there was a loud explosion, followed by another, as the delayed charges exploded and destroyed the two forts. Yellow sheets of flame leapt up into the sky before subsiding into a macabre dance. Soon the dark silhouette of land began to recede until all I could see was a red glow as the flames continued to consume the pirates' lair and then they too were gone and the Lion and Penelope were alone upon the sea. Soon the grey light of dawn came up and the night, gathering up its all-enveloping garments, gave way to a new day as the sun emerged on the eastern horizon and began its daily climb.

"But as it did so on this day, its rise was mirrored by the hope and excitement that arose in the breasts of those who had been rescued. After years of submission and toil with no end in sight, here at last was a future restored to them."

"During the voyage to Gibraltar, the crew of the Lion from Captain Lynch down to the lowliest sailor showed us nothing but kindness, as did the men of the 58th. The Royal Navy was not renowned for the quality of its victuals, which they gladly shared with us, but compared with the food we had had to endure it tasted like the repast of the gods and we greedily gobbled it down. On that first day, having consumed a breakfast of 'burgoo' (Oatmeal porridge), I lay on the upper fo'c'sle deck and fell into a deep slumber. I awoke to a deep blue sea and sky with occasional wisps of cotton cloud drifting slowly past, propelled by the same gentle breeze that was mischievously filling the canvas of the Lion and then dropping away as she sought to use it to progress through the water. Overhead the sun beat down upon us, the same sun which had mercilessly beaten down on us as we had rowed in the Meshuda, but now a very different sun: there to warm and caress those very same bodies as they luxuriated in their ability to move or not to move as the fancy took them. That night as the darkness arose to reconquer the heavens, we were fed salt pork and pea soup, before settling down to await the appearance of the moon and stars to dance their light upon the tranquil sea.

"I awoke the following morning before dawn. I had not slept well, as the full realisation of what had happened to me had begun to sink in. I was a free man, but free to do what? It was many years since I had left England in the Litchfield. Should I return to the land of my birth? But return to what? I had no family to return to, no home to welcome me, just memories of a hard and miserable life. Might I be recognised and held to account for the death of Samuel Clegg, despite my innocence? Joe, despite the dangers that might await him, wished to return to Gozo and see his parents, if they still lived, and to seek revenge on Georgi for betraying us. He urged me to come with him, but Katarina was no longer of this world and there was little reason for me to return

153

and face the risk of being captured by the knights. So sadly we agreed that we should part when we arrived in Gibraltar.

"Two days later, as the sun set in the west, the Lion's forward anchor splashed into the sea as we arrived at Gibraltar. Captain Lynch was immediately rowed ashore to report to the admiral and the governor. Joe and I, along with the other rescued galley slaves, remained on board, while the men of the 58th disembarked. As they did so, we heartily cheered them for their bravery that had won our freedom. The following morning, we were addressed by Captain Lynch: the Lion, he told us, was ordered to sail to England once she had taken stores on board. Any of us who were British were offered passage home in her if we wished. Alternatively, we could remain in Gibraltar along with those of other nationalities (most of the rescued being sailors) and find employment or passage home on one of the many merchant vessels that called into Gibraltar.

"I had thought to sign on as a sailor on a vessel from the American colonies and to make a new life for myself there. But something within me was driving me to return to the land of my birth and following the address from Captain Lynch, I and some thirty others informed his secretary of our desire to return to England. As the Lion was to sail in two days' time for Portsmouth, I decided to go ashore along with the others who were going to seek passage to other lands. As I walked with Joe up the narrow main street that I had last seen all those years ago, I passed by the Albion, half expecting to hear the raised voice of Mr Hawksworth booming out. But all was of course quiet, for that gruff voice was now silenced within the breast of its owner, sleeping soundly with the fishes in the warm enveloping waters of the Mediterranean. Joe and I walked on before entering a small tavern, 'The Pillars of Hercules', near the dockyard gate, where we toasted our freedom along with others who had been rescued with us. As we sat there reminiscing, we soon got into conversation with sailors from all parts of the globe, including the crew of a small brig from Sicily which regularly traded to and from Malta. Within a short time, Joe had arranged to take passage with them early next morning to Sicily and from then onto Valletta. Thus it was that, later that night outside the Pillars of Hercules, in tears as we parted, I embraced Joe; the kindest and most loyal friend a man could ever have had.

"Two days later in the early morning, the anchors of the Lion were hauled by the capstan up from the muddy embrace of the harbour bottom, her sails were unfurled in a light wind and she began her voyage home to old England. As the silhouette of the great rock faded from sight, a deep melancholy fell over me as I began to wonder what I should do and where to go when I arrived."

RETURN TO ENGLAND

"The voyage across the Bay of Biscay was mercifully calm. On the second morning I was pleased on coming onto deck to see Sgt Dodd. He was returning to England along with some twenty other members of the 58th who had completed their engagement in the army and were returning to civil life. I soon entered into conversation with him: he had served twenty-seven years in the 58th and was now returning to Chelveston, where his wife was the landlady of the Star and Garter pub they had purchased some ten years previously. As the Lion approached Ushant the weather changed as the winds increased and a heavy sea got up. Lashed by heavy rain and with poor visibility, Captain Lynch was forced to take in sail as the Lion was tossed and buffeted by the elements. The weather continued like this for almost a week, during which time the Lion made slow progress. Gradually, however, the wind abated and the Lion was soon in the 'chops of the channel' and the hearts of all on board lifted as the sun came out and decks and cordage started to dry. At the same time, the ship's cooks, whose galley fires had been extinguished during the storm, managed to relight them and a hot meal was served for everyone.

"I now spent all my time on the port side, straining for a view of England. The winds were now light and our progress was slow, when at about four in the afternoon a cry rang out from the masthead: "Land ahoy!" Some twenty minutes later, I managed to catch a glimpse of the southern tip of the Lizard. As the Lion made her way slowly up the channel the coast became clearer and the excitement within the crew and passengers alike grew. I struggled with my emotions: I was excited to be returning, but returning to what? Certainly not in my case to home, I knew of no such place. Sgt Dodd, noticing no doubt how subdued I was, questioned me as to why I was not excited as all the others were. When I told him that I had nowhere to go, he kindly invited me to travel with him to Chelveston where he assured me he could find work for me and provide a bed. I accepted his kind offer and my spirits started to rise, for at least I now had somewhere to go.

"We continued to make slow progress towards Portsmouth and the mood of everyone turned from excitement to frustration as familiar landmarks came into and passed out of view. At long last, however, we approached Portsmouth. Once again there was frustration as the Port Admiral signalled us to anchor at Spithead. The anchors were uncatted and our promiscuous anchors rattled out of the Lion and embraced the sandy bottom. The Lion came up with a start and remained stationary, riding on her anchors. We were home.

"Within a short period of time Captain Lynch was rowed ashore to report to the admiral. He did not return until the following morning during which time most of us had slept badly, full of excitement at finally going ashore. When we awoke next morning we waited anxiously on his return, hoping that we would soon be put ashore rather than having to spend another night on board. On his arrival, we were informed that those who had been rescued were to go ashore the following morning, where we would be welcomed by the admiral and a number of the dignitaries of the town, thus we had to spend a final night on board the Lion. In the meantime, I said goodbye to Sgt Dodd who disembarked that afternoon along with the other members of the 58th. They were to make their way immediately to the regimental depot in Northampton, where they would be discharged from the army. As he climbed over the side, Sgt Dodd repeated his invitation to me to make my way to Chelveston.

"I awoke the following morning to a gentle breeze blowing through the anchorage and the smell of skillygalle (a tasteless oatmeal gruel) and scotch coffee (boiled burnt bread in hot water sweetened with sugar). The ship's cooks prepared breakfast for the crew and then at last we climbed down the wooden walls of the Lion and into a jolly boat. Within a short time, at the call of a midshipman, the boat's crew dipped the blades of their oars into the Solent and commenced the long row into Portsmouth. I lay back in the boat and watched as Portsmouth Point came into view. Soon we were past the Round Tower and into the narrow mouth of the harbour with Priddys Hard and Gosport on our port side. Once through and into the harbour crammed full of sailing vessels as far as the eye could see, the midshipman steered us sharply to starboard and within a short period of time the jolly boat's painter was securely tied to an iron bollard in the Camber Dock and I set foot in England for the first time in many a year.

"Once ashore and along with those others who had been rescued, I passed out of the dockyard to an area of open land beside the 'Domus De' (an old hospice and almshouses) where a platform had been erected. We were then welcomed by the Mayor of Portsmouth and the Port Admiral and presented with new clothes to replace the rags supplemented by the ill-fitting garments that the sailors of the Lion had presented to us from the slop chest on our liberation. The mayor also presented us each with fifteen shillings to tide us over until we reached home or found work. Once the address was over and the Mayor and the admiral had departed, we were led to some nearby tents where we sat down to hot broth, large slices of pigeon pie, beef and mutton pudding, bread and cheeses and pints of ale. Gradually as they finished their meal my companions started to drift away, mostly to the nearby public houses to spend their new-found riches. I very quickly realised that the time had come when I must once again fend for myself.

"I had no desire to return to the sea and I quickly resolved to leave Portsmouth. The more difficult question was, however, where should I go? I had of course the offer to go to Chelveston, but I had never been there and the only attraction it had was that I knew Sgt Dodd would be there. It was then that I thought of my old friend Bounce and his home in Lee. Here at least I knew the area, though there would no doubt be many changes. Accordingly, I resolved to make my way to London and if there was nothing there for me to make my way to Chelveston. Thus it was that in the early evening I turned my back on the sea and started to walk out of the town. That night I slept under the stars in St James's Churchyard in Milton. It was a quiet spot, the inhabitants being in a far deeper sleep than I. The sun came up on a bright spring morning and I was soon on my way and off Portsea Island and on the London road. I walked all day, stopping only to buy a loaf of bread and some cheese at a roadside cottage. After years in the heat in the Mediterranean I enjoyed the lushness and tranquillity of the countryside. That night, weary and footsore, I lay under the stars in a quiet copse off the London road on a soft bed of young bracken, falling asleep to the night call of a pair of tawny owls as they set out to look for breakfast. The following morning, I bathed in a cool stream and recommenced my journey, still marvelling at the beauty of the countryside through which I was walking: fertile meadows, cool woodland, all such a contrast to the squalor into which I had been born and to which I was now heading. It was in this frame of mind, as I reached the top of an incline and saw the open road sloping gently away ahead of me towards an inviting public house in the distance, that I resolved that this was a place where I would like to stay for a while and with this in mind, I stopped at midday under a warm sun at the entrance to the Talbot.

"On entering, I called for a pot of ale and a mutton pie. Pulling up a chair close to the window, I soon got into conversation with a carter and a number of farm labourers all of whom confirmed to me that there was farm work available in the area and helpfully where I might go to find it. So it was that later that day, I found employment as a farm labourer and here, as you all know, I have remained ever since."

With the story of his early life now recounted, Sawson looked about him at his family and said: "De Montagnac regards me as his property. He will not rest until he has either captured me or killed me. He is a ruthless man and will not let anything stand in his way. I have no doubt that he will be back soon, accompanied by a band of murderous ruffians, eager to do his bidding, for he will pay them well. We must prepare ourselves for a violent attack launched by those who will show no mercy." As he said this, he looked up at his family gathered around him:

Molly and Anne had turned deadly pale and the colour had drained from the cheeks of Robert and Ben. Deep inside, Sawson's heart dropped a beat, for though he was still as strong as an ox and shaped by the horrors of his early life, he knew that his gentle family could be no match for the sweepings of the seas and ports who were about to descend upon the lonely farm and inwardly he cursed its isolation: that blanket of seclusion he had sought might now be his shroud and that of all his family, but he dare not let them know how hopeless he believed their position to be.

For the rest of the day, Sawson, Robert and Ben took such steps as they could to secure the farmhouse. The shutters were firmly closed, the rear doors to the scullery and the kitchen were firmly barred and the heavy furniture piled up against them. The fires were stoked up and as much water as possible was set to boil. From the farm building, bill hooks, pikes and scythes were gathered up, along with a collection of knives, axes and hammers. From behind the kitchen dresser, Sawson and Robert took out and loaded two old muskets that they occasionally used to shoot magpies. Robert then positioned himself at the barricaded kitchen door. Finally, Sawson went to an old chest in the dining room and took and primed an old pair of flintlock pistols that old Jack Cowper had previously owned. In the midst of all this activity, Molly Ben and Anne kept watch from upstairs over the front and back of the house, but nothing stirred. Then at about three in the afternoon Molly called out that she could see someone coming down the lane. Everyone ran into the house and the front door was secured. Sawson peered out into the farmyard through a crack in the shutters. At first he could see nobody, but soon a man emerged into the farmyard looking around in surprise at seeing or hearing nobody about in what was normally a busy farm. Sawson suddenly relaxed as he recognised old Billy the pedlar, a regular caller at the farm.

Old Billy was a stickily-built man with long, flowing grey hair and a wispy white beard. He had sharp blue eyes set in a red, leathery cheeks and a beaky nose. He always wore a black canvas coat and trousers tied around the waist by stout piece of rope. This clothing, along with his dirty yellow stockings, gave him the appearance of an upright crow. On his head he wore a battered stove hat which he had never been seen to take off. Though of advanced years, he was still immensely strong, as he needed to be to carry the immense pack that he carried on his back. When he opened his mouth to speak, which he did in a sing-song voice, the recipient of his speech was greeted by a single tooth standing firmly to attention at the front of his upper jaw. It was said that in his early days he had been a soldier, but where he came from or where he went to, nobody knew. When he called at Malsters he would normally, given its isolation from his next port of call, spend the night in the barn and leave before sunrise.

Sawson questioned him closely as what he had seen in his travels, whether he had seen anyone as he approached Malsters, but he had no news to tell. He had noticed nothing unusual on the road or indeed off it. Sawson felt obliged to tell him of the danger that he and his family were in and to warn him that he might be in danger if he slept in the barn that night or indeed if he left the farm now, as anyone watching might think he was carrying a message. On hearing this, Old Billy thought for a moment before saying that he was going to stay, provided he could sleep on the farm in a place of his own choosing. Sawson, grateful for any assistance, agreed that he could, but urged him to come into the house. But Old Billy refused, saying that he had not slept in a house for fifty years and he was not going to start now. He was not however, it has to be said, averse to going into the kitchen for a slice of pigeon pie washed down with a tankard of ale, following which he strolled out into the farmyard and looked about before making his way across to the pigsty, where a large sow and her eight young piglets were settling down for a good night's sleep. He stopped by the gate to the sty and put down his pack before sitting down on the ground. Anyone watching would have been surprised to see what happened next: He quickly opened the pack and took out a short piece of chain, which he transferred into one of his numerous pockets. Delving again into the pack, he drew out a cruel-looking knife with a long tapered blade. This was swiftly followed by a heavy wooden cudgel. Within seconds, both knife and cudgel were concealed in his clothing. He finally rummaged into his pack and took out a ball of rough twine. Then he secured the pack, before placing it inside the pigsty, between the pigs and the entrance. Once he had done this, he stood up and looked carefully around as a soldier might survey the ground before a battle. After a minute or two he walked over to a low-lying stone wall adjacent to the farmyard gates, which Sawson had just chained. He attached the end of the ball of twine securely to the wall and then walked slowly backwards to the pigsty keeping the twine at about six inches above the ground. On reaching the gate to the pigsty he opened it carefully still holding the twine tightly. He then sat down on the ball of twine and proceeded to remove his right boot to reveal five filthy toes, who, if they could have spoken, would no doubt have expressed bewilderment about their exposure to the light after their many years of incarceration. They would also have expressed surprise as to what happened next as Old Billy took out the knife and severed the taut twine from the rolled ball and tied the end to his five toes. He then placed the knife back in his pocket and the ball of twine in the pack and closed the gate. Having completed his preparations for the night, he threw himself down on the floor in the pigsty with the twine securely attached to wall and toe. Within a few minutes he fell fast asleep and very quickly was engaged in a melodious duet of snores with his new found piggy bedfellows.

Whilst Old Billy was preparing himself for his slumbers, Sawson did what he could to prepare for the anticipated attack: the outbuildings were secured and a variety of objects were scattered about the farmyard in the hope that any intruders would trip over them and thus alert him and the family to their presence. Having done this, he stood gazing at the front of the house for a good ten minutes, following which he went to the back of the large barn where the hen coop was. Moving carefully into the nearby grass, he suddenly stopped and made safe a gin trap that he had previously placed there in order to catch any fox that was out looking for a meal. He then lifted the trap up and walked to the front of the house. He stopped in front of the dining room window on the left hand side: here he thought was the most likely window that any intruder might approach, due to there being a privet hedge directly in front of it that would give a degree of cover to anyone approaching. Bending down he placed and concealed the trap with its evil serrated jaws directly below the window. This done, he drew himself up and walked around the farm for one last time before going into the house and securing the front door, just as the wind and rain began to get up. Inside all was quiet, save for the comforting tick from the longcase clock that sounded louder in the unusual prevailing silence. Sawson was ready.

THE ATTACK ON MALSTERS

Gritting his teeth in the face of the icy rain, the boy, George Pearce, eldest son of Joan and Bob, at last reached the road and turned right. Buffeted by the wind that was blowing directly in his face, he made slow progress towards the track on the left that led to Malsters. There he would have the sad task of telling Molly that her father, old Dick Garvey, had taken a turn for the worse and was not expected to last the night. At this time, George was sixteen years old and tall and muscular for his age. For as long as he could remember, he had his assisted his father with the sheep up on the Downs. He was light and nimble of foot and but for the weather, he would already have reached Malsters. There is a curve in the road just before the turn to Malsters and as he approached, he thought that he heard a raised man's voice. Instinctively he turned off the highway through some bushes and stopped and listened and this time he heard the distinct sound of a horse neighing, followed by an oath. Suspicious as to why anyone should be out on the highway on such a night without good reason, George made his way stealthily across the field. As he did so, he heard more voices: clearly there were a number of people nearby.

On reaching the edge of the field, George went down on his stomach and slowly inched his way towards the hedgerow that divided the field from the sunken track that led to Malsters. On reaching the hedgerow, he was able to peer through it into the lane below. As his eyes adjusted to the light, he was able to make out the silhouette of a carriage, stationary in the mouth of the track just off the Portsmouth road. But for his acute hearing honed by years of sheep tending, he would have turned into the lane directly where the carriage was. Near the carriage he could make out at least nine men and a number of horses tethered to the trees on the edge of the lane. He strained his ears to try and hear what was being said, but the wind and rain made it difficult. It soon became clear that the coarse, rough voices were not local to the area and at least two of the men (one of whom was over six foot in height) were foreign. As he lay and listened, it soon became clear to him that the men were armed and not there for any innocent purpose, and that the object of their attention was Malsters. He gave thanks that he had not stumbled upon them from the highway, for as a result of what he could see and hear, he realised that his arrival would not have been welcomed.

George realised quickly that there was even more reason now to get to Malsters as quickly as possible. He carefully crawled away from the lane at the same time wondering how to approach Malsters. He was concerned that if he entered the lane further down closer to Malsters he might meet some of the men, for he had no idea whether other members of the gang might have already advanced down the lane before he had commenced his observations. With this in mind, he resolved to keep well away from the lane and approach the rear of Malsters from across the fields. Once he was a safe distance from the lane, he got up and ran as fast as he could across the fields and through bushes and ditches. The ground was uneven and unfamiliar and as he ran, on occasions blinded by the icy rain, he tripped and stumbled and fell to the ground. Unfriendly bushes and branches vied to make contact with him, tearing at his clothing and scratching his face. Eventually he found himself, covered in mud and scratches, at the rear of Malsters. He stood still: apart from the wind and the rain and the beating of his heart he could hear nothing. Taking comfort from the fact that he had reached the farm before any attack, he quickly climbed over the orchard wall and ran to the kitchen door and banged heavily on it.

Within the farmhouse, Sawson and his family were startled by the loud knocking at the kitchen door. Thinking that the attack had begun, Sawson, pistol in hand, advanced to the door shouting: "Who is it?" George shouted his name, but the reply was lost in the wind. Sawson shouted out again: "Who is it?" At the same time, Robert, who had gone upstairs to look out of one of the bedroom windows, leant out of the window intending to fire at the intruder and heard George shout his name. Recognising his cousin, he shouted out to Sawson to hold his fire. Quickly joining his father, they pushed the piled-up furniture away from the door and within seconds the exhausted George was pulled into the house and the door re-secured.

Sitting down at the kitchen table with a bowl of hot broth before him, George blurted out his reason for coming and what he had seen on the way. Sadly, in the circumstances, everyone realised that Molly would not be able to leave to be with her father when he died. More chillingly, everyone realised that they might well die before the old shepherd went to meet the Good Shepherd and his flock. George's news, however, brought them a little relief: for there was now the certainty that the attack would come that night. Sawson then went to one of the shuttered front windows of the house and peered out into the deserted farmyard, whilst the rest of the family watched anxiously. Meanwhile Old Billy slept soundly, his snores drowned out by his newfound companions.

Just up the lane out of sight, a group of nine men stood silently. At a nod from the tall man that George had noted earlier, one of the group, a small thin man, moved forward and crawled on his hands and knees towards the chained gate that was the entrance to the farmyard. Pressing himself against the side of the lane he slithered on his belly until he reached the right hand stone pillar of the gate. From there he had an uninterrupted view into the yard and the front of the house. All was quiet, the wind had dropped and the heavy rain had turned to a light drizzle. To the east the sun was sleepily preparing to begin its daily climb. The man looked about and gave the lightest of whistles, which was unheard in the house, but immediately heard by a number of his companions around the corner, well used to breaking silently at night into houses in London. On hearing the whistle, five more men moved carefully forward and joined the thin man whilst the remaining three, including the tall man, went a little way back up the lane to join another of their number, who was with the tethered horses they had brought down the lane earlier. The three men including the tall man each took a horse by its bridle and stood still.

At the farmyard gate, the thin man pressing his body close to the ground, crawled along the bottom of the secured gates to where they met at the middle. He then stopped and took up a pair of bolt cutters which had been strapped to his right leg. Sawson had anticipated that any intruders might try to cut the chain and had selected the heaviest shackles that he had on the farm. The thin man soon realised that not only was his tool inadequate for the job, but that even if it had been adequate, there would be considerable delay, given the manner in which Sawson had tied the chain. The thin man therefore continued to crawl to the further pillar, following which he stood up with care and wriggled onto the top of the adjoining wall. From there he gave two short low whistles, that were acknowledged in the same manner by one of his companions. The thin man then lowered himself down into the farmyard. In doing so, unbeknown to him, his right leg came into contact with the twine that Old Billy had attached to the wall.

Old Billy awoke with a start and looked around. He quickly realised what had happened and, moving with surprising speed and agility for a man of his age, he crawled out of the pigsty door and lay behind the wall that divided the sty from the farmyard. As he lay there, he was startled by a low whistle from nearby and an answering whistle from further away. He raised his head slightly and peered over the wall just in time to see the thin man crawling in the direction of the sty. Old Billy ducked down. The thin man, unaware of Old Billy's presence, reached the wall of the sty and sat down with his back pressed against the wall to observe the house, which was only twenty yards away. He leant forward to get a better view. It was the last thing he ever did, as Old Billy sprang up and in a flash brought his chain down over the thin man's face and around his neck pulling him backwards and choking out any cry. Old Billy continued to pull and twist the chain with all his might. The thin man kicked out, but it was no use and he ceased to move. As Old Billy released his grip, he fell lifelessly forward. Old Billy, not sure whether the thin man was dead or had merely lost consciousness, glanced about him before taking out his knife and cutting the thin man's throat, following which he slipped back behind the wall.

A minute or two later, Old Billy heard a further low whistle as one of the thin man's companions tried to make contact with him. All remained quiet and Old Billy lay still. By the gate, the remaining five men stayed still, at a loss as to what to do. Eventually the man who had been returning the thin man's whistle got up and made his way to the wall. He was stockier in build than the thin man and had greater difficulty in climbing the wall but he managed to do so. On entering the yard he moved gingerly in the direction that the thin man had gone. Old Billy listened intently. All of a sudden he heard heavy breathing, as the heavier man approached. The heavier man suddenly caught sight of the body of the thin man. He crawled forward quickly and bent over him. As he did so, Old Billy hit the back of his head with his heavy wooden cudgel. He screamed out in agony. As he fell forward, Old Billy swiftly plunged his knife three times into his back and the man screamed no more. Old Billy, wiping his knife, disappeared into the pigsty with the pigs.

The remaining four men, having heard the scream, immediately ran forward and started to climb over the wall and the gate. Sawson and the rest of the household, alerted by the screams, looked out. Sawson, quietly opening the shutter of the window, watched as the men came towards the house, tripping on and cursing at the items he had strewn over the yard. As the men came in close range, Sawson took careful aim at the nearest one with his pistol and fired. An almighty scream was heard and the man fell dead on the ground. Sawson slammed the shutter shut and the three attackers sought cover, before firing at the house. As Sawson had anticipated, the three men then approached the dining room window under cover of the hedge. On gaining the window, they smashed the glass and began to chop at the shutters with axes. At the same time, they ignited brushwood bundles they had brought with them and thrust them up against the splintered shutter. Sawson roared at his family to keep back for fear of the assailants firing into the dining room. Meanwhile Ben and George ran to an upstairs window with saucepans of boiling water that they poured down on the men below. The attackers managed to avoid most of the water, but all of a sudden there was a terrible scream as the gin trap snapped tight on the left leg of one of the men as he jumped back to avoid the water. As the man struggled to free himself, the jaws of the trap bit deeper into his leg and his screams increased, unnerving his two companions, as they struggled to get through the window and into the house. As the first of them swung his body through the broken shutters he cried out in agony and fell back on his companion, as Robert thrust a billhook into his side. With that, the second man took hold of him and the two of them retreated out of the farmyard and up the lane, leaving their companion in the gin trap cursing and screaming.

Whilst the attack took place at the front, the other three attackers, leading their horses, had circled around to the back of the farm and had reached the wall of the orchard. Securing two of the horses to an old tree, they surveyed the back of the house. All was still quiet. At a nod from the tall man, one of the others, a tall swarthy young man who answered to the name of Ned, mounted his horse and rode up to the wall where he was joined by the two other men who were still on foot. The tall man stood at the head of the horse, holding its bridle securely. This done, Ned stood up in his stirrups and with the assistance of the remaining man, he stood up on the horse's back and climbed with ease onto the top of the wall. Once there, his companion threw him a stout rope that he tied around his waist, throwing the other end of the rope back to his companions, who held it tightly and took the strain as Ned lowered himself quietly down the wall into the orchard. On reaching the ground, the youth quickly untied the rope and crawled to the orchard gate. Within seconds, he slid back the upper and lower bolts; the middle bolt was secured by a rusty padlock and chain. The chain was not nearly as thick as on the farmyard gates and taking out a pair of bolt cutters, Ned quickly cut the chain and opened the gate and the two remaining men, leading the horse, silently entered the orchard and looked about them. Everything was still quiet.

As the three men advanced into the orchard, the silence was shattered by the shot that Sawson had fired at the front of the house and the shouts and screams of the attackers and the besieged. Taking advantage of the attack at the front of the house, the three men, one still leading the horse, quickly ran across the orchard and reached the back of the house, whilst the attention of Ben and George, who should have been keeping watch, was diverted. Once again the tall man nodded and Ned climbed onto the horse that the tall man then led to just under the main upstairs bedroom window. Their luck continued to hold, for just as Ben and George in response to a shouted command from Sawson were about to return to their posts, the scream of the unfortunate man in the gin trap rent the air and Ben and George froze before running to the front window. As they did so, Ned, once more standing on the horse's back, threw a grappling iron onto the roof. It held securely and taking hold of it, he pulled himself onto the window-sill above. On reaching the sill, he let go. The tall man threw him an axe and Ned kicked and broke the window glass before wielding the axe at the shutters that gave way. With a blood curdling shout, Ned, cutlass in hand, jumped into the bedroom, whilst at the same time the tall man who had now climbed onto the horse's back took hold of the grappling iron and started to pull himself up. The third man remained holding the horse.

Startled by the sound of the broken glass, Molly and Anne screamed. George and Ben, who were both armed with billhooks, ran towards the intruder, but they were no match for him. Ned swung his cutlass viciously at Ben with such force that he knocked the billhook clean out of his hands. He lifted the cutlass again to bring it down on Ben's head, but as he did so, George managed to drive his billhook into Ned's left thigh. The wound, though not that deep, was sufficient to cause Ned to curse and lose his balance and to deflect the downward course of the cutlass, which caught Ben on his right upper arm, causing a deep wound. Ben screamed out in pain and fell to the floor. As he did so, Robert, who had abandoned his post at the kitchen door and run up the stairs, pointed his musket at Ned and fired. Ned took the full force of the shot in the chest and fell mortally wounded. The discharge of the musket coincided with the arrival of the tall man through the window, armed with pistol and a scimitar. He immediately took aim at Robert, who threw himself down on the stairs. Mercifully the shot missed. At the same time, George pulled Ben into a nearby bedroom and proceeded to barricade the door with furniture.

The tall man, hearing the sound of women screaming, ran towards the room from which it came. He kicked open the door with ease. Sawson meanwhile, hearing the sound of battle, ran from the front of the house, pistol in hand, up the stairs. As he bounded up them he beheld a sight that far exceeded his worst dreams. At the top of the stairs stood the tall man holding little Anne, his right arm was tight around her throat and in his left hand was a scimitar. Sawson froze, there was no mistaking the livid scar: it was Hamidou.

"Drop the pistol!" screamed Hamidou. "Or the maid will not see the dawn!" As he spoke, he slowly moved the scimitar across Anne's throat; his meaning could not have been more obvious. Sawson stood transfixed, his worst nightmare had come to life: the centre of his life, all that he held dear, was held firmly in the arms of the man who epitomised all the misery that he had suffered since he had been sold into slavery… The pistol dropped from his hand and fell noisily down the stairs onto the stone floor.

"Tell your men to put down their weapons!" snarled Hamidou, who was clearly under the impression that there were more defenders in the house than just Sawson and his family. Sawson shouted out to Robert to do what Hamidou required and Robert reluctantly laid the musket down, which he had by now reloaded.

Hamidou called out for his companions, but other than an acknowledgement from the remaining man in the orchard with the horse there was no reply or sound other than the screams and curses of the man in the gin trap. Hamidou glared at Sawson. Notwithstanding that he held little Anne, he was clearly thwarted in his desire to 'recapture' the Count's escaped slave that was Sawson. His piggy eyes glared angrily at Sawson. "She will fetch a high price in Algiers!" he bellowed. "Or maybe we will keep her for ourselves!" He grinned horribly. Sawson in a rage leapt forward. "Get back!" roared Hamidou. "Or she dies!" Sawson, who had witnessed countless ruthless acts of cruelty by Hamidou, stopped in his tracks and retreated. "Do not try to follow us!" shouted Hamidou. "If you do, you know what the consequences will be!" And once again he drew the scimitar across Anne's throat. With that he bounded towards the window with Anne held tightly in his arms. He quickly lowered her out of the window into the arms of the man below, before jumping down onto the back of the horse below. As soon as he left the room, Sawson bounded to the window just in time to see the two men and Anne reach the orchard gate. He scrambled out of the window closely followed by Robert, but it was too late, as Hamidou and his companion reached the two remaining tethered horses. Hamidou climbed onto one, whilst his companion held Anne. He then pulled her up onto the saddle and galloped off, followed by his companion who had released the spare horse, smacking it on the rump, causing it to run off so that nobody could mount it and follow. Within seconds they had gone. All was quiet, save for the cries of the man in the gin trap. All of a sudden he let out a blood-curdling scream which ended abruptly as Old Billy arrived and drew his knife across his throat.

THE AFTERMATH AND THE PURSUIT

The sun came up over Malsters to reveal a scene of devastation: In the farmyard four of the attackers lay dead, whilst upstairs Ned still lay where he had fallen. The attackers had paid a heavy price, but it was nothing compared to the price that Sawson and his family had paid. Ben's wound would soon heal, but the loss of little Anne, now far away in the hands of Hamidou and the Count, was felt deeply by one and all and a deep sadness and emptiness filled the hearts of all the family. Sawson stood alone at the gates of the farm with tears falling down his tanned and leathery face and swore he would not rest until he found and rescued Anne. He composed himself with difficulty before returning to the house to console Molly, devastated by the loss of Anne and the news of her father that George had brought, not to mention the wound that Ben had suffered. There was, everyone knew, little time to lose. If Anne was to be found, it was necessary that Sawson should leave as soon as possible before the trail went cold, but to leave Molly at the time that she needed him most was almost too much for Sawson to bear.

On entering the house, Sawson gathered his family around him in the sitting room. They sat in silence, punctured only by the reassuring tick of the longcase clock. Sawson, looking at their sad and tearful faces, almost reverted to tears himself but (knowing as he did how important it was that he should remain strong and comforting in their hour of need) managed to control himself and addressed them: "I have to go after them at once," he said. Molly and his sons looked at him and nodded. "Robert, you must stay here and look after the farm and Ben, whilst your mother and George go to Dusters." Robert started to protest, saying he wanted to accompany his father, but he quickly saw the sense in what his father suggested and fell silent. At this, to everyone's surprise, George spoke: "Uncle let me come with you," he said. "I am sure you will need help." Sawson was about to decline when Molly said: "I agree, I can make my own way to Dusters and I should feel better knowing that there are two of you trying to rescue Anne." Sawson remained silent for a moment and then agreed.

Molly quickly set about preparing a breakfast, whilst Sawson gathered together a few things that he needed for the journey, not least the flintlock pistols. He then emerged into the sunlit farmyard, where Old Billy was calmly sitting on the pigsty wall whistling whilst securing his pack, giving no indication that a short time earlier he had killed three of the besieging ruffians. Sawson approached him and took him by the hand: "But for you, Billy, we would all be dead or carried away. I can never thank you enough. My house will always be your house. Stay as long as you like; I will be in your debt forever. Old Billy looked at him and smiled, his single tooth sparkling in the sunshine. "I thank ye," he said. "Perhaps one day when I cease my wanderings, but for now the open road calls and I must follow her, once I have had a bit of breakfast."

Sawson, blinking back his tears, took him back into the house where a hasty breakfast was consumed, following which Sawson, Robert and George carried Ned's body from upstairs to the field beyond the orchard, before taking the four bodies from the farmyard to the same location, where they were placed under an old tarpaulin pending their transportation to the old churchyard. This completed, Sawson and George, each leading a horse and accompanied by Molly, Robert and old Billy, walked slowly out of the farmyard and waving goodbye to Ben, turned into the lane and out of sight.

It was a fine, clear, cold morning. The wind and rain had stopped, droplets of water on the bushes twinkled in the weak morning sun. The little party walked slowly and quietly up the lane, each of them lost in their thoughts about what had happened in the previous few hours. The silence was occasionally broken by the harsh cries of the rooks and crows in the tall trees at the top of the lane. A magpie darted out from a low-hanging branch. Sawson's heart missed a beat; 'one for sorrow' as the old rhyme said and hoped for another 'two for joy' and with that, as they rounded a bend, two more rose squawking from a puddle where they had been taking a drink; 'three for a girl'. It was but little, but Sawson in his grief saw it as a good omen, as no doubt the others did, but nobody said anything. Just before reaching the last bend in the lane before it reached the main highway, they were startled by the whinnying of a horse nearby. Everyone save Sawson froze. He bounded forward round the bend, only to find four of the horses that had been tethered there earlier on that morning, awaiting the return of their owners, now asleep under the tarpaulin in the field beyond the orchard.

They moved on and reached the junction with the main highway. There Sawson knew he had to decide whether to turn left towards Portsmouth or right towards London. It was, he knew, a critical decision: if he got it wrong, there was every chance that they would never see little Anne again. It was, mercifully, an easy decision to make: the heavy rain of the previous night had left the ground muddy and the marks of the carriage wheels turning into the lane and coming out of it were plain for all to see. Peering at the marks with his long experience of life on the road, Old Billy confirmed Sawson's decision that the carriage had driven off in the direction of London. There could be no doubt that Anne would have been placed in the carriage by Hamidou, for he would not have dared to ride with her on a horse along the highway and take the risk that she might call out to other travellers on the highway. As they stood at the top of the lane, Old Billy noticed something else that Sawson and the others had not noted. "Look!" he cried. "Blood!" Sure enough, a number of spots of blood could be seen on the ground. Sawson gave thanks that the rain had stopped and the spots had not been washed away. The man that Robert had stabbed with the billhook had clearly been badly wounded and it seemed likely that the blood spots marked where he had been placed into the carriage. At this discovery, Sawson's spirits rose, for it would clearly be easier to follow the trail if the attackers were having to attend to a badly wounded companion who needed treatment.

It was the parting of the ways. Old Billy turned left in the direction of Portsmouth, promising to call in at the Talbot, for if they were wrong in deciding which way the carriage had gone, those at the inn would know and he would get word back. It was, he said, his intention to go to Portsmouth, which again was a relief to Sawson, for if in fact Hamidou and the Count were making for the port, then there was little doubt that old Billy, who did not miss a trick, would soon find out. Sawson embraced Robert who then returned down the lane to collect the tethered horses and lead them to their new quarters at Malsters, before going out into the fields beyond the orchard to recover the loose horse that had been set free when Hamidou and his companion had ridden off with Anne. Sawson, Molly and George turned right and soon after Sawson took a fond farewell of Molly, who turned off to the left and Dusters. Sawson watched her until she was out of sight, at which point with her departure he and George mounted their horses and set off in the direction of London.

For the next few hours Sawson and George rode in silence along the London Road. Eventually they arrived at the Red Lion at Petersfield. Sawson quickly dismounted and went into the old inn which was busy making preparation for the arrival of the Portsmouth Mail. His questions of everyone he asked as to sightings of a carriage heading for London met the same answer: "No sir, no carriage has been here for the past four hours." Sawson began to wonder whether Old Billy might have been mistaken and that Hamidou and his companions had in fact headed in the direction of Portsmouth. His doubts were soon, however, cast aside with the arrival of the Portsmouth Mail, whose guard confirmed passing a black carriage, accompanied by three horsemen, heading towards London some two hours ago. Buoyed by this news, Sawson and George rode on in pursuit.

Soon after they left the Red Lion, the sky turned black and it began to rain heavily. Their progress slowed as the rain lashed their faces and the wind buffeted them as they sat in their saddles. When they reached the Old Anchor at Liphook they were soaked to the skin. Dismounting from their steaming horses, Sawson and

George went into the inn and stood before a blazing fire thawing out, whilst the bar maid set about preparing them a hot meal of mutton, potatoes and turnips. As she placed the piping hot bowls before them, Sawson inquired of the carriage and the horsemen. "Yes," she said, they had been here and one of their number was not well, as they had inquired if there was a doctor nearby. The doctor, she had told them, had gone to Guildford that very morning for a wedding and she could not say when he would be back. The carriage had left soon after. Sawson questioned her about the person who was ill and who was in the carriage, but she was unable to help any further, she told him, as although she had gone out to the carriage and offered to help, her offer had not been accepted and she had not seen inside the carriage. She had, however noted that the carriage was unusual, in that individual spokes of its wheels were not painted one colour. Instead, each individual spoke had been painted: a third red, a third green and a third yellow, whilst the wheel hubs were painted blue.

Refreshed and with their horses fed, Sawson and George galloped on. Clearly, the man wounded by Robert's billhook was in a bad way and his condition was slowing down his party, as they tried to get medical help for him. They rode on past the lonely Hutts Inn and the Devil's Punchbowl, through Godalming and across Peasmarsh Common and then to Guildford, stopping to make inquiries about the carriage, but all to no avail. It seemed as if Hamidou and his companions had vanished into thin air. Then about four miles from Ripley their luck changed for the better, when they came across a farmer on horseback accompanied by two farm carts containing squealing piglets. He had good cause to remember the carriage, for it had come around a bend in the highway at speed and almost collided with him and his carts. An argument had followed, in the course of which he and his labourers had been threatened by some London ruffians led by a scar-faced foreigner if they did not quickly manoeuvre the carts out of the way.

Riding on, Sawson and George soon arrived at the Talbot in Ripley, a fine old coaching inn, far larger than the Talbot at home. Sawson soon learnt that the carriage had left there about an hour ago and had left one of its passengers, who was bleeding heavily, so that he might be seen by a doctor. The passenger had been placed in an upstairs bedroom and the doctor's arrival was awaited. Sawson had to act quickly: should he attempt to see the passenger and lose time? Or continue immediately with the pursuit? He quickly decided that it was better to try and 'have a word' with the passenger and having persuaded the landlord that the passenger was known to him, he was soon bounding up the old wooden staircase and at the door of the passenger's bedroom.

On the other side of the door, the passenger, a thin foxy-faced man, whose given name was Peter but known to one and all as 'Snout', was lying on the bed in pain. He had lost a lot of blood and was lapsing in and out of consciousness. A period of conscious coincided with the arrival of Sawson. As the door flew open and then was shut heavily and bolted, Snout did not need telling that it was not the doctor who had arrived. He tried to lift himself up, but Sawson was quickly upon him and his huge hands were around his throat as his angry eyes bored into him. Snout's life might have ended there and then as Sawson, beside himself with anger, squeezed his throat tightly. A shout from George brought him to his senses and Snout fell back onto his bed.

"Where are they taking her?" Sawson demanded. Snout replied that he did not know. Sawson's hands once again tightened around the unfortunate Snout's throat. Sawson repeated his question, but again Snout denied all knowledge of the destination of the carriage. Sawson then demanded of Snout how he had come to be involved in the attack on Malsters. Snout, fearful for his life, rapidly told him everything he could. He and two companions had been drinking, as was their wont, in the Bugle Horn in Charlton village, when they were approached by a man with a severely pox-marked face and asked if they were interested in a 'job' out of town. It was to be an attack on a lonely farmhouse, whose owner, they were told, had fallen out with a man who was called the 'Count'. They were promised that they would be well paid for their 'work'. All that the Count wanted was that the farmer be captured and taken to the Count in London, the pox-marked man did not say where. They were assured there would be little resistance and that they could take whatever they wished from the farm, the Count only being interested in the capture of the farmer. Snout and his two companions agreed to go on the job and to meet the pox-marked man in two days' time at the stables of the Catherine Wheel coaching inn in Borough High Street near London Bridge.

Two days later they went to the stables, where they were joined by others that the pox-marked man had recruited. It was there that they were first introduced by the pox-faced man to Hamidou, who had arrived in the black carriage owned, they were told, by the Count, though they did not see him. After further discussions about money, they had set off without the pox-marked man to Malsters. "Where" demanded Sawson, "was the Count's residence?" Snout could not say. Had he ever seen the pox-marked man before in the Bugle Horn? "Once or twice," said Snout. "Where does he live?" asked Sawson. Snout did not know, but he volunteered that Hamidou, on departure, had said to the pox-marked man that he would see him at the 'Watch House'. "Where is that?" demanded Sawson, but Snout did not reply and started to slip back into unconsciousness. Certain that they would learn nothing further, Sawson and George left the room, passing the doctor, who had just arrived, on the stairs. Without a word they passed out of the inn and into the stables and once again mounted their horses and rode out onto the highway.

It was late at night when they arrived, tired and mud splattered, at the Bear at Esher. Their horses were exhausted and in need of a rest. Once they had been fed and watered and left in the charge of an elderly ostler, Sawson and George went into the busy inn. There was no news to be had of the carriage from anyone within. It had been a long and eventful twenty-four hours and once they had partaken of a hasty meal of stew and dumplings, washed down with tankards of ale, they made their way up narrow stairs to a cosy chamber. Within minutes, despite his worries for little Anne, Sawson fell into a deep sleep, as did George.

They awoke the next morning to the sound of a cockerel crowing in the garden at the back of the inn. A ray of sunshine between the shutter doors illuminated the chamber.

Opening the shutters, Sawson looked out over the lush countryside behind the inn. A young boy was lazily driving a herd of disinterested cows towards a farmhouse to be milked, whilst in the distance two ploughmen were slowly leading their magnificent horses to the fields to begin the day's work. A pigeon called from a nearby tree in response to a blackbird piping his morning song. It was in truth a lovely morning, but its beauty was lost on Sawson whose sleep had been disturbed by his concerns over little Anne. Dressing quickly, they made their way down into the dining room of the inn. Here it was anything but quiet, as passengers awaiting the mail coaches partook of breakfast, calling out their orders to the serving girls. The doors to the kitchen swung to and fro as trays of breakfasts were carried in to feed the hungry diners, whose numbers increased and decreased with the arrival of the coaches. Outside, the horns of approaching and departing carriages summoned the ostlers, who led out teams of fresh horses to be harnessed to the coaches, whilst others of their number let the tired and weary horses who had arrived back into the large stables to be fed and watered. Coachmen and guards came into the dining room to announce the imminent departure of their respective coaches, causing passengers to bolt their food or curse the kitchens for the non-arrival of their ordered breakfasts.

Sawson and George descended into this maelstrom of activity. George, who had never been beyond the world of shepherding up in the downs, stood as if transfixed by the frenzied human activity. When asked by Sawson what he wanted for breakfast, he was dumbfounded by what was on offer. There were smoked herrings, young split salmon fried or baked, grilled kidneys and bacon, sausages, mashed potato, beef or tongue in a mustard sauce, roasted chicken, eggs scrambled, boiled, fried or poached, crusty white breads and rolls and nutty brown breads, jams and marmalades, fresh butter and cheeses, porridges with treacle or without, tea or coffee, small beer, apples and pears. Eventually having consumed vast dishes of bacon and eggs with bread, butter and marmalade and a number of cups of tea, they paid their bill and walked out of the inn to the stables. Their horses, duly refreshed, were led out to them and climbing onto the mounting block, they swung themselves into the saddle and trotted out of the inn onto the London road.

AN OLD FRIEND FOUND

Since the night before, Sawson had been considering what to do in the morning. The trail of the carriage by now was cold. There was no doubt that Hamidou and his cronies were heading towards London, but they could have entered the city by a number of routes, so there was little point in making any further inquiries until the outskirts of London were reached. Where in London was the question? London was a big place. They had no idea where the 'Count' was residing, nor did they know where or what the 'Watch House' was. It was unlikely that they would learn much at the Catherine Wheel, as it appeared that it was simply the place where the ruffians had gathered. They did know however, that the pox-marked man had been to the Bugle Horn more than once and it seemed sensible to start their inquires there.

They set off in an easterly direction through the rich countryside that lay to the south of London, passing isolated farms, small hamlets and villages. Their progress was slow, as there was no direct route: The main roads all headed north in the direction of London like spokes on a wheel converging on a single hub. It was therefore necessary to follow the small lanes and bridle ways that led from one village to another. It would, in other circumstances, have been a pleasant ride, but the concerns as to little Anne's fate continued to prey upon Sawson's mind to the exclusion of everything else. Having forded the River Wandle at Mitcham, they soon found themselves on Mitcham Common.

The sun by now was high in the sky, the only sound being the lowing of the cattle that grazed on the rough pasture there. The air was fragrant with the sweet smell of gorse, which was so abundant here that it was being harvested by a number of men with carts to be sold to local bakers who valued it because it burnt fast and furiously. On they rode, passing through the lavender fields for which the area was famous. They crossed over the London to Brighton road at Thornton Heath, stopping to let the horses drink deeply at the large pond at the entrance to the isolated farm a mile beyond the crossroads. On reaching Collier's water they skirted to the south of Whitehouse Wood and Beggar's Wood before emerging onto Penge Common with Gretton House to the south.

Their route then took them through to the hamlet of Kent House, west of the parkland surrounding Beckenham Place. They were soon riding through the lush meadows bordering the River Pool south of Bell Green. They stopped again for their horses to drink and then walked them through the bubbling, chattering river as it flowed north to meet its big brother, the Ravensbourne, that in turn flows into the Thames at Deptford. Scrambling up the riverbank they rode on and in the late afternoon they crossed the Ravensbourne River itself and the London to Bromley road near the Green Man in the hamlet of Southend. They continued to ride east before turning north at the entrance to the lonely, isolated Grove Farm. Jackdaws and crows, who had observed their approach from the west from the clump of elms at the farm entrance, welcomed their approach with threatening cries and as the sun started to set, they pressed on anxiously. Soon they were past Burnt Ash Farm perched on the hill of the same name. The road now fell away in front of them heading north. On either side, fields of vegetables stretched as far as the eye could see. Two farm labourers trudging wearily from the fields, heading in the same direction as Sawson and George, gazed curiously at them, but said nothing. Smoke slowly climbed skywards from the chimneys of small cottages around the inn that stood on the north western corner of the approaching crossroads like chickens around a mother hen, whilst on the right hand side in the distance the ancient timber-framed Lee Green farmhouse with its crooked cockerel weather vane stood in splendid isolation, surrounded by its fields. On the left hand side, half a dozen inquisitive bullocks, chewing contentedly in the Bright field, regarded the two horsemen with interest. Sawson looked ahead and smiled as the familiar sight of the Old Tiger's head, with its large maypole outside, came into sight.

Arriving at the inn, Sawson looked about him. The inn had been extended slightly to the north facing onto the road that led to Blackheath. There was also a new stable block to the rear which bordered onto the Quaggy River. Otherwise nothing had changed since he had last been there. George and Sawson dismounted and handing the reins of their horses to a youth who had emerged from the stables, with a request to feed and water them, they entered into the inn through the front door. They immediately found themselves in a large and airy room with a large bar and comfortable wooden settles, chairs and tables. At one end of the bar a small group of weary farm labourers, tradesmen and carters were busy supping their ale, smoking their pipes and putting the world to rights. Behind the bar a jolly red-cheeked stout man with greying hair was engaged in keeping their pots charged, whilst joining in the general banter. On seeing Sawson and George the conversation subsided for a few seconds as the speakers glanced at them, but they quickly returned to the issues of the day. Meanwhile the red-cheeked man, who had moved down the bar towards the travellers, inquired of them how he could be of assistance. Sawson ordered two pints of ale and as the red-cheeked man drew the ale from the barrels on the stillages behind the bar, he looked closely at him.

The red-cheeked man placed the ale before them and inquired whether there was anything further that they required. Sawson smiled gently: "Durst thou not know me, Bounce?" he said. The red-cheeked man looked at him quizzically. "The old Litchfield?" said Sawson. Bounce (for it was indeed him) stood transfixed. "Sawson!" he whispered, "We thought you were drowned!" With that, he heaved himself over the bar and within seconds the two old shipmates were tearfully embracing each other.

It was not until the early hours of the morning that Sawson climbed up the stairs to the comfortable chamber that Bounce had put at his disposal. There had been so much to talk of between the two as they sat in the company of George and Bounce's wife and family in the small private dining room at the back of the inn over plates piled high with succulent whitebait from nearby Greenwich, followed by a steaming steak and kidney pudding and then bowls of fresh fruit and cream, washed down by the best ales and brandies that the inn could provide. They spoke of their lives since they had last met.

Bounce's mother and uncle were long dead. He had inherited the inn and the Bright field, but he had expanded both businesses.

He had extended the inn to provide extra accommodation and stabling for those travelling between London and Folkestone, while continuing to grow fruit and vegetables in the Bright field for the London market. With the profits he had made, he had purchased Lee Green Farm and its fields as well as the two large fields immediately opposite the inn to the south of the Folkestone road. In all these fields he grew vegetables and fruit. He had additionally set up his own Carter's business to carry his produce and that of neighbouring farmers and estate owners into the London market. The carthorses were kept in two large fields on the east side of the Blackheath road opposite the inn and bordered by the gurgling Quaggy River. In the early hours of every morning except Sunday, the front of the inn was a scene of feverish activity with the arrival and loading of fresh produce onto six large carts bound for London.

Bounce was assisted in the running of the businesses by his family. His wife Martha ran the Inn, assisted by his seventeen-year-old daughter, Bess. His two sons, Sam and Tommy, went with the carts each morning into London and dealt with the wholesalers there. There was not much happening in the Lee area that Bounce was not involved with or aware of.

Bounce listened carefully as Sawson explained what had happened to him since they had last met and why he had had to travel to London. He knew nothing of the Count, Hamidou or the 'Watch House', save that he wondered whether the 'Watch House' might be in Clerkenwell, the watch-making area in London. He knew nothing of the pox-marked man, but he knew Jeb Butler, the landlord of the Bugle Horn, well. When Sawson had finished speaking, Bounce took up a sheet of paper and wrote a letter to Jeb Butler, asking for any information he might have of the pox-marked man and in particular his whereabouts. Having written the letter, he placed it in an envelope which he sealed. He then called for a young stable boy called Alex and handed him the envelope with instructions that it was to be handed to Jeb by eight o'clock the next morning and that he was to wait for an answer. On noticing that Sawson appeared concerned and guessing rightly that the concern was that the inquiry might become public knowledge and alert the pox-marked man that he was being sought, Bounce placed his hand on Sawson's sleeve. "Don't worry," he said. "Jeb is safe." Sawson realised that Bounce had his fingers in many pies, some of which perhaps he shouldn't. That was of no concern to him, for Bounce with all his contacts, was exactly the ally he needed if he was to ever find little Anne. Bounce went on to say that Sam and Tommy would let it be known to their contacts in London that they were looking for a carriage with the distinctive painted wheels that the maid at the Old Anchor had described. It was agreed additionally that they would make discreet inquiries at the Catherine Wheel public house in the Borough.

Sawson, whose chamber was situated at the rear of the inn, slept soundly that night. Not so George. He had spent the evening listening to Sawson and Bounce, whilst at the same time shooting furtive glances at Bess, who sat at the end of the table. Glances which he was happy to see were reciprocated. As he lay in his small chamber he found it difficult to sleep, despite the events of the day. Just as he was about to succumb to the embracing arms of sleep, the stillness would be punctured by the distant sound of an oncoming horse rider or carriage, slight at first but becoming louder as it approached the inn and then fading away slowly after the rider or carriage either stopped at the inn or continued past into the dark night, before being replaced by the next oncoming sound. When he eventually managed to fall asleep, it was not for long before he was awoken from his slumbers by the sound of creaking carts and heavy horses at the front of the inn.

Climbing out of his bed and peering out of the window, George gazed out at a busy scene below. The sun was not yet up but men were busily loading up large wagons with vegetables and fruit. Sacks of carrots, potatoes, cabbages, turnips, onions and leeks along with boxes of plums, apples and pears were piled high onto the carts and heavy tarpaulins were then thrown over them and lashed securely to the sides. While this was going on, pairs of large carthorses were led quietly out of their field and looked expectantly on at the carts as if assessing the weight, they were going to have to pull that day. Once the carts were loaded, the horses walked slowly forward and then backwards before standing patiently as they were harnessed to the carts. A sweet smell of fruit and vegetables wafted gently up to him in the cool morning air. The process of loading and harnessing the horses was carried out with precision under the watchful eyes of Sam and Tommy. A shout from the darkness and the sound of a cart approaching denoted the late arrival of a fat farmer with a cart full of parsnips which needed to be distributed between the wagons, amongst much shouting and swearing as tarpaulins were untied and then retied.

George watched transfixed. In his sheltered life on the Downs, he had seen nothing like this. These carts were going to London. He had never been there! He ran down the stairs and asked of Sam whether he could come with him. Permission was immediately granted and within a few minutes he was seated high up alongside one of the wagon drivers, having told Bess to tell Sawson he would soon be back. At a shout from Tommy, the first wagon pulled out of the forecourt of the inn and turned right in the direction of Lewisham, followed by five others. The heavy wooden axles of the carts groaned as if in rebellion as the cart horses, placid as ever, took the strain and began their daily plod to London along the muddy and rutted road which led to Lewisham. It was still dark as the convoy crossed the Ravensbourne at Lewisham and the horses started to take the strain as they pulled the wagons up the incline on the far bank with loom pitt hole on the left hand side. The wooden wheels and axles continued to complain as the heavily-laden wagons approached the top of the incline. The driver had no need for a whip, the horses knew the route well and stoically continued to pull encouraged, only by the voice of the driver. Soon the summit was reached and the road fell away towards New Cross where it joined the London to Dover road in front of The Marquis of Granby Inn. On arriving at the inn, Tommy called a halt for fifteen minutes for the horses to drink and to have their nosebags full of hay attached.

The sun was coming up as they left the Marquis and passing through the New Cross turnpike they turned into the Kent Road bordered by fields and orchards and a large brickfield. The road was busier now. Just before the halfway houses, their progress was slowed by cattle that had left the pens at the Red Cow Inn earlier that morning and were being walked by a gang of Kentish drovers along the final part of their journey from deep down in

Kent to the meat market at Smithfield. After much shouting, the wagons slowly rumbled by. Kent Road now became Kent Street and passing the Church of St George in the Borough, they turned right into the Borough at its junction with Blackman Street. As the wagons trundled slowly up the Borough, George marvelled at the shops, warehouses and coaching inns which lined the road on either side, but it was the press of people and the noise that impressed him most. On all sides his ears were assailed by the sounds of the city: pie men, flower sellers, vendors of all types called out their wares; carriages, carts, horsemen, sedan chairmen and pedestrians all trying to weave their way through the narrow streets with much shouting and swearing. He could smell the city: a mixture of sweaty people, cooked food, horse dung, sewage, vegetables all combined to assault his nostrils. Ahead of him the great tower of Southwark Priory slightly to the left loomed over the mean housing warehouses and wharves, all clustered together on the south bank of the Thames. The convoy continued northwards for a short distance and turned left into Stony street. From there it was but a short distance to their ultimate destination in Dirty Street, where Bounce rented a small yard to unload the carts. On their arrival, it was organised chaos as the carts were unloaded and the vegetables and fruit disappeared into Borough Market.

GEORGE'S ADVENTURE

George remained by the carts as they were unloaded. Tommy and Sam, who had both kept an eagle eye on the unloading, collected payment, issued receipts and recorded the details in their ledgers. Whilst this was going on, the carters and their assistants had a quick breakfast and fed and watered their horses. Once this was completed, five of the carts were driven to the stables of the King's Head in the Borough to be loaded with horse manure to be conveyed back to be spread on the fields in Lee. Tommy and Sam, along with George, travelled in the remaining cart to the Catherine Wheel to make inquiries about the pox-marked man. Before doing so, Tommy had put the word about to the market workers as they came to unload the carts and to a number of street urchins that he and his brother were interested in the whereabouts of a carriage with the distinctive painted wheels that they described.

On arrival at the Catherine Wheel, Tommy and Sam went into the inn, leaving George in charge of the cart whilst they conducted their inquiries and no doubt other business that they did not want him to be privy to. As he sat up on the cart and surveyed the busy throng of people flowing up and down the street, George froze. A tall man dressed in a heavy coat and a large hat emerged from the Dog and Bear across the street. Despite the hat and coat there could be no doubt, there was no mistaking the scar, it was the man that George had last seen coming in through the upstairs window at Malsters. It was Hamidou. As George watched, Hamidou walked up the Borough towards London Bridge. George had seconds to decide what to do. Should he run into the Catherine Wheel and find Tommy and Sam in which case Hamidou might disappear? Or should he follow him at once. There could be no doubt what to do and George immediately jumped down from the cart and started to follow Hamidou.

Hamidou strode purposefully up the Borough before turning right into Tooley Street and then into St Olave's street and then left into Morgan's lane. He then crossed Pickled Herring Street and walked down Pickled Herring Stairs, where he joined a queue waiting for a waterman to be rowed across the Thames. George, who had kept him in sight, had to think quickly. If he joined the queue and waited for his turn Hamidou would be over the river and out of sight before he managed to land. He did not know how far away the next stairs were, but he guessed that if he ran as quickly as he could, he could reach them before Hamidou had embarked. He ran to the east along Pickled Herring Street and reached Dancing Bridge Stairs. He was in luck and calling out to a passing waterman, he was in the middle of the Thames just as Hamidou set off from Pickled Herring stairs. Noting that the boat that Hamidou was in was heading to the Iron Gate Stairs on the north bank of the Thames, George instructed the waterman to land him there, which he did without difficulty. He then ran up the stairs into St Catherine's Street. Crossing the road, he darted into the entrance of a narrow alleyway which opened out into the street. Concealing himself there, he looked back across the street and observed the entrance to the stairs that he had just run up.

Within a short period of time, Hamidou emerged into the street and turned left. George came out of the alleyway and followed at a safe distance. Hamidou strode on, crossed into Pillory Lane before turning into Maudling's Road. He stopped halfway up outside a mean-looking house next to a butcher's shop. George at this stage was at the entrance to Maudling's Road and immediately ducked back to avoid being seen. As he did so, he saw Hamidou, before he entered the house, look directly across the street and raise his left arm as if in greeting. He then entered the house.

George stopped and thought. Was it a signal? And if so, who was it to? And to what purpose? He resolved not to enter the street from the same end as Hamidou had done. Instead he walked on for a short distance and then turned left and left again and reached the opposite end of Maudling's Road. As he stood on the corner, a young washerwoman turned into the road. George immediately engaged her in conversation, asking for directions to the Iron Gate Steps. As she walked down the road telling him the way, he glanced to the right of the street and noted a foreign-looking man standing at the upstairs window of the house directly opposite the house that Hamidou had gone into. There could be no doubt that the house was being watched, a view that was reinforced when he noted a curtain flick at the downstairs window of the house opposite. Hamidou was clearly aware that the house was under observation, as his wave to the man in the upstairs window demonstrated. Clearly those watching the house were in fact guarding it and there could be only one reason for that: Those in the house had something to hide and that something could only be one thing: little Anne was there.

George waited for half an hour and then returned to Maudling's Road. He walked up the road and entered the butcher's shop. Noting that the butcher had no sausages for sale on the rough wooden counter, he inquired of the butcher if he had any. The butcher replied no, but that if George cared to wait he would make some. George agreed and whilst the butcher busied himself in preparing the sausages, George carefully observed the house opposite: the man at the upstairs window was still there. George then turned his attention to the rear of the shop he was in. He noted that there was a small room at the back, beyond which he could just see a small yard with a low wall to the side which separated it from the yard of the adjoining house that Hamidou had gone into. Having collected the newly-made sausages, George went back out into Maudling's Road. Out of the corner of his eye he could see that the man was still at the upstairs window. George made his way slowly down the street. He knew that there was nothing that he could do on his own; he needed to tell Sawson what he had found so that they might return with reinforcements. Once he had reached the corner, he ran as fast as he could, back the way he had come earlier that morning. He did not make the journey back as quickly as he had done earlier for the streets were even more crowded than they had been. Arriving at the Catherine Wheel, there was no sight of Tommy and Sam or the cart, they clearly must have set off back to Lee. It dawned on George that here he was alone in London, a city that he had never been to before and a city in which he knew nobody. The information that he had was, however, crucial and there was no choice: he would have to get back to Lee on foot.

Sawson had awoken that morning after a refreshing sleep. Descending for breakfast, he was told by Bess that George had gone to London with the wagons that normally returned in the mid-afternoon. It did not cause him any concern, as he knew George would be looked after by Tommy and Sam. He breakfasted with Bounce and strolled with him to see the stables. Alex returned in the late morning with a letter from Jeb Butler. He knew of the pox-marked man, but he had not been seen for a couple of weeks. That was not, however, unusual and he promised that he would send any news that he had of him or his whereabouts as soon as he received it. He further promised to make discreet inquiries of his customers as to where the pox-faced man might be found.

The news was disappointing, but not unexpected. What was unexpected, however, was the return of Tommy and Sam without George. They told him they had left George in charge of the cart and had returned to find the cart abandoned and George nowhere to be seen. Sawson knew that George would not have just run off, he had either seen something or he had been taken. Whatever had happened, it was essential that he be found and found quickly. He called for his horse and within ten minutes Sawson, together with Tommy and Sam, were galloping towards London.

George meanwhile had set off on foot for Lee. As he retraced the route that he had taken earlier that day, the skies darkened and soon it started to rain. The road underfoot was rutted and full of potholes. As the rain continued, it started to become muddy, the carts and carriages and horseman passing by threw up the mud and soon he was splattered all over with mud and soaked to the skin. The rain increased, but he knew that his discovery was of such importance that there was no time to find shelter. So he plodded on through the mud, but his progress was slow as he stumbled along the road. At one point he lost his footing and fell face down in a puddle of muddy water. He picked himself up just in time to avoid being trampled on and run over by the huge hooves of two heavy carthorses pulling a covered wagon. The driver of the cart, after swearing at him to be more careful, took pity on him and invited him to sit up with him. George gratefully accepted. The cart was fully loaded, carrying uniforms and coats (as the driver, chewing on a quid of tobacco explained) for the artillery garrison at Woolwich. The stout horses pulled with all their might, their giant quarters glistening and steaming in the rain, but the cart proceeded at no more than walking pace down the middle of the road, as the driver sought to avoid driving into the deepest ruts and potholes and breaking an axle.

When they were about half-way down the Kent road, the conversation between George and the driver was interrupted by shouts and oaths from behind to clear the road. The driver, a thickset man, stoically ignored them and continued to chat to George. The shouts became louder and the verbal abuse increased. Still the driver, chewing on a straw, ignored them, despite the obvious anger being expressed. There came a point where the road widened and a carriage started to pull level with them from behind. A coachman shouted at them in a foreign accent to get out of the way. "Bloody frog," muttered the driver, who still made no effort to move his cart and gazed fixedly ahead. The carriage pulled ahead of the cart and cut in front of them.

The driver spat a mouth of tobacco juice onto the road and remarked: "Think they own the road between here and Greenwich; that's not the first time they have done that!"

George was not listening properly, instead he was staring at the coach open-mouthed as it raced away. For the individual spokes of the wheels of the carriage were painted one third red, one third green and one third yellow, whilst the wheel hubs were painted blue. Realising what the driver had just said, he questioned him closely, but all he could tell George was that he had seen the carriage a number of times travelling between London and Greenwich and back again. George asked him if he knew a place called the Watch House but he did not.

Gradually the rain eased, visibility improved and it was just as well that it did, for just as the driver was explaining to George that their destinations diverged at the Marquis of Granby, three horsemen came galloping along the road in the direction of London. "Bloody idiots galloping along this road!" exclaimed the driver. "A horse could easily break a leg with all these potholes." George said nothing, but stared intently at the oncoming riders. As they approached, he immediately recognised Sawson, who was staring grimly ahead as he sought to get to London as quickly as possible. George shouted out to him, but Sawson heard nothing and galloped past. George stood up and shouted and despite being covered in mud, Tommy recognised him and drew his horse to a halt, whilst Sam galloped on, calling on Sawson to stop, which he did. Thanking the driver, George jumped down onto the road where he was soon reunited with Sawson.

THE BIRD HAS FLOWN

George lost no time in telling Sawson of what he had seen in Maudling's Road and of having seen the coach recently travelling towards Greenwich. Sawson decided that they should go to Maudling's Road directly. He hoisted George up on to the saddle in front of him and they were soon on their way to London. On reaching the Borough their progress was slowed by the press of people and it became clear to Sawson that it would be quicker to proceed on foot. They left their horses at the yard in Dirty Street. Before leaving for Maudling's Road, Sawson pointed out that they were but four and they did not know how many of their enemies there might be. Tommy and Sam soon recruited four burly market porters who armed themselves with staves and cudgels. Thus having doubled their numbers, they followed the route that George had taken earlier that day.

On reaching the entrance to Maudling's Road they paused. It was now early evening. George once again walked slowly up the street. On nearing the butcher's shop he glanced up across the road as he had done before: there was nobody at the upper window and he continued up the street before walking back down. Once again there was nobody in the window. George joined Sawson and the others and informed them of what he had seen. Sawson calmly gave his orders and the eight men, in groups of two and three, slowly made their way up the street in the direction of the butcher's shop. As they neared it, the foremost group slowed down their pace and they all started to bunch together. Then Sawson shouted: "Now!" At which George and three of the porters charged into the butcher's shop, past the astonished butcher and into the yard. They were soon over the low wall and into the yard of the adjoining property thus preventing any escape to the rear from anyone in the house.

If the butcher was surprised it was nothing to the surprise experienced by Harry Peters as he dozed before his fire in the downstairs room of the house. He was a thin weasel-faced man now some sixty years of age. In his youth he had made his living by rolling drunks in the streets and relieving them of their purses, pilfering goods in the docks and house breaking. If there was any dishonest work going, he was your man. An unfortunate fall through a roof of a large house he was 'visiting up town', followed by an encounter with the jaws of a bull mastiff who was 'on duty' at the time had left him with a crippled leg which had put paid to his youthful pursuits. He then made his living by receiving stolen property and selling it on at a profit. He maintained that he had now 'retired', but the number of furtive knocks on his door in the hours of darkness gave the lie to that. The knock he got to his door that evening, causing it to come off its hinges, was the biggest he had ever received. The shock that he received as the door fell in was nothing however to the shock that followed as Sawson roared into the room and hoisted him by his throat to his feet.

"Where is she?" Sawson roared as his companions followed him into the house and started to search it. "Who?" squawked Peters as the pressure around his throat began to squeeze the life out of him. "The girl!" shouted Sawson. Peters gave an incomprehensible reply. Sawson shook him as a terrier might shake a rat and threw him to the ground where he lay in undisguised fear looking up at the giant of a man that was Sawson. "There is no girl here," he whimpered. "There is nobody else here," called out one of the porters and "nobody got out the back." Sawson stood still whilst Peters squirmed on the ground. George confirmed there was no sign of little Anne.

"You were visited this morning by a foreign man with a scar," said Sawson. "What was his business?" "He wanted to sell me a silver candlestick," said Peters. "Why was a man opposite keeping an eye on your front door?" demanded Sawson. "I don't know," said Peters, now growing in confidence. "I didn't see anyone," he said as he pulled himself to his feet. "Get out of my house!" Sawson stood still and then turned slowly in a daze towards the broken door, his hopes of finding little Anne dashed. On reaching the door he turned to look back just as Peters took out a handkerchief to mop his brow.

Sawson stopped and marched purposefully into the room. "Where did you get that handkerchief?" he demanded. Peters gulped. "I bought it," he stammered. Sawson grabbed hold of Peter's hand and pulling his fingers back with such force as to cause Peters to call out in pain, he took the handkerchief from him. He looked at it carefully. There in the right hand corner were the embroided initials AS. It was little Anne's. He had given it to her one Christmas and she had embroidered it. Once more he demanded, "Where is she?" Peters made no reply. Sawson repeated the question. Peters began to whimper. "I don't know who you are talking about," he said. "I bought it!" Sawson said nothing. He picked Peters up and threw him over his shoulders as one might pick up a rag doll and marched with him out of the door and into the adjoining butcher's shop. Pushing the astonished butcher to one side, he threw Peters down onto the butcher's block. "Hold him there," he said calmly. George and Sam did so while Sawson reached up and took down the butcher's saw. "I will ask you once more," he said. Peters, who was by now a blubbering wreck, said nothing. Sawson took hold of Peter's good leg and ripped his trouser leg off and then taking the saw in one hand he drew it across his lower leg sufficient to draw blood. "Speak!" he shouted. Peters said nothing. Once again he drew the saw across his leg. Peters screamed and then he spoke: "Stop!" Sawson stopped and waited. "Where is she?" he demanded. "They took her this morning," he cried. "Where to?" demanded Sawson. "They spoke of a Watch House," he blubbered. "Where is the Watch House?" asked Sawson. "Greenwich, that's all I know," said Peters. And despite further encouragement with the saw, that is all that Peters could tell them of little Anne's destination.

Under further questioning, Peters confessed that he had been approached by Hamidou, with whom he had had dealings in the past. He was clearly terrified of Hamidou and his ruffians and he had agreed that they could keep little Anne at his house for a few days, whilst plans were made to move her out of London. Two of Hamidou's henchmen had remained in the house to guard her, whilst two others had taken a room across the street to keep the house under observation. That morning Hamidou had come to the house and an hour later a carriage had drawn up and little Anne had been placed in it.

There seemed little doubt that when the coach had been seen by George in the Kent Road, little Anne had been inside. But where she was now, nobody knew.

Sawson and his companions left Maudling's Road, taking Peters with them. Such was his obvious fear of Hamidou, that Sawson had little doubt that if given his liberty, he would reveal the presence of those searching for her as being in London, which would no doubt result in Hamidou taking additional steps to keep her secure. Sawson was assured by the porters, no doubt sensing that there was money to be made, that they 'would look after him' until he gave them the word. Sawson, desperate not to let the Count and Hamidou know of his search and thus lose any element of surprise, readily agreed terms with them.

Sawson, deep in thought, together with his companions made their way back to Dirty Street. He was mightily disappointed that they had not found little Anne but at least if Peters was to be believed, they knew that she had been taken to somewhere in Greenwich. On their arrival at Dirty Street, his spirits were lifted by the news that awaited them there: a small freckled-faced boy called Danny, who could have been no older than six, was sitting on a wall outside the yard. He jumped down at their approach and came running excitedly towards them. "Mister! Mister!" he shouted, addressing Tommy. "I've seen the coach!" Whilst Peters was taken away, the boy explained that he and a companion called Jerry, who was older, had seen the coach about an hour before crossing London Bridge into the city. They had followed it as far as Fleet Street, when it had stopped outside the Cock Tavern. There a man had got out and walked down Middle Temple Lane and the coach continued on towards the Strand. Jerry had followed after it, shouting to Danny to go back to the yard and tell Tommy what they had seen. Danny described the passenger who got out as being an old man with swarthy dark skin and a hooked nose. There could be no doubt that it was the Count.

It was now getting dark, but Sawson resolved to wait for the return of Jerry. Leaving word with Danny as to where he could be found he, George, Tommy and Sam walked to the Catherine Wheel to take refreshment, for it had been a long day for all of them, particularly George who was struggling to keep awake. Indeed, they had no sooner sat down to meat pies and ale, when he fell fast asleep at the table. George was awoken from his slumbers some two hours later by the excited arrival into the inn of Danny and Jerry. Jerry was breathing heavily, as well he might give the distance he had travelled. Once he had recovered his breath and swallowed several mouthfuls of pie and ale he managed to blurt out his news.

JERRY'S NEWS

Jerry said that the carriage had continued along Fleet Street and then stopped at Saint Clement Dane's Church, where there was room for carriages to wait. A bald-headed man (no doubt Hamidou) had got out and spoken to the driver. After about an hour, the old man with the hooked nose who was now carrying a sheath of papers, walked up to the carriage and got in, as did the bald-headed man. The carriage then set off with Jerry in pursuit. The traffic was so heavy that he had little difficulty in keeping up with the carriage, which eventually stopped outside 27, Grosvenor Square. The old man, still clutching the papers, and the bald-headed man got out. They were welcomed by a footman with a big dog and went into number twenty-seven. The footman and the dog remained outside by the door. He was quite certain that nobody else had got out. The carriage then drove off slowly to some mews in Mount Street. Jerry had walked by as the horses were being put into the stables; glancing into the carriage, he confirmed that it was empty. Following that, he had run back to the Borough as fast as he could and here he was. Sawson thanked him warmly and rewarded him and Danny generously. He asked them both to keep him informed as to the coach's movements.

Sawson now knew where his enemies were and he had little doubt that his small army of street urchins would watch carefully every movement the coach made and report it to him or to Tommy or Sam. He still, however, did not know what he most desired to know, namely the whereabouts of little Anne. A further 'interview' of Peters by the porters had gained no further intelligence, save that he, Peters, was now even more frightened of Sawson than he was of Hamidou.

It was agreed that Sam would remain in London that night, so that he could make inquiries in the morning about the occupants of number 27, Grosvenor Square, whilst Sawson, George and Tommy would return to Lee so as to be better placed to make inquiries in Greenwich. As they rode silently down the Kent Road, Sawson reflected on recent events and agreed with George that they had learnt a lot in a single day.

The moon was already high in the sky and the owls calling to each other across the fields, as the welcoming sight of the Old Tiger's Head came into view. Climbing stiffly down from their horses, which were led away for a well-earned rest, they entered the inn. After relating the events of the day to the anxious Bounce, the little party went swiftly to their chambers. Within a short period of time they were all wrapped in a refreshing and enveloping sleep.

Sawson awoke early the following morning. It had rained in the night and the air outside was fresh and cool. Dressing quickly, he went downstairs, the market carts had long since left, but the inn was busy with coaches arriving and leaving. Descending into the bustle and taking a mug of sweet cold milk and a hunk of buttered bread he made his way out into the rear of the inn and sat in the garden beside the stable block and gazed at the sparkling water in the Quaggy River as it danced its way excitedly west to the Ravens-Bourne and then on to the Thames. Whilst sitting there, he was joined by Bounce, who informed him with a wink that he had sent two 'likely lads' who 'knew what they were doing', to seek news of the coach and the Watch House. There was nothing more that Sawson or George could do, other than wait. This Sawson found difficult, whilst George for some reason seemed quite happy to while away the time helping Bess.

The wagons returned at two in the afternoon, accompanied by Tommy. On hearing them return, Sawson dashed to the front of the inn, but there was no news. The journey to and from London had been uneventful. Sam had not returned by the time they left. All Sawson could do was to sit and wait and talk to Bounce who could see how difficult it was for Sawson to be inactive. Then at about eight p.m., everything happened at once. Firstly a young horseman came galloping up to the inn: vaulting off his horse and throwing the reins to the ostler, he ran into the inn and sought out Bounce, who was sitting with Sawson in a private parlour at the back of the inn, where he liked to carry out 'business' away from prying eyes. Entering the parlour, he looked questioningly at Sawson before turning to Bounce. Bounce gave him a quick nod at which the horseman sat down. As he did so, Sawson could not help but notice a pair of pistols tucked into his waist. Bounce introduced him as Will Butler, the son of Jeb Butler of the Bugle Horn. Will was not interested in the life of a publican, preferring instead to ride (for he was a magnificent horseman) on the King's highway and in the Hanging Wood to the east of the Bugle horn, relieving travellers of their purses.

Sawson had no interest as to how Will made his living. He was, however, very interested in the news he brought. The pox-marked man was back: indeed, Will had seen him within the hour, drinking in the Bugle Horn. Sawson jumped to his feet and called for his horse. It was with difficulty that Bounce persuaded him that it would be better not to confront the pox-marked man. Rather, it would be better to follow him, for with any luck, he would lead them to where little Anne was. It would be better, Bounce said, if George were to go with Will, for George had already showed himself adept at following people. Sawson should, he suggested, remain and await the arrival of Sam with news of 27, Grosvenor Square and its inhabitants, so as to be able to immediately plan his next step. Sawson, despite his natural desire to be involved, saw the sense of this. Thus it was that within ten minutes, George found himself galloping in the darkness towards Charlton in the company of Will.

George and Will had been gone for only about fifteen minutes before Sam came galloping up to the inn. He was soon seated in the same parlour recounting what had occurred that day. He had arrived at 27, Grosvenor Square early in the morning. Through idle chat with some of the tradesman in the square he had found out that the property belonged to the Ashley-Cooper family. They had rented it out for the past six months to a foreign gentleman, whose description matched that of the Count. Of the Count nobody knew much, but they all spoke of a mean, nasty, scar-faced man, much given to shouting, who appeared to be the Count's right hand man. Sam had strolled slowly up to the house on the pretext that he had newly established a silver shop in the area and would be happy to call on the occupants to show his wares. The footman was also foreign with little English, but with what little English he did have, he made it perfectly clear that

Sam's presence was not welcome, a view echoed by the chained mastiff nearby. As he was leaving, a butcher's cart drew up and delivered a quantity of meat to the house. Following the cart, Sam managed to strike up a conversation with the butcher's boy, who informed him that he had only delivered enough meat for three days as the inhabitants were leaving on Saturday, today being Wednesday.

Sam had remained around the square but saw nothing of note. At about four in the afternoon he saw a young man waiting outside number twenty-seven. After a while, a young housemaid came out and walked off with the young man. Sam followed them out of the square and eventually saw them enter a public house. Waiting for a few minutes, he went into the public house and eventually struck up a conversation with the couple, in which the housemaid revealed that she worked at number twenty-seven along with two other maids, a housekeeper, a cook and a butler and two footmen who were foreign. The inhabitants of the house consisted of a man she called The Count, a bald-headed man with a large scar on his face and two others. Despite discreet questioning by Sam, she made no mention of any girl or woman living there. She finally confirmed that the Count was going abroad on Saturday, having completed the purchase of a large piece of land, though she did not know where.

This was news indeed and reinforced the sound advice that Bounce had given, for now Sawson could start to make plans. He still did not know where little Anne was, but the Count and Hamidou or the pox-marked man would lead him to her.

Whilst Sawson was listening to this latest piece of news, George was still galloping towards Charlton. Unlike Will, who had grown up with horses and who in many ways was more at home in the saddle then on his feet, George, living up on the

Downs, was not an experienced horseman, and indeed the ride to London with Sawson had been an experience in itself. Will was galloping at speed, spurring his horse on and it was as much as George could do to keep him in sight. Soon, however, Will slackened his pace as Charlton House came in sight and the two of them rode abreast of each other as they approached the house and St Luke's Church and graveyard. "Get down now and hide in the churchyard until you hear the owl call three times," he said, before proceeding to realistically mimic the call of an owl. "When you hear it, make your way to the lychgate and I will join you there." George dismounted and Will, taking the reins of George's horse, rode quietly on and turned into the stables behind the Bugle Horn. Once there, he rode up to one of the stables and bending down opened the half door and shepherded George's horse inside and closed the door. He then rode slowly down the line of stables until he reached the end stable that adjoined the inn. If George had been present, he would have seen how Will, the highwayman, could vanish into thin air: quickly he dismounted and removed his saddle, bridle and reins, which he hung up in the tack room across the yard. Then returning to his horse, which stood obediently by the stable, Will climbed up onto its back, reached up and pulled open the small door to the hay loft above. The loft appeared to be full of hay but when he pushed at, it became clear that the loft behind was empty. Standing up on his horse's back, Will pulled himself up into the loft. Once in, he gave a low whistle and his horse trotted away into the open field at the back of the inn. Will pulled the door closed and replaced the straw. He then made his way across the loft to a spy-hole from where he had a clear view into the bar below. They were in luck, the pox-marked man was still there, supping ale with two unsavoury looking individuals. Will watched him intently, as he had on many occasions watched unsuspecting travellers that he was to meet later. After half an hour or so, he saw handshakes being given and other signs that the pox-marked man was about to leave. Closing the spy hole, Will descended from the hayloft the way he had come. Within a minute George, who was not enjoying being alone in a dark and silent graveyard, heard the welcoming calls of an owl. He made his way to the lychgate and was soon joined by Will. Crouching down and concealing themselves behind the graveyard wall, they had a clear view of the entrance to the inn.

As they crouched behind the wall in the darkness, the wind started to increase, clouds started to obscure the moonlight and within a short time it began to drizzle. It promised to be an unpleasant night to be out. A noise suddenly came from the front of the inn and the pox-faced man emerged, carrying a lantern in his right hand. Turning left out of the inn, he walked towards the churchyard. Their hearts were pounding, for if he came into the churchyard he would surely see them. Once more they were in luck as he turned right into Charlton Church lane and started to walk downhill towards the Woolwich Road.

FOLLOWING THE POX-MARKED MAN

The descent down the lane was steep. George was grateful to have Will with him for the area was completely unknown to him. The rain increased and the lane underfoot was muddy and slippery. Several times George slipped and almost fell. On each occasion, his collar was grabbed by Will's strong hand and he was restored to his feet. Silence was essential. Ahead of them the lantern of the pox-marked man danced in the darkness, guiding them on. Without it, their task would have been even more difficult. Soon they found themselves in a sunken part of the lane that was so overshadowed by trees that they found themselves in total darkness. A fox barked. George jumped and Will chuckled. They proceeded on, Will moving lithely ahead as might a panther. Gradually the lane became less steep as it joined the Woolwich road near Lombard's Wall on the southeast corner of the East Greenwich Marsh.

They saw the lamp turn left ahead of them as the pox-marked man turned west towards Greenwich. The rain started to ease off and soon the clouds above were scudding by with the moonlight increasing. They needed to become more cautious now and they dropped back, their eyes set on the dancing light ahead. They passed the secluded East Coombe farmhouse on their left and Horn Lane which led out to the east side of the marsh and the common sewer and the King's sluice. On they went past Vicar's Lane and Hawk's Marsh on the right. Soon they reached the oddly named Catt's Brains Fields on their right. All of a sudden the lamp disappeared as the pox-marked man turned into Marsh Lane. "He's going out onto the marshes!" exclaimed Will. "We must be careful where we tread!" Turning into Marsh Lane they could see the light about one hundred and fifty yards ahead. They proceeded with caution, the marsh was no place for the unwary, with muddy fields and large drainage ditches on both sides of the lane. Passing Pond Meadow, a bullock bellowed, causing George to shiver with fright. Suddenly the light ahead disappeared. Will ran forward: the lane turned sharply to the left by Foster's Hole and Lady Marsh. He called out, "Quickly!" to George, who soon joined him. They were now in Blackwall Lane. The lantern ahead continued to guide them. Passing the Great Pitts and the Further Pitts on their left, they saw the light turn sharp right off the lane. Hurrying to the spot where it had left the lane, they found a small turning ahead of them through the fields. On an old wooden board attached to a stake they could just read in faded white lettering 'The Watch House'. The light had now disappeared. They walked very slowly down the turning with fields on both sides. Soon a row of stunted trees came into sight behind which they could just make out the lines of a building. Throwing themselves to the ground and crawling on their stomachs, they reached the trees. A cloud floated away and there, bathed in the moonlight, they saw a large two-storey building with outhouses. They had found the Watch House, isolated and hidden away at the top of the marshy peninsular.

As they lay there a dog barked loudly. Whether it had sensed them was not clear, but it was immediately joined by at least two others. The canine choir was clearly heard by someone in the house, for a door was flung open and they could clearly see a man illuminated by the light within. He came out and stood looking about. George and Will froze. Eventually the man shouted at the dogs who quietened down, save for the odd whimper The man went back into the house and slammed the door shut. They remained still for about five minutes and carefully slithered away until they judged it safe to stand. On reaching Blackwall Lane, they retraced their steps. All of a sudden Will stopped still and listened with the acute ears of a highwayman. "Quick," he said and pushed George to his right into Pond Meadow. They threw themselves to the ground and into a ditch, where they lay still. They did not have to wait long before they could hear quite clearly the approach of a carriage and horses slowly coming up the lane. Louder and louder it came. They pressed themselves further on down into the ditch. As they peered upwards to the road, the carriage went past and they could see clearly in the moonlight the distinctive red, green and yellow spokes of its wheels. If they had any doubts as to the significance of their find that night, the sighting of the carriage caused them to fade away.

They lay quietly in the ditch for the next ten minutes and then when they judged it safe to do so, they emerged back onto the lane. Walking at a fast pace they soon reached the safety and anonymity of the Woolwich road, where they stopped to catch their breath and decide what to do next. It was clear that they must get to Lee as soon as possible and tell Sawson what they had discovered. They had followed the pox-marked man on foot and it was now the middle of the night. Rather than continuing west and then ascending to the wastes of Blackheath, where they might meet footpads, cut-throats or other unsavoury characters (as Will well knew), they retraced their steps back to the Bugle Horn. After refreshing themselves with pots of ale and bread and cheese, they were soon back in the saddle and galloping back towards Lee, reaching the Old Tiger's Head just before the sun rose. The area outside the inn was just as crowded as it had been when George had first set off to London. Jumping from his horse, he ran between the carts and into the inn and went bounding up the stairs to Sawson's chamber, banging loudly on the door and shouting at the top of his voice. He aroused Sawson from his peaceful slumbers and informed him of what he and Will had discovered.

Sawson, dressing himself rapidly, bounded down the stairs and within a short time he, George, Will, Bounce, Sam and Tommy were all gathered together in the private parlour at the back of the inn where this latest piece of news was digested. It was now Thursday morning; they knew the Count was leaving 27, Grosvenor Square on the Saturday, but where was he going to? Was he staying in this country or going abroad? What was the significance of the Watch House? Was, as seemed likely, little Anne being held there? These questions had to be answered and answered quickly. Sawson spoke: "Now that the Watch House has been found, it has to be watched and watched closely." Bounce nodded in agreement. It would be no easy task, given its isolation out on the marsh, where few people had any need to or desire to go. "Leave that to me," he said. "I know just the man to do it: Silas Yardley. He has been a ditch man on the marsh these last forty years." That resolved, it was agreed that Sam would return to London and try and find out where the Count was moving to. There was nothing further to be done. Sam and

Tommy left with the carts for London, whilst Will and George retired to sleep after their night's exertions.

Sawson and Bounce, having breakfasted well, went to the stables and within a short time they were riding up Lee road with the grounds of Wricklemarsh House to their right. The road ascended gently until it reached the junction with the road to Lewisham to their left. On reaching the junction they stopped: ahead the road sloped steeply down towards Blackheath. They rode forward, descending the slope with care to a small stream that they crossed, before beginning the gentle ascent up onto Blackheath, where they stopped and looked about them. In the distance they could see carriages and carts moving slowly on the London to Dover road. To the east, Shooters Hill stood out, reflected in the rising sun. Sawson sat quietly on his horse and gazed about. He had not been there since the death of Samuel Clegg and the memories of what had occurred here all those years ago came flowing back. He shivered and rode on, anxious to cross the heath and escape the nightmare that had returned. On reaching the Dover road, they turned right in the direction of Shooters Hill. They followed the road for a short distance before turning left towards Moys Hill. At the top of Moys Hill they looked down: laid out before them they could see the peninsular of East Greenwich marshes, bordered to the left and right by the River Thames which flowed like a silver necklace from west to east. At Blackwall point at the tip of the peninsular, two sailing ships were slowly edging their way around the point en route to Gravesend and the sea. At the bottom of the hill the Woolwich road ran busy with traffic in both directions.

Bounce looked out intently from their vantage point. Having got his bearings, he pointed out a large field at the bottom of the peninsular on its western flank. "That is the great meadow," he said. "Just above it you can see Bendish Sluice, which opens out into the Thames. The building beside it is called the New Magazine. That's where we shall find Yardley." They descended down Moys Hill with care. On reaching the Woolwich road, they turned right and rode east, with the marshes opening out on their left. Sawson, aware that his enemies did not know of his presence in London and anxious to retain the element of surprise, was keen to avoid the road and suggested turning off it and riding across the marsh to the New Magazine. Bounce however counselled him against such a course, for though Rayle Meadow and the Great Meadow looked inviting in the mid-morning sun, the ride would be anything but easy: the ground was always extremely muddy and bisected by drainage ditches and their way would be barred by the Bendish Sluice. They rode on and then turned left into Marsh Lane and started to ride north. It was quiet out on the marsh, save for the sound of birdsong and the call of seagulls that had been driven inland by a storm at sea. In the meadows on either side, cattle grazed peacefully; there was no sight or sign of human activity anywhere. On reaching the start of the common sewer on their left, they stopped and dismounted, before turning left onto a narrow path with the sewer to one side. Leading their horses, they walked in single file along the path. After about five minutes, their progress was halted by an enormous bramble hedge. Turning to their left, they followed a narrow track for about thirty yards before a gap in the bush appeared on their right. Pushing their way through the gap they entered a small area of open land and there directly ahead of them was the New Magazine. It had been in a previous century the Government Powder Magazine. Gunpowder from various mills had been brought here, tested, stored and then distributed. It had been a convenient location for both the Royal Artillery depot and the dockyard in Woolwich. The dangers of gunpowder and the behaviour of the soldiers who had garrisoned it had caused the inhabitants of Greenwich to petition successfully for its removal to Purfleet on the northern bank of the Thames further downstream. Though the soldiers and the gunpowder were long gone, the abandoned, now derelict, buildings had not. They stood as they had been left, the wind and the rain and the passage of time had taken their toll on them. It was a scene of desolation: doors hung off hinges, roofs had fallen in and dark holes in the walls marked where windows had once been. They were not, however, totally abandoned, for Silas Yardley had lived there on his own for over forty years.

They entered a muddy, overgrown courtyard filled with rubbish and looked around. Seeing nothing, they followed a well-worn path towards what appeared to be the only building with a closed door. As they did so, a high-pitched voice from behind screamed out: "What's your business here!" They turned quickly as Silas Yardley emerged from behind a large bush. He was a small, leathery-faced man with a lantern jaw, piercing green eyes and a snub nose. A dirty brown clay pipe was gripped tightly in the left side of his mouth. His head was adorned with an old stove hat from under which wisps of grey hair peeped out. He was dressed in a smock made of sacking, the arms of which were tied around his wrist by pieces of string. His leggings were made of the same material held up by an enormous belt. His right foot was encased in a large black leather boot which reached up to his knee. Its brother had clearly gone missing for his left foot was contained in a brown ankle boot giving him a lop-sided appearance. In his right hand he carried a long-handled shovel. He advanced upon them slowly, the spade held out in front of him as a soldier might hold a musket with a bayonet. As he approached, he recognised Bounce and lowered his spade before turning to face Sawson, who towered over him. "He is a friend of mine," said Bounce. At this Silas nodded. "I watched you come onto the Marsh," he said. "What can I do for you?"

Looking carefully about him Sawson asked: "What can you tell us about the Watch House and a man with a pox-marked face?" Yardley took the pipe out of his mouth and spat violently on the ground. "That be Black Jack Whitfield and his thieving nest of rats. Been there for years they has, more's the pity. If there is any mischief in these parts, you can be sure they are involved! The house used to belong to Hatcliffe's Charity as did most of the fields around it. They employed Black Jack to maintain the river wall at the top of the marshes and to keep the ditches clear and in return they gave him the lease of it in order that he might carry out his duties the better." He spat again. "He's never done a day's work in his life, nor have his three sons," he said. "The ditches are blocked and the river has extended the great breach that occurred after the great storm." As he said this, he pointed up and along the west bank of the peninsular where a large indentation in the river wall could be seen. "He keeps a small boat there," he said, "so that he can get off the marsh unobserved. Many's the time I have seen small boats from the shipping in the river rowing to and from the great breach. What they are up to I don't know and I don't ask, but if Black Jack is involved you can be sure that they are not coming there for a social call, if you get my meaning."

"You said it used to belong to Hatcliffe's Charity. Who owns it now?" said Sawson.

Yardley looked at him in a pitying way. "Don't you know?" he said. "Most of the marsh has been sold to a foreign gentleman. He has bought parts of it from the Drapers' Company, the Mercers' Company and from Morden College. It has taken some time, but now he owns nearly all the northern part of the marsh, though what he wants it for I don't know." "What does the foreigner look like?" asked Sawson. "I have never seen him," replied Yardley, "but he has an assistant who has an ugly scarred face. He frequently travels here in a black coach." "That will be Hamidou." said Sawson.

Sawson was anxious to get as good a view as possible of the Watch House without being seen, so Yardley agreed to take them further onto the marsh. Leaving their horses tethered at the magazine, Yardley guided them up towards the western bank of the peninsular. His strange footwear acted as no impediment to him and it was with difficulty that they managed to keep up with him. Within a few minutes, they reached the top of the western wall of the peninsular: To their left, the land fell away to a large muddy area known as the Great Pitts, which extended north to the Further Pitts, whilst to the left the fast-flowing waters of the Thames at Blackwall Reach lapped against the shore. In the distance, the spire of St Alphege's church in Greenwich stood out against the westerly sun. Not a soul could be seen, the only sign of human activity being a number of hoys on the river and a heavily-laden East India Company ship sailing slowly towards London and the docks. All was quiet save for the occasional mooing from the cattle on the marsh and the gulls swooping down onto the river. Soon they reached the Great Breach, where the river had broken through the bank. The tide was just starting to come in through the breach which now extended about a hundred yards into the land. They stopped and lay down so as not to be silhouetted against the sky, as the sun began its descent to the west. Looking into the breach, Yardley pointed out a number of small rowing boats pulled up onto the land well away from the high tide mark. "Those are Black Jack's," he said, before pointing further to the east where a thin wispy stream of smoke could be seen reluctantly ascending to the sky. "That's the Watch House," he said.

Sawson gazed intently. The building was obscured by the stunted trees that George and Will had noted, but he continued to look at it for some twenty minutes, committing every detail he could to memory. He then transferred his attentions to the breach and the boats. At last, satisfied with what he had seen, he nodded and they made their way back to the Magazine. On their arrival, Sawson placed a purse of coins into Yardley's hand. "That is for your troubles," he said. "There will be more to come if you will keep the Watch House and the Great Breach under observation and get word to me of anything you see." Yardley agreed that he would and it was arranged that he would go to the Bugle Horn with any information that he had. With that, Sawson and Bounce took their leave and made their return to Lee.

PLANS ARE LAID

On reaching the Old Tiger's Head, Bounce called for a hot meal and within a short period of time, he and Sawson were seated in the back parlour devouring steaming bowls of lamb stew washed down by tankards of foaming ale before a roaring log fire. Tom had returned with the wagons, but there was no news of Sam. The two old friends chatted happily before the fire until, exhausted by their day's adventure, they fell asleep in their chairs. Outside the wind got up and it started to rain heavily. The old inn was still and quiet as if it too had gone to sleep. Every so often the quiet was disturbed by the distant noise of a coach approaching, shouts as horses were changed and then the decreasing sound of the coach disappearing into the night, but Sawson and Bounce continued to sleep heavily. They were eventually awakened from their slumbers in the early hours of the Friday morning by the arrival of Sam with news from London.

Seated in the warm parlour, the fire newly-piled with logs which spat and crackled as the long tongues of fire caressed them before taking hold and enveloping them, Sawson, George and Bounce waited patiently for Sam to remove his wet clothing and eat and drink. At last having refreshed himself, he told them what he had discovered: he had reached Grosvenor Square to find four carts stationary outside number twenty-seven. With much shouting and swearing, boxes, trunks, caskets and furniture were being taken out of the house and loaded onto the carts. Sam strolled up to them and stopped to watch the loading. As he did so, a particularly heavy trunk was being lifted onto the back of a cart. The two men engaged in the manoeuvre were having difficulty and it seemed the trunk was too heavy for them. Sam immediately went to their assistance and with his help, the trunk was securely loaded onto the wagon. The two men duly thanked him before going back into the house. They emerged a few minutes later with a trunk of a similar size.

Sam, who had remained standing by the cart, once again assisted them. With this, one of the men inquired of him that if he, "had nothing better to do, did he want a day's work loading the wagons?" Sam accepted with alacrity and was soon in the house helping with the removal. As he did so, he chatted with the men and learnt that the occupier of the house, described as a 'foreign toff', was going abroad and that most of his belongings were to be taken to Duke Shore Stairs at Limehouse to be loaded on a Dutch ship.

As they continued to load the wagons, the footman that Sam had previously seen arrived at the front of the house. Sam took the opportunity to ask the man whether he was travelling abroad with the Count and if so, were his belongings to be loaded onto the wagons and taken to the ship? The man replied shortly that he was going on the ship, but not until he had travelled with his fellow footman and his master to his master's new estate. What little belongings he had, he would carry himself onto the ship later, when he and his master joined her down river. Sam, as a result of what he had learnt, determined to find out more about the ship and when she was to sail. Once the loading had been completed and the wagons were ready to leave, the driver in charge of the wagons took out his purse to pay Sam for his labour. Sam quickly remarked that he had a sweetheart in Wapping and could he travel with the carters to Limehouse? In return for the lift, he offered to help unload the carts. Pleased with the assistance he had given, his offer was swiftly accepted and within minutes he was sitting up with the driver as the wagons lumbered slowly out of Grosvenor Square.

The journey through the crowded streets of London was slow. Carts, carriages, horsemen and pedestrians struggled to make their way through the throng. The heavily-laden wagons moved slowly through a cacophony of street cries, cursing drivers cracking their whips, street urchins dashing into and across the narrow streets. At times the convoy would come to a total standstill, as traffic coming in the opposite direction refused to give way, before eventually doing so amid much swearing and shouting and shaking of fists. The giant carthorses would then slowly take the strain and the wagons would creak and lumber forward to meet the next obstacle to their progress and the whole process would start again. Eventually having passed through the centre of the city, the press of people, horses, carriages and carts lessened and the speed of the convoy increased slightly. Thus it was that at six in the evening the convoy entered into Narrow Street and eventually stopped near the top of Duke Shore Stairs.

Walking down the steps with the carter, Sam looked out to the mass of shipping on the London river, silhouetted against the setting sun. It looked to be a scene of chaos. Ships of all sizes were anchored in the river: It seemed to Sam that it would be possible to walk across the river over the banks of ships that lay there, straining against their anchors. Alongside the sea-going vessels, there were small boats into which cargoes were being discharged, whilst from other small boats cargoes were being loaded. The carter hailed a waterman and inquired of the whereabouts of the Dutch ship, Zwalluw. The waterman pointed out a bluff-bowed ship, anchored in the middle of the river. "Wait here," said the carter, who was then rowed out to the ship. He returned half an hour later in a ship's boat from the Zwalluw and then Sam and the others began the difficult task of unloading the wagons and then man-handling the trunks, boxes, caskets and furniture down the steps to the bobbing boats from the Zwalluw. It was back-breaking work and the steps were slippery and narrow. It took over two hours, as the loaded boats were rowed by the dutch seamen out to the Zwalluw where the cargo was then hauled aboard, before the boats returned to the stairs to collect a further load. In the course of the loading, Sam struck up a conversation with one of the sailors in which he learnt that the Zwalluw was to sail for Amsterdam on the Saturday morning tide, which was at two in the morning. They would lose time however, complained the sailor, as they had to pick up passengers as they sailed downstream. Armed with this information, Sam had taken his pay for the day and left.

Sawson and Bounce reflected on this information. There was clearly little time to lose. It seemed quite clear now that that the Count, Hamidou and at least two others of the Count's retainers were going to embark on the Zwalluw as she made her way down the Thames towards the sea. Given the position of the Watch House and the observations of Silas Yardley, the obvious point of embarkation had to be the Great Breach. The obvious question in everyone's mind was why was it necessary for the Count and his party to leave the country in this way rather than to embark at the Duke Shore Stairs. There could only be one reason: the count had something to hide and that, everyone agreed, must be little Anne. Her rescue clearly would not be easy: the Count's party would be made up of at least four who were to leave the country, if not more. Added to them would be Black Jack and his three sons and any other scoundrels he had recruited. The rescuing party would consist of Sawson, George, Bounce, Sam and Tommy, along (they hoped) with Will. Silas Yardley they hoped would assist, but he was not the strongest of men. It would be clearly necessary to recruit additional assistance and soon. "Leave that to me," said Bounce with a knowing look. "I know just the lads." With that, they all retired for what little was left of the night.

TO THE WATCH HOUSE

The following evening at five p.m., Sawson and his companions assembled in the back parlour of the Old Tiger's Head. The room was crowded, for in addition to Will who had ridden over from Charlton, there were ten men that Bounce had recruited. The newcomers, who were mainly farm labourers, were not the type that you would like to meet alone in a dark alley in the middle of the night, or putting it another way they were just the type of companion you would like to have by your side if you were passing through some of the rougher and more dangerous parts of London. Their rough hands and weather-beaten faces gave confidence to everyone in the room. Sawson briefly addressed the party as to what was required of them. Three of Bounce's men, led by a stout man with a lived-in face, were to make their way to the New Magazine where Silas Yardley would be waiting for them. They were then to be guided by Yardley to the Great Breach, where their task was to stove in any boats they found on the shore and to prevent any boat from the Zwalluw landing. The rest of the party were to join Sawson in entering the Watch House and finding and releasing little Anne. The approach to the Watch House was to take place very quietly under cover of darkness at midnight, some two hours before the Zwalluw set sail. Thus it was that at six p.m., as the sun was setting, Sawson and the others mounted their horses and set off to the East Greenwich Marshes. They were armed with a variety of weapons; flintlock pistols, knives, short and long swords, cutlasses and cudgels, each man carrying the weapon he was comfortable with.

It was a clear and dry evening as the party of men rode across Blackheath and they chatted quietly amongst themselves. As they rode down Moys Hill the weather took a turn for the worse and by the time they reached the Woolwich road a light drizzle had set in. Soon they had turned into Marsh Lane where they dismounted. They walked quietly up the lane, leading their horses. As they did so, mist began to rise from the marshes. They did not dare to light a lantern for fear that a gap in the mist might alert the inhabitants of the Watch House of their approach. It was with relief that when they reached the common sewer, Silas Yardley emerged silently out of the mist. Rather than take the risk that the three men assigned to him would get lost, he had come up the lane to meet them. Leaving their horses with the main group, the three men followed Silas into the all-enveloping mist and they were soon lost from sight.

Sawson and his companions walked slowly on until they reached the Pond Meadow on their left. Turning into the meadow, they found that stakes had been driven firmly into the ground by Yardley so that they might secure their horses, for the approach to the Watch House was to be made on foot. With the exception of Will, they all tethered and hobbled their horses and waited. Meanwhile, Yardley and his companions had made good progress through the mist. Such was his knowledge of the marsh, gained over the past forty years, that Yardley could have found his way with his eyes blindfolded. The others struggled to keep up with him, but soon they were onto the Great Breach and setting about looking for the boats that were normally beached there. It did not take them long to find them and to knock their bottoms out. Once done, they settled down to keep a watch on Blackwall Reach and the arrival of the Zwalluw.

It was now nearly nine p.m. in the evening and rather than set off and spend over an hour lying on their stomachs on the damp marsh for over two hours, Sawson decided that they should wait with the horses for an hour before moving off towards the Watch House. It was just as well that they did so, for as they stood shivering in the meadow, Will once again with his keen hearing called out for all to be quiet whilst he quickly swung himself into the saddle. They all strained their ears and soon heard distinctly through the mist the distant sound of a carriage and horses coming slowly up the lane. Will rode his horse a little further up the lane so that he was obscured by the mist, Sawson and the others quickly threw themselves down into the ditches on either side of the lane and waited. You could feel the tension as each man waited for the coach to arrive. The sound of the approaching coach increased slowly as the driver strained to see the road ahead of him. After what seemed an eternity, the sound of hooves, jangling harness and creaking wheels became very loud and a light could be seen emerging out of the mist as the coach came closer. The coach could only be going to one place and indeed it could only be one coach. Suddenly it was upon them. From just up the road Will, still hidden by the comforting and all-embracing mist, shouted, "Stand and Deliver!"

The startled driver of the coach pulled heavily on the reins and the coach, which was in any event moving at a snail's pace, came to a sudden halt. As it did so, the window on its right side was pulled down and a man looked out ahead into the mist from where Will was slowly emerging. All of a sudden he thrust his hand holding a cocked pistol out of the window. On seeing it, those in the ditch on that side of the road let out a cry, which no doubt startled the man who pulled the trigger. There was a loud bang as the pistol ball aimed at Will's face passed harmlessly by. The man did not get a second chance as those by the road rose up in unison. Both doors of the carriage were wrenched open and the two passengers inside were pulled out onto the grass and cuffed into submission. Sawson, meanwhile, had reached up and taken hold of the left leg of the startled coachman who he pulled down onto the ground, whilst at the same time George and Sam took hold of the horses' halters and prevented them bolting away with the empty carriage.

The two subdued passengers and the driver were bundled into the meadow where Bounce began to interrogate them. They were sullen and uncooperative in their replies to the questions he put to them, but they began to sing like canaries when Sawson took the passenger who had shot at Will into his bear-like grip and shook him like a rag doll, as he whispered into his ear, so that all could hear, that he would tie him to one of the stakes and shoot him if he didn't talk. The man did, as did his companion and the driver: Yes, they were going to the Watch House. Yes, the Count was there and yes they were going to join him and row out to a ship as it came down river and finally, after Sawson had introduced his enormous hands to the throat of the unfortunate man, yes, there was a young girl being held by the Count who was also to be taken abroad.

It was with a sense of relief that Sawson let the man fall to the ground. Little Anne was close by, the ship was not yet due and if Silas Yardley and his men had done their work, those in the Watch House would not be able to reach the ship through their own endeavours and they would require the assistance of the Zwalluw's crew. There was still, however, a lot to do. Little Anne was still in the hands of the Count and his ruffians at the Watch House and it was still necessary to get into the house and rescue her. His original plan had been for himself and the others to creep up to the house as far as they could without alerting the dogs and then to storm the house. He was now concerned that the element of surprise might have been lost if those in the house had heard the pistol shot. On the other hand, the capture of the coach gave them a different option, for using it, they could drive right up to the house without detection. A further meeting of Sawson's giant hands and this time the windpipe of the coachman elicited that the coach was not expected at any particular time, as long as it was before midnight.

A search of the coach was carried out and under a pile of cushions Tommy found a small casket of gold sovereigns, no doubt to pay Black Jack and his family and the coachman for their troubles. They also found a number of letters from influential people in the City of London, expressing interest in the Count's plan to drain part of the marsh and to drive a canal through the peninsular, with secure warehouses on its banks in which ship owners could land their cargoes without fear of the endemic pilfering which occurred on the London river. The casket and the letters were 'confiscated' by Sawson and placed into the safekeeping of Bounce.

It was now getting on towards eleven p.m. The coachman was relieved of his hat, gloves and cape, before he and the two passengers were bound tightly together and then secured to the stakes with the horses. As an added precaution, their legs were also tied to the horses' hobbles. This done, Sawson, who had donned the coachman's garments, climbed up onto the driver's seat and took hold of the reins. Bounce climbed up beside him, whilst the others, with a mixture of muffled light-hearted oaths and jokes, either climbed into the coach, onto its roof or held onto its back. Slowly the coach started to move along the road, preceded by Will on his horse. It was raining heavily now and progress along the misty lane, which had now become Blackwall Lane, was slow. Nobody spoke, for sound travelled across the marsh. In the distance a dog yelped and then all was quiet, as they approached the Watch House.

At last they reached the turning to the right which led to the Watch House. All was quiet, the rain started to ease, but the mist remained thick. They all stood by the coach and waited for Sawson to speak. This was the moment that Sawson had thought about ever since he had observed the house in company with Bounce and Silas Yardley. He divided his forces; he would drive the coach with Bounce beside him. Sam and Tommy along with four of Bounce's recruits were to travel in the coach, while George was to lead the three remaining recruits on foot around to the back of the Watch House to cut off any retreat from that quarter. Will was to remain mounted midway down the lane to prevent anyone escaping down the lane to the Great Breach. Once everyone had been briefed as to their role, Sawson climbed back into the driver's seat and the horse and carriage turned slowly into the narrow lane. Midway down the lane Sawson halted the coach and spoke to George and his party. "We will give you half an hour to get behind the house then we will drive the coach to the front and gain entry," he said.

George and his three companions moved down the lane and were soon lost in the mist. After about thirty yards, they struck off to their right into the Howze field. Their progress was slow due to the mist, but by keeping close to the boundary of the field and the lane they eventually made out the silhouette of the house. A yellow light from a downstairs room acted as a marker for them and keeping themselves as far away as they could from it, but without losing sight of it, they stealthily made their way around to the back of the building and lay down on the grass, before crawling forward to a position so close to the building that they could, despite the mist, make out the rear door and windows to the property. They lay still and listened intently. Straining their ears, it was not long before they heard the approach of the carriage.

Once the half hour had elapsed, Sawson flicked the reins and the horses obediently moved forward, pulling the carriage behind them. There was now no need for silence, and as the carriage neared the house he called out to the horses as any driver might as he neared his destination: "Steady now, not far now. Well done my beauties, almost there." The sound of the carriage's approach did not go unnoticed. The main door of the house opened and a man holding a bulldog on a chain stepped out of the light into the dark and misty courtyard. It was Black Jack; he advanced towards the coach and shouted angrily. "You're late! Where have you been?" Sawson gave a muffled reply, causing Black Jack to come even closer. "What did you say?" he growled. He received no verbal reply to his question, for in a flash Sawson jumped down from the coach onto him and he fell to the ground, where a club from Bounce to his head ensured that he would take no further part in the night's proceedings. At this, the doors of the coach flew open and those inside, led by Sam, raced for and into the open door. They were quickly followed by Sawson and then by Bounce, who had secured the chain of the incredulous bulldog to the coach. On entering the house, Sawson and his companions found themselves in a large hallway which was empty, save for a number of packing cases ready, no doubt, to be carried to the river. To the left, a wide flight of stairs led up to the second storey of the building.

The speed of the attack and the entry into the house had taken the inhabitants by surprise, but they were quick to rally. Suddenly a door at the end of the hallway opened and three men emerged from the kitchen, followed quickly by George and his companions, who had forced the rear door. Seeing Sawson and his party in front of them, one of the men raised his arm, a pistol cracked and one of the recruits shouted out in pain as the ball shattered his arm and he fell to the ground in agony. At this, one of the other recruits threw a heavy-handed dagger at the man with the pistol. It caught him full in the throat and he gave out a horrid gurgling sound before falling to the ground. Whilst the remaining attackers closed with the two remaining men from the kitchen and incapacitated them, Sawson looked about. There was no sign of anyone else. "Search the house!" he roared. Just as he did so, a girl's scream could be heard from upstairs. Sawson recognised it immediately as being little Anne. He turned and looked back at the staircase just in time to see Hamidou emerge at the top, closely followed by the Count. He was pulling little Anne, who was screaming loudly.

Hamidou, quickly seeing that there was no escape down the stairs, turned in a flash and he, the Count and little Anne disappeared. Sawson, a short sword in hand, bounded up the stairs after them, followed by George. Forcing open a door at the top of the stairs, he found himself in a large room that ran almost the width of the house. Glancing to his left, he was just in time to see little Anne, who was now gagged, struggling as she was forced down another staircase by the Count. In an instant she was gone, but not so Hamidou, who stood at the top of the stairs, barring the way. Sawson ran swiftly towards him, the pent-up anger, built up over so many years, coursed through his veins. Here was the chance at last to confront on equal terms the man who had lashed and violently beaten him and his fellow galley slaves, the man who had violated his home and kidnapped his daughter. As he approached, Hamidou pulled out an evil-looking scimitar and advanced towards Sawson, swinging it in front of himself in exactly the same way as Sawson had witnessed him do in countless acts of piracy. Sawson checked his pace and as the scimitar passed from right to left in front of him he lunged at Hamidou with the short sword. Hamidou, moving quickly for a big man, jumped backwards, leaving Sawson exposed as the scimitar flashed back from left to right, coming within inches of his right arm. As Sawson pulled his arm back, he pretended to slip to his right, at which Hamidou raised his scimitar, as Sawson had seen him do many times in battle, in order to bring it down on Sawson's head and shoulders. As he did so, Sawson, in a single movement, slipped to his left, whilst at the same time lunging upwards with his short sword, causing its blade to penetrate deep into Hamidou's torso. So quick was the movement that it did not check the downward swing of the scimitar, which grazed Sawson's right arm, causing him to lose his grip on the sword on which Hamdou was now impaled. Sawson moved quickly backwards and as he did so, Hamidou drew himself to his full height and, as if oblivious of the sword blade deep within him, advanced upon the defenceless Sawson still swinging the scimitar. Suddenly he stopped, a look of incredulity came over his cruel face, he staggered forward and fell heavily, never to rise up again. He, who had so cruelly taken so many lives under the blue Mediterranean sky, had lost his on a dark, damp and misty night on East Greenwich Marshes.

INTO THE BREACH

Sawson stood and gazed down on the body of Hamidou. He was joined by George and Bounce. They both knew what this moment meant to Sawson, but they all knew that things had not really changed. They had come to rescue little Anne from the Count and that had not yet happened. There was no time to lose; swiftly they ran to the staircase which led down to what originally had been the servants' quarters when the house was built. Immediately in front of them a wide-open ground floor window revealed where the Count and little Anne had gone. Sawson looked about himself but could see nothing to indicate in which direction the Count had gone: the mist still lay heavily over the marshes, which were dismally quiet. He was quickly joined by the rest of the attacking party, who confirmed that there was no-one in the house. There was no doubt that the Count had escaped with little Anne out onto the marshes.

Will, meanwhile, had remained as instructed halfway down the lane. He was wet and cold, he had heard shouts and the pistol being discharged in the house, but what had happened he did not know. He sat still on his horse and listened keenly. For a while he heard nothing and then there came the sound of movement down the lane coming towards him. He had been in this position many times, but on those occasions he was usually aware of what was coming. He cocked his pistol and waited. As the sound came closer, he clenched the reins of his horse tightly causing it to snort loudly. Ahead in the mist the Count clearly heard the horse and taking a primed pistol from his waistband, he advanced cautiously down the lane before going into a field to the right, pulling the struggling little Anne behind him. Will, who had been peering intently down the lane, suddenly heard movement in the field to his left. He turned quickly, but he was too late as the Count fired at him through the mist. Fortunately, perhaps because of the mist, the ball missed, but the sound of the discharge so close caused the horse to rear up in fright and as a result Will dropped his pistol as he struggled to remain in the saddle. In the confusion, the Count, still pulling little Anne, made his escape down the lane.

The discharge of the pistol was heard by Sawson and the others at the house. It was clear to them in an instant that the Count had gone down the lane with little Anne. "He's making for the Great Breach!" shouted Sawson. "Quickly, after him!" They made their way into the narrow lane and moved as quickly as they could, though severely hampered by the mist. They soon came upon the rueful Will, who confirmed what had happened and the direction in which the Count was travelling. They pressed on, Sawson wracked by the thought that after all that had happened, the evil Count might yet escape with little Anne. It all now depended on Silas Yardley and his three companions having damaged the boats and positioned themselves so as to prevent the Count reaching the water. Soon they were back on Blackwall Lane and ready to cross the Further Pitts to reach the Great Breach. Sawson paused and instructed his companions to advance in line, ten yards apart. He positioned George at the northern end of the advancing line and Sam at the southern end, with instructions that when they reached the Breach to continue onto it, keeping in line and wading out into the river, before turning in towards the centre. Once everyone was in position, the line started to advance slowly towards the west.

Having completed their task on the Great Breach, Silas Yardley and his three companions had settled down to keep watch, two of them looking out into the misty river, whilst the other two looked towards the land. At about three in the morning the sound of an anchor being dropped could be heard in the river and the hazy light of a ship's lantern could just be seen through the mist. Twice they heard the sound of gunshots and then all went quiet. They lay still and waited. Nothing happened, until Silas sat up with a start. His keen hearing, honed by a life of isolation on the marsh, had detected the sound of someone or something approaching from the land. The four of them quickly made their way to the water's edge and lay down on the ground. The sound gradually came closer until the Count, pulling little Anne, came into view. They remained lying on the ground. The Count looked around carefully before making his way with little Anne to the upturned boats. It would have been the work of but a moment to turn one of them over and drag it to the water's edge before forcing little Anne into it and making his escape. It was not to be however, for Silas and his men had done their work well; the boats were useless and the Count let out an audible expletive before advancing towards the water's edge.

Silas and his companions lay still on the ground. The Count stopped some twenty yards from them and looked out into the river. He no doubt saw the hazy light flickering through the mist and he hailed the vessel that was clearly the Zwallow. His cry was answered and the Count responded by requesting a boat to be launched to pick him up. At this Silas and the others stood up and showed themselves. The Count, clearly shocked by their appearance, reacted quickly by pulling out a large knife and holding it to little Anne's neck. Silas and his companions stopped dead in their tracks, as the Count retreated slowly up the beach in the direction he had come from. At this point Sawson and his line of men emerged from the mist, cutting off his retreat. The Count turned towards Silas and his men and threatened them: "Let me through or she won't see the dawn," he growled. They had no choice and the Count, still pulling little Anne behind him, passed through their ranks and waded out into the river, shouting for the boat to hurry up.

By the time Sawson reached the water's edge, little Anne was some twenty yards from him but she might as well have been twenty miles away. There was nothing he could do. In desperation he moved forward, but a shout from the Count that he would use the knife if he came any further, held him back. The sound of oars and voices heralded the imminent arrival of a rowing boat. The water was now halfway up the Count's chest and to little Anne's shoulders as the boat suddenly came into sight. To the men on the beach all was lost. Sawson groaned inwardly, but then the Count seemed to lose his balance: George had reached the river a little earlier and following Sawson's instructions, had waded into it up to his chest, before turning south. As he progressed silently, he found himself level with the Count and little Anne. Dipping down under the water, he worked his way behind the Count who was looking to his left at the shore and to the right for the boat. Coming up close behind the Count he held his breath; he again went underwater and took hold of the Count's legs. The Count stumbled and let go of the knife which fell into the water, as George grappled with him. Seeing this, Sawson ran into the water and reached the protagonists just as the Count was trying to drive George away by threatening to drown little Anne. Stretching out his mighty arm, he grabbed the Count around the neck, causing him to let go of little Anne, who was seized by George and taken to the shore. As Sawson struggled with the Count, the boat approached. Seeing this, Bounce and the rest of the party, concerned that those on board would assist the Count, dashed into the river and the boat swiftly turned, disappeared into the mist and was seen no more.

Sawson, aware that little Anne was safe, wrestled with the Count. The anger that he had felt with Hamidou was as nothing compared to that which he felt towards the Count who had organised the attack on his home, kidnapped his daughter and caused him to be branded and to have his ear docked all those years ago. They wrestled violently with each other in the river. Slowly his hands tightened around the Count's throat, as he gradually pushed him down under the water. The Count continued to struggle, his legs kicked out, but his efforts soon ceased and he kicked no more. Sawson released his grip and as he let go, the Count's body drifted away on the tide and with it an enormous weight was released from Sawson's shoulders. The Count De Montagnac was no more. He turned slowly and looked towards the shore where little Anne stood safe in George's arms. A ragged cheer rang out as he started to make his way slowly towards the land, a great physical tiredness swept over him, but his heart was bursting with joy as he walked up the Great Breach and little Anne ran into his outstretched arms. Once again, he burst into uncontrollable tears as he had that day on Gypsy's Fall when his nightmare had started, but this time the tears were of happiness and joy, as the unspoken burden that he had carried since his flesh had sizzled under the branding iron was lifted. He was free at last; the threat to hunt him down whatever happened uttered by the Count at Sidi Ferruch was lifted. He could live out the rest of his days without looking over his shoulder.

It was a tired but happy body of men that made their way off the marshes that morning. On reaching the Pond Meadow, they recovered their horses and untied the coachman and the two passengers from the coach, with a warning that they should not move for an hour and then it should be towards the Watch House, where the coachman would find his coach and horses. Sawson mounted his horse, swung little Anne up in front of him and they all rode off into the lane. As they reached the Common Sewer they stopped for Silas Yardley who, not given much to dialogue with his fellow man, preferred to return to the New Magazine rather than to the celebrations that were to occur at the Old Tiger's Head. Sawson shook him warmly by the hand before he left into the rising mist, calling out his thanks in his high-pitched voice for the pocketful of gold sovereigns from the casket that Sawson had given him.

Dawn broke as they reached the Woolwich road and as their horses carried them up Moys Hill, the first rays of morning sunshine started to break through. On reaching the top of the hill they looked back, the marshes below were still enveloped as if in sleep in the mist, but ahead of them, illuminated in the early morning, lay Blackheath. They rode quietly across it, each man engrossed in his thoughts of the night before.

Soon they were riding in high spirits down Lee Road towards the welcoming sight of the Old Tiger's Head. Dismounting from their horses, it was a very weary party that strode into the inn to be welcomed by Martha and Bess, who immediately took charge of little Anne, who was exhausted by her ordeal. A chamber was quickly prepared for her and within a short time she fell into a deep sleep. Her rescuers made their way into the back parlour and slumped onto the chairs and benches. Martha quickly set about organising a large breakfast of eggs, bacon, sausages, liver, kidneys and chops, bread, cheeses, pies and fruit for them. Having eaten their fill, they all retired to the chambers upstairs and slept soundly until the early evening.

That night Bounce hosted a party such as had never been seen at the old inn. The tables were piled high with loaves of freshly baked bread, bowls of creamy butter, a large tongue and a ham, pickles, great joints of roast meats, pies and puddings and bowls of steaming vegetables, chickens, ducks and two suckling pigs turned slowly on the giant spit in the kitchen. Once they had eaten their fill of meats and vegetables, the tables were replenished with bowls of fruit and jugs of cream and cheeses. All this was washed down with as much ale, brandy, wines and gin as anyone wanted. Midway through the meal they were joined by little Anne, whose rescue was immediately toasted by the company and continued to be throughout the night as more drink was consumed. The tables and chairs were then pushed to one side, two fiddlers struck up and the dancing commenced, led by little Anne who pulled her father onto the floor. Sawson was not a good dancer (in fact he could not dance) but he did not care, for his heart was almost bursting with happiness as he danced with his little Anne. The dancing went on until well into the night. As they sat drinking and watching, Bounce and Sawson could not help noticing and remarking to each other that George and Bess, who had spent much of the evening dancing together, had disappeared outside and that Will was dancing a lot with little Anne. Finally, late in the night the party began to break up. As it did so, Sawson presented to all who had taken part in the rescue 'their share' of the Count's sovereigns.

Soon only Bounce and Sawson were left in the parlour. The two old friends sat up reminiscing. Sawson was to leave in the morning for home and they agreed that they would keep in touch and that Bounce would come and visit Malsters in the next few months. That settled, they made their way wearily to bed.

HOME

The following morning Sawson, despite his late night, rose early. On going downstairs, he found little Anne and George who had already breakfasted. Little Anne was excited and eager to set off home to see her mother and brothers. Sawson sensed that George was not as keen to depart as his cousin and drew him into conversation. "I want to stay here with Bess," George said. Sawson, who had anticipated this might be the case, replied gently that he understood, but that he should come home with him, for it seemed certain his mother had just lost her father and without doubt he should be there to comfort her and to help his parents with the forthcoming lambing. To soften the blow Sawson added, "I have spoken to Bounce and he has agreed that there will always be a place for you here if you want to come back." This made things slightly better for George, but not for Bess who wept bitterly as George prepared for his departure.

A little later that morning, having said fond goodbyes to Bounce and his family, Sawson mounted his horse, swung little Anne up in front of him and started off for home, accompanied by George, whose departure caused Bess to run upstairs in tears, where she was eventually comforted by Bounce, who promised to take her with him on his forthcoming visit to Malsters.

The journey home was uneventful. Anne chatted away happily, whilst George in the beginning was rather subdued, before reverting to his old happy self. Eventually the following day, they turned off the Portsmouth Road down the old, familiar, sloping lane to Malsters. They rode peacefully between the high banks, the only sound being a croaking welcome from the crows busy overhead. Midway down the lane, Sawson reached inside his jacket and blew on an old hunting horn. Hearing it, Molly flung open the door of Malsters and along with Robert and Ben she raced across the farmyard, reaching the gate as Sawson, Anne and George arrived. There, at the entrance to their home, he and his family were reunited.

Walking behind his family and George towards the comforting entrance to the farmhouse, Sawson looked about him: nothing had changed, everything was as it had been, but everything had changed. He was a free man. He answered to nobody. That was something that everybody else he knew took for granted, but up until now not him. It was a precious feeling and worth more than all the jewels and money in the world. Delighting in it, he slowly entered the house and closed the door. He was home, he was free.

EPILOGUE

George remained at Malsters overnight, before returning home the next day to a warm welcome from his parents. But missing Bess and having tasted the delights of London, the life of a shepherd did not appeal and two months later he returned to the Old Tiger's Head to be with Bess. He is still there working alongside Sam and Tommy.

Strangely, Will has not, we believe, returned to his old ways, but instead has started to help his father at the Bugle Horn. Three months ago he travelled with Bounce to Malsters to visit Sawson, though he spent most of the visit around little Anne!

Sawson remains with his family at Malsters. He is happy and contented. He has been known to visit The Talbot Arms more frequently than in the past, where he will sit and chat and enjoy the company of others. Now though, he never bothers to keep an eye on the Portsmouth Road.